The Beach Party

NIKKI SMITH

PENGUIN BOOKS

PENGUIN BOOKS

UK | USA | Canada | Ireland | Australia
India | New Zealand | South Africa

Penguin Books is part of the Penguin Random House group of companies
whose addresses can be found at global.penguinrandomhouse.com.

First published 2023

001

Copyright © Nikki Smith, 2023

The moral right of the author has been asserted

Set in 12.5/14.75pt Garamond MT Std
Typeset by Jouve (UK), Milton Keynes
Printed and bound in Great Britain by Clays Ltd, Elcograf S.p.A.

The authorized representative in the EEA is Penguin Random House Ireland,
Morrison Chambers, 32 Nassau Street, Dublin D02 YH68

A CIP catalogue record for this book is available from the British Library

ISBN: 978-0-241-99722-2

www.greenpenguin.co.uk

To women who have each other's backs

The Beach Party

'He who helps the guilty shares the crime.'
– Publilius Syrus

Prologue

The blowflies find it first. A throbbing hum that feasts rapidly, knowing they won't be alone for long.

A vulture circles on a thermal of warm air above the limestone cliffs, the surface of the Mediterranean Sea shimmering in the heat that accompanies the start of the tourist season. An updraught lifts the bird higher and the Mallorcan villa comes into view below: a rectangle of terracotta roof tiles, a flash of a turquoise swimming pool, a blaze of cerise-pink bougainvillea. There's no sign of the occupants who arrived here last week: no boat moored by the jetty, no streaks of blood on the marble floor, no evidence to show how easy it is to separate flesh from bone.

The vulture circles once more, then drops down and lands on the dirt track that leads away from the villa and the ocean, through the shade of the pine forest and out to the main road. Its four talons gouge out marks in the red earth. The flies lift off in a black cloud as the vulture struts over, examines the bloody remains on the floor and begins to feed.

Chapter 1

Nina – Now

Nina's phone vibrates with a text letting her know her driver has arrived. She's set her mobile to silent so as not to disturb Hugo – her husband doesn't appreciate being woken up when he doesn't have to leave for another hour and a half. She shuts the door of their Mayfair apartment, walks two flights down the communal staircase and out of the main entrance, the black-painted heavy double doors opening out on to a pillared stone porch, a set of four shallow steps leading to the pavement, where the car is waiting for her.

The driver gets out to hold the rear door open. Nina doesn't acknowledge him as she slides inside and he shuts it behind her. Their morning routine doesn't involve chit-chat; he's picked her up enough times to know that.

She places her Mulberry handbag beside her and settles back against the cream leather, adjusts her cashmere throw around her shoulders as she presses the button to turn on the heated seat. It's supposed to reach twenty-four degrees today, but the chill of the early-morning start makes it feel at least five degrees colder. At least it's not raining. She hates being wet even more than she hates the cold. She stares at her phone, already typing a response to one of the dozens of emails that are waiting in her inbox, all sent after she last looked at eleven thirty last night, every one of them marked as urgent.

The Tesla Model S is practically silent as it slides past the pavements of Grosvenor Square, past the green lawn of the central gardens and the memorial to the victims of the September 2001 terrorist attacks; most of the occupants in the various apartments behind the black iron railings are not yet awake. The driver hesitates at the T-junction.

'The traffic's bad along Shaftesbury Avenue,' he says. 'They're doing roadworks at Holborn. Do you want me to cut down and go along the Embankment?'

Nina hesitates, her fingers hovering over the screen as she finishes reading a message sent by her associate at 2 a.m. explaining why the amendments to the contract won't be waiting for her when she gets in. *Get them to me by eight at the latest*, she types.

'How much of a delay?' she asks.

'Six minutes, according to the satnav.'

She knows the London Eye, Blackfriars Bridge and the Shard will still be blurred silhouettes in the dawn mist across the expanse of dark water. The river is less than fifty metres from bank to bank, but thirty people drowned in it last year. She tucks a loose strand of blonde hair behind her ear.

'No,' she says. 'Stick to the usual route.'

Thirty-five minutes later, Nina steps out of the Tesla as it pulls up outside the vast building with blacked-out glass windows that is home to over six thousand employees. She smiles briefly at the security guard as she swipes her pass over the turnstiles, from force of habit rather than in acknowledgement, then walks across the polished granite floor and presses the button for the lift.

Her office overlooks the trading floor. She can see most of the desks are already occupied; the odd empty space will soon be filled by those who are currently still in the gym, an area illuminated by green and white neon lights that takes up almost the entire basement of the building; rows and rows of exercise machines as far as the eye can see, a place full of grunting and sweat, the competitiveness almost as fierce as on the trading floor itself.

She glances at the clock. Still an hour and a half to go before the London markets open at eight. Enough time to answer some emails and mark up comments on the press release that is due to go out later today.

Her phone buzzes and she swipes up to open the new email that has appeared in her inbox, the sender's name unfamiliar. She clicks on it, half expecting spam, and reads the words addressed to her. A line of cold sweat pricks the skin between her shoulder blades – the first intimations of a feeling she hasn't experienced in years.

Her forehead creases, despite her three-monthly injections of Botox. She reads the email again.

Unless you want everyone to find out what you did that summer, you must return to the villa. Saturday after next, 6 p.m. I'll be waiting.

How did they find her?
She walks quickly over to her office door and pushes it shut. Her legs give way beneath her and she collapses back on to her chair, time slipping away in an instant.

Has it been sent to any of the others?

Not Claire, obviously – she's no longer in a position to be able to read emails – but what about the rest of them? Her contact details are the only ones shown, but that doesn't mean anything.

She braces herself, then clicks on the attachment at the bottom of the email, any concerns about security breaches forgotten as the image downloads on to her screen. She swallows as she enlarges the photo with her fingers.

Oh fuck. This isn't good. This isn't good at all.

Red streaks flash through her head and the smell of diesel burns her nostrils. Were they really so naïve thirty-three years ago to think it wouldn't catch up with them?

Chapter 2

July – 1989

Aiden pushes his fringe out of his eyes and looks again at his green Swatch, scanning people's faces as they walk across the tiled floor of Gatwick's South Terminal. They should be here by now.

He glances at the queue building up ahead of him at the check-in desk, where a tanned passenger service agent hands a woman her boarding pass with an accompanying flash of white teeth. The split-flap departure board whirrs round and his Britannia Airways flight disappears then reappears nearer the top. He rubs his neck and turns up the volume on his Sony Walkman, hiding his anxiety in the heavily synthesized beat of Erasure's 'A Little Respect'.

When he thinks back to this moment afterwards, he realizes he should have seen it when they walked towards him. It was obvious, with hindsight. The two of them together, their hands almost touching, mirroring each other's movements in a way only those with a particular kind of confidence can manage. A self-assurance that suggested they could do *anything*, not because they'd just left university and had a bright future ahead of them, but because they'd done it before. And got away with it.

But he doesn't see it. He doesn't turn and run out of the airport as he should have; he's too busy trying to grab his headphones back from Seb, who has snatched them in one hand, his other arm around Nina's shoulders, trapping her long blonde hair, which she's found the time to crimp.

'Knew you'd beat us to it,' Seb says. He drops his Adidas holdall on to the floor. Aiden pushes his mother's blue suitcase with its thick straps further away with his foot, as if he can pretend it doesn't belong to him. Seb stares at him. 'Have you had your hair cut?'

Aiden shrugs. 'Just a trim.' He wants to ask why they are over an hour late, but doesn't want to be a killjoy. Will is the worrier in their group, not him.

'Looks like you're channelling Tom Cruise,' Seb says as he reaches out and ruffles Aiden's hair.

'I don't look like fucking Tom Cruise.' Aiden pulls away and runs his hand over his head, smoothing out his dark fringe.

'Yeah you do,' Seb says. 'In *Rain Man*. It's a compliment, mate. Chill out.'

Aiden shuffles his feet as Seb points at the check-in queue and turns towards Nina.

'I told you we should have left earlier,' he says.

Aiden attempts to straighten out the tangled wire of his headphones, fitting the orange foam pad back over one of the earpieces where it has come loose. He breathes deeply, trying to imagine space in his mouth, as his speech therapist had advised.

Nina steps forward and kisses him on both cheeks. She's wearing Poison, a scent that had lingered in every room of their university house, and drags a wheelie bag behind her. Its tan colour and monogram are familiar; a real designer piece, not a fake.

8

If it wasn't for Nina, Aiden knows they wouldn't be going on this holiday at all. She'd offered up her parents' villa in their final term as casually as if she had been offering to make them a cup of tea. He'd known she was wealthy, but it was only after that conversation that he'd realized just *how* wealthy. Especially after she'd shown them the photos. A large sandstone property perched on the edge of a cliff overlooking the ocean, with rooms like something out of one of those boutique luxury hotels he'd seen in magazines. All pale colours and marble floors. Outside, there were teak sun-loungers covered in plump white cushions beside a huge pool where the mosaic dolphin design on the bottom was visible below the smooth surface of the aquamarine water.

'I love your hair, Aiden,' Nina says coyly. He smiles. Everyone smiles if Nina pays them a compliment; their faces light up as if she has flicked a switch. 'Where's Will?' she asks.

'He's going to meet us in the departure lounge,' Aiden replies. 'He said he had to do something for his mum before he left.'

Nina raises her eyebrows. 'Let's hope it doesn't take long. Shall we get in the queue, then?'

Seb lifts his holdall on to his shoulder and adjusts the cream cable sweater draped around his neck. He grins as he slaps Aiden on the back, his hand connecting with the image of Freddie Mercury's face on his leather jacket, making Aiden flinch.

'This is going to be so fucking ace, guys,' he says. 'All six of us, and two whole weeks in Mallorca. Thirty-six degrees and constant sunshine. Party time. Bring it on.'

He holds up his hand to high-five Aiden and pauses to allow a girl into the queue ahead of him, his eyes sliding over her tight denim shorts.

Aiden looks at the check-in desk and catches another glimpse of the tanned passenger service agent, remembering the way he'd smiled, the flash of his teeth.

Chapter 3

July – 1989

The palms of Zoe's hands are damp as she stands with her arms stretched out either side of her. Claire had walked straight through the metal detector – the buzzer had only gone off when Zoe stepped under the arch, the sharp noise making her jump. She can see Claire up ahead, standing by the conveyor belt with one hand tucked into the back pocket of her acid-wash jeans, her newly permed curls bouncing as she turns her head to watch her bag approach the X-ray scanner.

The officer pats down Zoe's T-shirt, reaching under her armpits. Zoe glances at the clock: 2 p.m. An hour and a half until their flight. If she gets a move on, there's still enough time to pick up a gift for Nina in Duty Free. Claire said she'd already got something – no doubt having spent double what Zoe can afford – but Zoe doesn't want to arrive empty-handed.

She moves her feet apart so the officer can reach her ankles. Claire still hasn't admitted that her plan had been to get the Gatwick flight with the others, that she'd only abandoned the idea a couple of days ago when it became clear she couldn't change her booking from Manchester. Nina had told Zoe on the phone and the words had stung, like rubbing lemon juice into a cut. *Didn't you know?* she'd asked. *No, I didn't,* Zoe had been forced to admit, the three words souring the start of her trip.

The officer tells Zoe to put her arms down and asks to see her passport. Zoe takes it out of her pocket, feeling the indents of the gold printed design beneath her thumb. She smiles briefly as she hands it over, flinches as the woman bends back the brand-new burgundy cover. The officer looks at her, then at her photo, then at Zoe again, her face expressionless. Zoe fiddles with her earring, disentangles a strand of her red hair from where it has wound itself around the gold hoop.

Claire had talked about nothing other than the holiday all the way to Manchester airport, her words spilling out frantically, like she'd half pressed the fast-forward button on one of her mix-tape cassettes. Zoe had responded at what she'd hoped was appropriate intervals with 'God, yes' and 'I know' and 'Did she?' while Claire babbled on, oblivious, the dimples that Zoe was so envious of never leaving her cheeks.

Zoe had been thinking about her mother, wondering whether the carer had been in, whether they'd found the instructions she'd left out. She can't shake the feeling she's forgotten something. She'd picked up her mother's prescription from the doctor's and topped up the electricity meter. There wasn't anything else. Was there? *Forget about it. You're supposed to be on holiday. Enjoy it while you can.*

The officer hands back her passport and tells her she can go, beckons the next passenger forward. Zoe looks over at the conveyor belt and watches as Claire turns towards her, a crease between her eyebrows, her lips fixed in a small smile. Something inside her falls away, as if someone has sliced through her intestines with a sharp pair of scissors. She's seen that look before. Whenever Claire walked into a club on a night out at university, slipping past the bouncers without having to empty her pockets. She swallows, hoping the security guard hasn't noticed the line of perspiration on her upper lip that she wipes away with her hand as she tells her feet to move from where they are currently stuck to the floor.

Claire wouldn't be that stupid – would she? Zoe remembers the way she'd held on to her rucksack in the passenger seat of her Ford Escort this morning, refusing to put it down on the floor. She had assumed it was because the mat was littered with sweet wrappers she hadn't had time to clear up, crumpled pieces of red foil left over from the chocolate strawberry creams her mum liked. The only ones soft enough for her to eat. Now she wonders if it had been anything to do with the state of her car at all.

Claire looks at the scanner, her gaze fixed on her bag. Zoe holds her breath as her face burns, paranoia painted in flushed circles on her cheeks. The security officer is staring at her. She thinks of her mother, of how she's only booked the carer for two weeks, of spastic limbs with no one to massage them, of red sweet wrappers, and a hundred other things that rise up and whirl around inside her head. A loud, rushing noise echoes in her ears.

Claire's rucksack moves along the belt and into the X-ray machine. The scanner operator stares at the TV screen in front of him and frowns. Zoe's vision blurs.

There is a sudden commotion from the other side of the conveyor belt and Zoe instinctively turns to look – a man in a Guns N' Roses T-shirt is shouting at one of the

security officers, who tells him to calm down as he empties the contents of his bag on to the counter. Other
passengers pretend they haven't seen, shooting sideways
glances at him as they walk past. Another security officer
heads over to the fracas, taking with him a large Alsatian
on a lead.

Claire's gaze switches from her bag to the dog, her face
white. The scanner operator turns and says something to
his colleague as the bag passes through the machine and
clatters down the conveyor belt. Claire steps forward to
retrieve it and grins at Zoe, the colour rushing back into
her cheeks, her tight curls bouncing behind her in her
banana clip as she walks off towards the departure lounge.

The passenger behind Zoe tuts at her to move, then
pushes past to reach their luggage. Zoe's bag appears on
the belt and she steps forward to grab it, fiddles awkwardly with the zip before pulling out a bottle of water
and swallowing a few gulps, her mouth suddenly bone
dry.

You're being paranoid.

Claire would have told her if she was going to do anything like that. They would have discussed it, and Zoe
would have told her not to be a fucking idiot. It's one
thing taking a couple of pills on a night out, but trying to
smuggle them through an airport is something else completely. And Claire isn't stupid; she'd graduated with a
First in her Law degree. Better than Zoe had managed for
Drama. She slides the bottle back into her bag and tightens the neon-blue scrunchie her mum had given her
before she came away.

She clears her throat as she walks over to the entrance

to the departure lounge, where Claire is waiting for her, tells herself she's being stupid. They've been friends since they met in halls, working in their first term behind the bar in the student union with Will and Aiden. They've shared a house as well as their secrets for the past two years. Claire had covered for her when it mattered most, and now they have two weeks in Nina's incredible villa to look forward to.

Don't think about his face. The way they'd dragged him out of the archway under the clock tower.

No one is going to find out. She adjusts her bag on her shoulder. Claire isn't the one who let them down. Of course Zoe trusts her.

Chapter 4

July – 1989

Aiden watches Nina shove her Ray-Bans on top of her shiny, blonde hair and glance at the departure board as their gate number appears.

'We need to go,' she says. 'Where the fuck is Will?'

Seb shrugs, not taking his eyes off his Nintendo Game & Watch. Aiden can hear the tinny bleeps and explosions coming out of the orange machine. He doesn't understand how Seb can play for hours; he gets bored after a few minutes.

'He said he'd meet us here,' Aiden says. 'I told him we'd be outside the entrance to Duty Free.'

Nina rolls her eyes.

'Well, he's late. And Claire and Zoe are going to be waiting for us in Palma.'

Aiden looks at her.

'You and Seb go. I'll meet you at the gate.'

'Are you sure?' Nina asks the question but is already raising herself off the metal seat.

'Yes,' Aiden replies, knowing that she doesn't need him to answer; Nina will go anyway. An unspoken agreement exists between them since that final term at university: if she asks him for something, he does it. The cost of fucking up and having Nina bail him out. A debt he's not sure he'll ever be able to repay.

Nina looks at Seb. 'Come on, dufus. Let's go.' She pulls on his arm, but he shakes her off.

'Don't call me that.'

She narrows her eyes. 'All right, chill out.'

He stares at her, his screen flashing. 'It's not funny, Nina.' She glances briefly in Aiden's direction, as if she's reminding Seb of his presence.

'Do you want us to get on this plane or not?' she asks.

Seb's cheeks flush as he snaps the plastic orange cover shut on his game of *Donkey Kong* and sticks the Nintendo in his bag. Aiden watches them head off towards the departure gate, the space between them a fraction wider than it was before.

Where the fuck is he? The departure board now shows 'Boarding' next to their flight rather than 'Go to Gate' and Aiden isn't sure how long he should wait. Or even if he should wait. Would Nina rather he just got on the plane? Or should he hang around for Will and try and get on the next one? He has no idea how to get to the villa from Palma airport; he doesn't even have the address, only a photo that Nina gave him so he could show his parents where he was going.

Jesus, Will. They are so close to sliding into the swimming pool, to lying on a lounger in the sun with a cold beer, but if he doesn't get his arse into gear they're going to miss out. Aiden adjusts his headphones around his neck and picks up the rucksack he's brought as hand luggage. He glances at the board again, then checks the time on his Swatch. He'll give him two minutes. If he's not here by then, he's going without him.

17

He's counting down the last twenty seconds when he catches sight of the back of Will's denim jacket in one of the phone booths next to Duty Free. It's emblazoned with a Smiths album cover: the face of a US Marine with 'Meat is Murder' written on his helmet. He had first seen Will wearing it three years ago, when he was serving pints in the student bar in Birmingham, had been drawn to the familiarity of the military connection, which had turned out to be nothing to do with the military but was Will's way of showing his support for being vegetarian. Now, he has to look twice to check it's actually Will who is wearing it. He's shaved his head. Aiden squints at him. It can't be much more than a grade two all over. If it wasn't for Will's lanky frame and pale skin, he'd fit right in with the recruits Aiden's dad trains every day at the barracks.

He walks up behind him, recognizes Will's familiar habit of chewing the skin beside the nail on his thumb.

'. . . I didn't think they could do that without telling you first.'

Aiden reaches out to touch his shoulder but hesitates when he hears the tone of Will's voice. Will's head drops forward as he taps a ten-pence piece against the metal slot before pushing it into the machine, then he sticks the rest of his coins back in his pocket.

'I'm sorry, Mum,' Aiden hears him say. 'I have to go. I've run out of change.'

Will's voice breaks, and the rawness of his emotion scrapes at Aiden's insides. He steps away into the safety of WH Smith and pretends to examine the shelf of best-sellers as he watches Will lower the receiver, rub his sleeve across his face and look up at the departure board, where 'Last Call' is now flashing for their flight.

Despite the way Will goes quiet or changes the subject when the others talk about their families, Aiden reminds himself that he shouldn't assume he knows everything about the person he considers to be his closest friend. There are things Will doesn't know about him either. Friends, even the best ones, don't tell each other everything.

Chapter 5

July – 1989

Zoe watches Will appear through the arrivals gate at Palma airport, pushing a trolley piled high with a jumble of bags balanced on top of a blue suitcase. For a moment it looks like the metal frame is holding him up as he leans on it, his face paler than she remembers. Something in her stomach rises and then falls when she thinks about their last conversation when they were still at university, his breath on her skin. She silently urges him to look in her direction, but he stares straight ahead.

Claire dumps her bag on the floor beside Zoe, squeals with delight and runs towards the others. Zoe watches her throw her arms around Nina and feels a stab of jealousy – as if the closeness they'd built up on the flight – downing shots of vodka, trashing photos of Elle Macpherson in *Marie Claire*, filling in the sex quiz in *Cosmopolitan* – had all just been a pretence. A brief flashback to how close they'd been in those first few weeks at university, when they'd worked together in the student bar, before Claire had decided to switch courses and started spending more time with Nina. Zoe had felt her pull away, Claire had given up her job and Nina had become the one who mattered most.

Didn't you know? Nina's words echo in Zoe's head and the handles of the plastic bag with the bottle of Malibu that Zoe had purchased for her in Duty Free cut uncomfortably into her hand.

Seb embraces Zoe, lifting her up, and she buries her head in his neck, checking to see if Will is watching as soon as her feet touch back on the ground, but he's looking in the other direction. A strand of her hair catches on Seb's gold signet ring as she pulls away. Her throat aches when she swallows. *Get a grip.*

'Cooper!' Seb grins, and she forces herself to smile back, her lips sticking to her teeth. 'How was your flight?'

'Fine,' she says. 'Or that's what Claire said.'

'Oh yeah, I forgot you've never flown before.' Seb puts his arm around her shoulders, but Zoe can tell he has already lost interest, his eyes focused on the others, seeking out more interesting conversations. She looks across to where Claire and Nina are holding hands, catches the words 'bag' and 'dog' among their snorts of laughter and swallows the lump she can feel forming in her throat. Nina waves at her, and she flushes.

Seb puts his other arm around Will.

'This guy,' he says to Zoe, 'spent too long in WH Smith and nearly missed the bloody flight, the dipshit.' Zoe stares at Will's hands, which are still gripping the metal bar of the trolley, his knuckles white. 'But then I thrashed him at blackjack on the plane to make up for it,' he adds.

'It's supposed to be a holiday, Seb, not a competition,' Will replies. He rolls his eyes, but Seb doesn't notice, has already disentangled himself from them and is walking away to join Nina.

'You shaved your hair,' Zoe says.

Will nods as he runs his hand over the layer of short stubble. 'Yeah. Less maintenance.'

She raises her eyebrows. ''Course it is.' She wishes she could take back the comment as soon as it leaves her mouth, but it's already too late; Will pushes the trolley past her and she's left feeling worse than she did before.

'All right, Zo?' Aiden kisses her on the cheek, and she squeezes his arm, his leather jacket soft under her finger-tips. The smell of his aftershave, fresh and simple, is so familiar she experiences a sharp pang of homesickness. She nods, unable to answer. 'You made it OK, then?' he adds. 'I told you there's nothing to this flying business.'

'It was fine,' she says, clearing her throat. She doesn't mention what happened at security. Doesn't want him thinking she's paranoid. 'Did Will really almost miss the flight?'

Aiden looks ahead to where Nina is walking out of the airport through a set of glass doors, side by side with Claire, who hasn't stopped talking, even more overexcited than usual. They watch Nina stretch out both her arms either side of her and tip her head backwards as the heat hits her like a wall, her outline silhouetted against the set-ting sun. Aiden frowns.

'What?' Zoe asks.

'She reminds me of something,' Aiden says. He shakes his head. 'A painting or a . . . I don't know. Doesn't matter. And Seb's exaggerating,' he adds. 'You know what he's like. Will just cut it a bit fine and the airline had to put out a final call for him.'

Zoe bites her lip. Aiden always defends Will. Even

when he doesn't deserve it. She pulls on the sleeve of his jacket.

'Aren't you going to be way too hot in this?' she asks.

He grins at her. 'Probably. But you know me, Zo. Style beats practicality every time.'

Zoe watches Nina tap her credit card on the counter and nod impatiently as the woman runs through the car-hire rental contract, her patter delivered in perfect English. Thirty seconds into her speech, Nina interrupts her mid-sentence and puts her card on top of the carefully prepared paperwork.

'Just add on any excess and I'll pay it,' she says, holding her hand out for the keys. 'I presume it's been cleaned?'

The woman nods, a polite smile fixed on her face.

'Would you like a receipt?' she says.

Nina shakes her head.

'How do you want to split the cost?' Zoe asks.

Nina waves her hand. 'Don't worry about it. My treat.'

Zoe's bag feels instantly lighter as she carries it over to the silver Jeep Cherokee and puts it with everyone else's in the boot. She breathes in the smell of warm tarmac, her stomach fizzing with anticipation.

Seb and Nina climb into the front seats; Zoe lets Claire go in ahead of her so she won't have to sit next to Will, the thought of their bare skin pressed up against each other almost unbearable.

'Fuck.' Will drops the metal clasp of the seatbelt and rubs the red mark that appears on his hand. Zoe can't remember ever feeling heat like it. It smothers them like a heavy blanket, burning her lungs each time she takes a breath. At home, any time past seven o'clock and goose-bumps rise up on her arms. This is dense, thick, something she can almost lean against. Manchester, with its grey drizzle, feels a million miles away.

'Just get in,' Nina says impatiently. 'And hurry up and shut the door unless you want to walk.' She turns around in her seat to stare at him, and Zoe isn't sure if she's joking. She can't always tell with Nina. The most difficult of them all to read. Would lend you fifty quid in a heartbeat but insists on things being done her way. Sometimes Zoe thinks Nina should have studied Drama, like her. She can convince people of anything; it's the only reason they all managed to graduate. The four of them shuffle along the back seat, their skin sticking to the plastic. Aiden wriggles out of his jacket and Zoe takes it, slides the lining under her legs.

Nina switches on the air-conditioning and a blast of hot air fills the car as she pulls out on to the main road. Zoe leans her head to one side and rests it on the window, shutting her eyes for a moment while she thinks about her mum lying under her new duvet cover, the one she'd bought her just before she left, the wildflower pattern a futile attempt to brighten up her bedroom and assuage the guilt she felt at leaving her behind in their shitty house. She'll phone her when they get to the villa. She glances at her watch. They're an hour ahead of the UK here. Her mum's evening carer won't have come in yet.

She sees Aiden looking at her, his eyebrow raised in an unspoken question, and she smiles briefly, then looks away. It's only two weeks. She deserves a break. Everything will still be there when she gets home. Her stomach shrinks at the thought. Maybe that's what she's most afraid of.

Seb turns up the volume on the radio and they start to sing along to the familiar pop song, the Jeep vibrating with noise. Claire reaches into her bag and pulls out a can of Quatro. She takes a swig of the green liquid, a burp escaping as the fizzy drink hits her stomach, her dimples appearing as she giggles. She offers the can to Zoe, who takes it and smiles back, genuine this time. Zoe lets their voices float in the warm air around her, thoughts of her mum fading until she's completely immersed in the moment.

Nina stops in front of a set of traffic lights and a loud banging noise explodes on the window beside Zoe's head. She shrinks away from it instinctively, watching Aiden's eyes widen as he stares at the glass.

'What the fucking hell is that?' he says.

Chapter 6

July – 1989

A face is pressed up against the Jeep window. Not a face – a black mask with a hook nose and two holes through which Zoe can see eyes staring out at her. Claire lets out a shriek. A couple of large, twisted horns with pointed tips, ends as sharp as needles, curve up out of its forehead. Zoe can hear whatever it is knocking on the door as if it's keeping time to a beat. It moves, turns towards her, spreads out its palms on the glass either side of its head. For a few seconds, Zoe thinks she is looking at a monster.

She watches Seb slam his hand down on the push button sticking out of his door to lock it as another figure, dressed in a red hood and wearing a similar mask, appears in front of the Jeep. Nina twists around in her seat and looks at everyone sitting behind her, her eyes wide.

'We're fucked, people.'

There's a silence, and then she laughs, a high-pitched screech that makes Zoe shiver, and she feels Aiden press himself further back against the seat. He grips her hand and his face drains of colour in the same way she'd seen that night at university. Claire stares at the glass, and Zoe feels something in her chest tighten as she notices how huge her pupils are.

'Can you see that?' Claire whispers.

Aiden nods.

Nina turns back around to the front, takes her hands off the steering wheel, holds them up in the air and shouts, '*Muévete del camino!*' at the windscreen.

The man standing beside Zoe's window tips his head from side to side, banging his palms on the glass like it's a drum. Zoe wants to shout at Nina to drive but can't seem to find her voice. Then he stops, suddenly, with a flourish, and the man in front of the Jeep bows deeply before stepping out of the way as Nina accelerates forwards. For a moment no one says anything, then Nina thumps the steering wheel with one hand and turns up the volume on the radio, the hard beat of Run DMC's 'Walk This Way' vibrating through the floor beneath their feet.

'Your faces!' she shrieks. Zoe hates it when Nina is like this. Revelling in the knowledge that she knows something they don't; a mean streak that slips out occasionally, like a sharp knife. 'They're harmless. They're just dancers practising for the Correfoc. The Fire Run. It's a festival to mark the summer solstice. They make a big thing of it out here.'

'What, by dressing up and scaring the shit out of people?' Seb says.

'It's all part of the tradition. My parents love it. The locals wear masks, play drums, let off fireworks. I went last time I was here; it's supposed to be the one night of the year when you can dance with the devil.' She lowers her voice at the end of the sentence, relishing the drama.

'Are we planning on going?' Claire asks, her voice tight.

'Not to the big one they hold here in Palma. But they'll do something to mark the occasion where we are. Usually a beach-party kind of thing. More of a chilled-out vibe.'

The song finishes and Nina flicks off the radio as the news comes on. The inside of the Jeep turns silent as they head out of Palma on the coastal road that runs along the west side of the island, the heat continuing to press against the windows. Zoe is conscious of the ocean stretched out below her, difficult to see properly in the creeping darkness. Every now and again she spots a light from a boat on the horizon, but the water is pitch black and she shivers, remembers the numbness she'd felt when it closed over her head in Birmingham, her feet sinking into the muddy silt of the canal until she thought she'd never touch anything solid again.

She puts her hand on Nina's headrest in front of her and leans forward to try to get more air in her lungs.

'Almost there,' Nina says. 'You're going to love it.' She pulls off the main road and heads down a long dirt track with dense pine trees either side, the Jeep bouncing on the bumpy surface. Zoe twists the handle to wind down her window, her face hidden by the shadows. The heat rolls inside the car in waves, making the palms of her hands slippery. She doesn't know how much longer she can stand it. She needs to get out.

She can feel Will staring at her but can't bring herself to look at him, won't let herself think about his hand reaching for hers in the water.

'Almost there,' Will says, repeating Nina's words. 'Just take some deep breaths.'

She wants to tell him that he's misunderstood, she

28

doesn't feel car sick, but doesn't want to have to explain in front of the others. She shuts her eyes and counts as slowly as she can to a hundred, telling herself she will get out and walk if they're not at the villa by then. At ninety-six, the Jeep hits a hard surface and the noise of the tyres on the dusty track turns to something quieter as they pull up in front of a set of large black metal gates. Nina leans out of the window, enters a code into a keypad, and they swing open.

Wrought-iron lights switch themselves on as they go down a long driveway, bathing everything in a warm glow. Nina stops in front of a garage and they all stare at the villa in front of them. Zoe thinks it's even larger than it looked in the photographs. A honey-hued building with a stone facade that stretches the width of the entire plot, covered in curved terracotta roof tiles. She can see ten sets of windows on this side alone, each with its own pair of green wooden shutters, all overlooking the front lawn, which is currently being watered by strategically placed sprinklers, the sound instantly reminding her of summers past. The place is stunning. She can't believe Nina's parents own somewhere like this to use for a holiday; it's about ten times the size of Zoe's terraced house.

'Oh my god, Nina, this is fucking incredible.' Claire runs over to one of the windows and squeals as she peers inside. 'Guys, there's another garden at the back. It's huge. I can see the patio! And the view from that side looks straight out over the sea.' She squeezes Will's arm.

'Well, if you hurry up, we can get in the pool,' Nina says as she heads towards the front door. 'There's a gate over there that you can use to get through to the back' – she points over towards the garage – 'but I need to unlock it from the other side.'

Zoe picks up her bag, the last one left, and shuts the boot of the Jeep as the others disappear inside the house. The air moves behind her, a whisper on the back of her neck, and she turns around, expecting to see one of them coming back for something they've forgotten, but there's no one there. She holds her breath, feeling as if someone else is holding theirs too. A shadow passes by the bushes in front of the gates and she squints, trying to make it out, but it dissolves into the greenery as all the lights go out.

'Nina?' she shouts.

There's a silence.

She calls out again, louder this time.

'Nina?'

Will appears at the front door, a silhouette against the light.

'You OK?' he asks.

'The lights . . .' She trails off.

'Hang on a sec, they're on a timer.' He presses a switch, and they come back on. Laughter spills out from inside the villa behind him. Zoe walks towards the sound more quickly than she usually would, her footsteps speeding up as the lights go out again, and then starts to run, her heart thumping as she imagines fingers reaching out and touching the back of her neck.

She reaches the safety of the doorway, her mouth dry, and pushes past Will to get into the hall.

'What's the matter?' he says.

'Didn't you hear that?'

He frowns. 'What?'

Zoe glances into the darkness before she slams the door shut behind her, cutting off the chirruping of cicadas and the noise of the sprinklers. *Breathe.*

'Nothing,' she says. 'I'm just being stupid.'

Chapter 7

July – 1989

Claire shrieks with laughter as Seb somersaults fully clothed off the side of the pool. Aiden grabs a handful of Will's T-shirt and pulls him into the water as he jumps in on top of Seb.

Will shakes his head and blows water out of his nose.

'Loosen up, Lawson,' Seb shouts as he surfaces. 'We're here to party.'

Will grins, then dives down, grabs Aiden's legs and pulls him under the surface before swimming for the side and jumps out before Aiden can reach him.

'You need to be quicker,' Will says, picking up a beer. 'You're losing your edge.'

Aiden laughs as Nina turns up the stereo in the living room and 'I Think We're Alone Now' blasts out through the patio doors.

Claire ignores the warm water that splashes over her feet from the boys' rough and tumble and walks across the patio, dragging Nina outside. She holds out a free hand towards Zoe as they emerge through the glass doors, beckoning her to come and join them. Zoe shakes her head as the two of them dance around on the wet tiles at the edge of the pool.

'Spoilsport,' Claire shouts, flicking water at Will as Zoe

heads back towards the living room. 'Where are you going?'

'To get us some drinks,' Zoe replies.

'There'll be stuff in the fridge,' Nina shouts after her. 'I told the housekeeper to stock up before we arrived.'

The beat of the music thumps in Claire's head. She wishes she hadn't had that last shot of vodka on the plane; it was too much on top of the half a tablet she'd swallowed in the departure lounge toilets.

She'd taken the bottle of pills out of her mother's bathroom cabinet before she'd left for the airport, emptying out the original contents and turning on the tap to wash them down the sink. It had taken a few attempts before they all disappeared, leaving her with an empty, coffee-coloured, transparent plastic container, the label wrapped around it listing the contents as estazolam.

Her mother kept numerous bottles of sleeping tablets on her shelf, all jammed in next to one another. Claire had taken an old one from the back, one she was sure her mother didn't use now that she'd moved on to more exciting pharmaceuticals with names like amitriptyline and doxepin, new prescriptions from a variety of different doctors that were supposed to improve her mood when it became clear she was suffering from something more than just a lack of sleep. None of them had worked, as far as Claire could tell.

She had filled the empty bottle half full with her tablets, the ones she and Nina had bought from Dan before they'd left Birmingham; enough to see them through the summer. When she got back, she was going to have to find another Dan nearer to where she lived, but that wouldn't be difficult. There were Dans everywhere; you just had to know where to look.

Nina had asked her to bring them, and Claire had done it without a second thought, until her bag had gone through the scanner. She'd been surprised the security guard hadn't been able to hear her heartbeat when that dog came out. She'd taken a half in the loos afterwards just to chill out, but as the contents of her stomach slide backwards and forwards, she's no longer sure it was such a good idea. She wipes a trickle of sweat off her forehead as Zoe returns holding a bottle of tequila, a knife and a salt cellar.

'Shots!' Claire squeals, and bangs on the table. 'I *love* tequila. Let's do it.'

Aiden puts his hands on the side of the pool and she watches him climb out, the water trickling off his body in small streams as he walks towards her, then changes direction and heads off across the patio to pick up one of the towels Nina has left in a pile on the outdoor sofa. She feels the thud of her heartbeat against her ribcage as she watches him dry himself off.

'We need lime wedges,' she says.

Nina points at one of the large terracotta pots that are positioned in various places on the terrace.

'There's limes and lemons. Help yourself.'

Claire picks a lime and slices into the bright green peel, the sharp tang of the zest making her salivate. Zoe walks into the kitchen again and comes out carrying a tray with six shot glasses. She holds one out to Will, and Claire sees their fingers touch as he takes it, Will's lingering a fraction of a second longer than he needs to. She looks at Aiden, but he is still standing with his back to her under the pergola, pulling on his T-shirt.

Claire takes a pinch of salt and sprinkles it on the back of her hand between her thumb and forefinger then licks it, grimacing at the taste. Zoe offers her a glass, but she waves it away and instead tips the bottle of tequila straight into her mouth and swallows.

'Lick, shoot, suck, right?' she says, and grins at Will before she bites into a lime wedge.

Nina doubles over with laughter, but Claire has turned away and watches Aiden as he walks across the patio, past her, and lies down on one of the loungers. The aftertaste of tequila burns in her mouth as Seb sits down next to him, blocking her view.

She passes the bottle over to Zoe and takes a long drag on her Marlboro Light, blowing the smoke out lazily in rings, her party trick. She watches Zoe fill up the glasses, then reach up and stroke Will's buzz cut. He ducks away, laughing, and she raises her glass towards his in a toast.

Claire runs her finger over the dimple at the side of her mouth and digs her nail into the small dent until she feels it pierce the skin. A combination of tequila, Ecstasy and frustration numbs the pain to the point she can barely feel it. It's almost as if Aiden has forgotten what happened in that final term. That without her, he'd have been completely fucked.

She cuts open another lime, presses down hard on the knife to slice it into quarters as she calls out to Zoe to turn up the music.

'Are we going to party, people, or what?' she shrieks.

She looks over at Aiden and he acknowledges her with

a brief smile before he turns away and grabs Nina, dancing with her in his wet boxer shorts.

It's only the first night.

Zoe cranks up the volume and the night begins to slip away into a blur. More shots. Swimming topless in the pool. Downing tequila straight from the bottle. Dancing on the table. Playing Truth or Dare. Lying on one of the teak loungers watching shooting stars. More shots. And then time stops being linear, turning instead into a juddering mishmash of random moments: flashes of images and isolated senses, the smell of jasmine, the taste of something bitter, the sound of hysterical laughter.

There's plenty of time.

Later, as she presses her finger against her cheek, relishing the sting of lime juice against the cut, she knows that no matter how many weeks she is here for, it won't be enough.

Chapter 8

July – 1989

The scream wakes Zoe up. She sits bolt upright and winces at the sunlight streaming through the gap in the long muslin curtains. For a few seconds she doesn't know where she is, lying in a four-poster bed, fully dressed in the clothes she was wearing last night. Her T-shirt reeks of stale perspiration, booze and smoke.

A sharp pain cuts into her head as she stares at the too bright white walls and dark wooden furniture, her tongue like a ball of cotton wool in her mouth. She staggers out on to the landing and swallows the hot liquid that rises up from her stomach.

Who was that?

'Claire?'

Her voice comes out as a croak as she walks clumsily down the staircase and into the huge open-plan living space where they ended up drinking last night when they came in from the terrace. It stretches across the entire back of the villa, at one end housing a large farmhouse-style kitchen with a twelve-seater dining table which is now covered in empty bottles and overflowing ashtrays. She has a sudden flashback to last night; holding hands with Nina on top of it while dancing to Whitney Houston.

She shuts her eyes briefly and takes a deep breath before walking past the two cream sofas in front of the stone fireplace. She squints at the painting that is hanging above the mantelpiece, a yellow canvas with lizards crawling over it, their small black eyes studying her intently.

More paintings hang on the walls and several alabaster sculptures of naked women sit on a wooden shelving unit. Their arms are flung out to either side as if they are falling, expressions of shock on their faces. She can't imagine ever owning somewhere like this. Every item has been carefully chosen, colour coordinated so nothing looks out of place, but still unique and original – rather than a room decorated with items chosen out of the Laura Ashley catalogue, which is about as upmarket as Zoe has ever seen at home. *Almost too perfect.*

Six sets of dark floor-to-ceiling double doors are spaced evenly at intervals along one wall, all leading out on to the patio area. One set has been propped open and she can see Nina and Claire lying on their backs on sun-loungers by the pool, the water a deep, clear turquoise that makes her want to slide into it and float on her back to ease the thumping in her head.

Will is sitting on one of the outdoor wicker sofas under the shade of the pergola that juts out over the patio. A discarded deck of playing cards is lying on the table in front of him. Zoe sees him looking at her and pulls her T-shirt down over her thighs, elongating the large black letters of 'CHOOSE LIFE' that are printed on the front.

'I thought I heard someone scream,' she says.

'That was Claire,' Nina says, raising herself up on one elbow. 'Seb threatened to tip her into the pool.'

'Afternoon, Cooper,' Seb says. 'Slightly overdid it on the tequila shots, did we?'

He's sprawled on the sofa opposite Will but turns his head in her direction, a trilby-shaped straw hat covering his damp blond hair. Zoe sits down in the only available space, next to Will, keeping as much distance between them as she can, wondering if she's going to throw up over Nina's patio.

Will pours a glass of water from a jug on the table, ice cubes clinking in the liquid, and pushes it towards her. Her hands tremble as she takes a sip and screws up her eyes against the sun, staring at the uninterrupted view of the sea and sky; endless shades of blue that stretch out ahead of her, merging together at some point in the distance.

'Gorgeous, isn't it?' Will says. 'Nina said they've got a gardener who looks after the grounds and another guy who does the pool.'

'Luis is our gardener,' Nina says. 'Comes in most mornings. And Mateo does the pool on a Tuesday. He's been with us since my parents bought the place. Barely spoke any English when he first started.'

Zoe looks around. The whole place is stunning and, if she didn't feel so awful, she'd be flat on her back on one of the sun-loungers. She can't remember the last time she felt this hung over, and it's not just the headache and the nausea. There's something else. A sense that she's forgotten something. *Last night is still hazy. What happened?*

She looks at Will. 'How come you're not suffering?'

He hesitates, his eyes not quite meeting hers. 'Because I didn't overdo it. I didn't want to feel like shit today,' he says. 'Nina has a big night planned tonight.'

Zoe's stomach turns over. 'Where's Aiden?' she asks.

'Probably gone for a run.' Nina rubs some sun cream across her forehead, then lies back down and adjusts her sunglasses. 'You know what he's like – never misses a day, even on holiday. Army life is going to suit him.'

'He's got a year or so before he starts all that,' Zoe says. 'He's got to qualify as a solicitor first.'

Everything in her head feels jumbled as she looks at the bougainvillea flowers, hundreds of pieces of crumpled bright pink tissue paper, and she has a sudden flashback to the sweet wrappers in her car. Shit. She forgot to call her mum. She glances at her watch. Twelve thirty. Eleven thirty in the UK.

'You going to come and sunbathe?' Nina asks. 'We've still got a few hours before we hit the town.'

'Can I use your phone first?' Zoe asks. Nina holds up her thumb in response. Zoe wonders whether her legs will support her if she tries to stand. She can feel Will watching her and wishes she could remember whether she talked to him last night and, if she did, what he said, but she can't; it's all a blur after the first few shots. She has another flashback to them all sitting in a circle on the living-room floor playing Truth or Dare, the three girls dancing, mascara running in inky trails down their faces in the heat, Claire holding out two tablets in the palm of her hand and Nina taking one. She chokes on a mouthful of water.

'You OK?' Will asks.

Zoe nods, coughing, and gets up slowly, sips on the clear liquid in her glass as she walks back inside, past one of the many herb-filled terracotta pots on the patio. The bitter liquorice scent of fennel fills her nostrils. She walks across the living room, quickens her pace on the stairs, then sprints into her en suite bathroom. She shoves the glass on the sink, throws herself down on her knees and empties the contents of her stomach into the pristine white toilet bowl, hoping no one by the pool can hear her.

'Did the carer remember to give you your medication?'

Zoe crouches on the landing by the phone, pushes her finger into the tight plastic spirals of the handset cord. She's wrapped in one of the thick, fluffy white towels that were hanging in her bathroom. It looks brand new and she tries not to think about the one her mum will have been dried with at home, threadbare in patches with a faded pattern and her old swimming badges sewn around the edge.

Her mum's voice sounds so much frailer than it does when they are face to face, the difficulty she has pronouncing words so much more evident when Zoe isn't standing in front of her, able to pick up on non-verbal cues. Despite her shower, she still feels grubby; the shame at not calling yesterday as she'd promised coats her skin in a layer she can't wash off.

'It's OK. No, not that big.' Zoe picks at the pink varnish that has chipped on her nail as one lie expands into another. There's no point in tormenting her mother with descriptions of something she'll never get to see.

'Yes, Claire and I are sharing . . . I'll try to take some

photos to show you when I get home. Nina brought her camera, I think. Look, I'd better go. I can't stay on too long. I'll call you tomorrow. Love you.'

Zoe hates the eagerness with which she puts down the phone. She shouldn't have left her. It makes it harder to go back now she knows what she is missing.

She peers out of the window, holding her towel around her, the ocean stretching away into the distance, its surface like sequins sparkling in the sun. The whole place is beautiful, despite her hangover. She grips the sill as her stomach contracts and tells herself it's the alcohol working its way out of her system rather than gnawing worry over what might have happened last night.

It's all still a blur.

She drops her towel and pulls on her bikini, her fingers trembling as she does up the clasp at the back.

Don't be stupid. Nothing happened.

She runs her hands through her hair, gathers it up into a ponytail and fixes it in place with her scrunchie before smiling at herself in the mirror.

'Nothing happened,' she repeats out loud. The words sound hollow, echoing in her head as she walks across the landing and down the stone stairs to join the others.

Chapter 9

Claire walks to where Nina is staring out over the bougainvillea-covered stone wall behind the pool. The villa is set on the edge of a cliff that drops away sharply, a hundred or so metres of grey rock dotted with pale green scrubland bushes until it reaches the sea that spreads out beneath them, teal at the edge, expanding through cerulean and cobalt, countless shades of blue that deepen the further out they go, until in the distance she can see they are almost black.

'What time did you crash?' Nina says. 'You look knackered.'

'Do I?' Claire adjusts her sunglasses. 'I don't remember. Not long after you.'

Nina touches Claire's cheek. 'You've cut yourself.'

'It's only a scratch. I must have caught it on something last night. Is that a jetty down there?' Claire points at something sticking out at the bottom of the cliff into the water.

Nina nods.

'You can get down to it by those steps.' She points at a gate further along the wall. 'But it's a trek back up again and there's no beach. It's where my parents keep their boat.'

'You have a boat?' Claire leans over the wall, stretching out to get a better view. Nina pulls on the back of Claire's bikini strap. Her fingers are cold from where she's been holding a drink, and Claire shivers.

'Careful,' Nina says. 'It's a hell of a drop.'

Claire walks over to the gate and slides back the bolt that's holding it shut. It's stiff and squeaks. Dozens of uneven steps carved into the rock fall away below her. There's a thick rope handrail attached to wooden posts on one side.

'Can I go down?' she asks.

Nina shrugs. 'If you want.'

The way she says it makes Claire hesitate, the patio stones feeling hotter than ever beneath the soles of her feet. She needs her flip-flops, but Nina is standing in her way. She leans to one side and lifts one foot off the floor a fraction, then switches to the other as Aiden appears from inside the villa.

'Want to come down to the jetty with me?' she asks.

'Already been,' Aiden says. 'I went early this morning, couldn't sleep.'

I know, Claire thinks. *I heard you.*

Nina stares at him. 'Did you?'

He nods. 'Luis . . . your gardener . . . said it was OK. I ran down, thought it would be a decent workout, but I had to walk on the way back up. You weren't kidding when you said it was steep. And I didn't have any music, which made it ten times harder. Have you seen my Walkman? I had it last night but can't find it now.'

'Nope.' They both say it at exactly the same time, but Claire doesn't meet Aiden's eyes.

44

He fiddles with the strap on his Swatch.

'Seb? Will? Either of you seen it?'

'No.' A resounding chorus.

Aiden rolls his eyes and disappears back inside the villa.

'You'll come down with me, Will, won't you?' Claire's voice has the whiny tone of a spoilt child, and Will shakes his head, engrossed in another game of blackjack with Seb.

Claire edges around Nina to retrieve her flip-flops from beneath her sunbed, defeated by the heat. She stands at the top of the steps that stretch out below her, the sun pressing down on her head, her desire to see the boat now shrivelled away into nothing. Nina is breathing heavily, as if she can't get enough air.

'Someone fell,' Nina says.

'What?' Claire sees Seb hesitate and glance at them over the top of his cards, shading his eyes under the brim of his hat.

'Years ago,' Nina says quickly. 'They think she must have slipped. They found her at the bottom of the steps. That's why my father had the handrail put in.'

Claire swallows, grips her flip-flops more firmly with her toes.

'Jeez, Nina. Did you know her?'

Nina shakes her head. 'It was just after my parents bought the place.'

'But to have someone die at your house . . . that's awful,' Claire says.

Nina shrugs. 'It was an accident. She shouldn't have been here.'

If it weren't for the fact Claire can see Nina is holding

45

on to the gate so tightly that her tendons have risen up on the inside of her wrist, she would question whether this is another one of her stories. Like the ones she used to tell at university when Claire was never sure just how much was truth and how much was embellished. How some guy who already had a girlfriend had been pestering her. How someone had followed her across campus back to their house and she'd had to wait in the dark until Seb got back. How she'd collapsed with stomach pains in the middle of a lecture and been rushed into hospital.

Claire had found out later that at least half the events Nina had told them about weren't true. She had never understood why Nina loved the *drama* so much. She already had all the attention anyone could wish for. She looks round as she hears Zoe come out of the patio doors, to a round of applause from Seb.

'She doesn't seem too bad, considering,' Claire says quietly.

Nina stares in her direction. 'I didn't think she'd drunk that much.' She hesitates. 'Although, to be honest, I don't remember much after we started playing Truth or Dare. I was hammered.'

'She wasn't drunk,' Claire replies. 'I dropped a half into one of her shots.'

'You didn't!' Nina's voice has that tone where Claire knows she's saying one thing but means another. She feels the warmth of her friend's admiration spread over her skin, dissolving the tension that was there before.

Claire smiles, the small scab on her dimple pulling tightly on her cheek. Nina isn't the only one who can make up stories. No one understands what she has had to sacrifice to be Nina's best friend – even changing degree course to be closer to her – but it's been worth it. Now people take notice of her. And she isn't going to let Zoe worm her way in.

She'd seen Zoe and Nina getting closer in those last few weeks of term, studying in the library and having lunch together, Nina fussing over her after everything that had happened with Will. Nina had even asked her *here*. But this holiday is going to put a stop to all that.

She feels Nina's hand on her arm.

'Let's go down to the jetty another time, yes? Maybe tomorrow morning, when it's cooler. Use the rest of today for a tanning session before tonight.'

Nina turns around, and Claire can't help noticing how she almost trips over in her eagerness to get away from the steps. She knows Nina doesn't remember what she'd said last night, doesn't realize how stories can become a confession, something to be stored away for later, to be told at the right moment.

Chapter 10

The taxi picks them up just as it's starting to turn dark. Stones pop and spit beneath the wheels of the Toyota van all the way up the track until they reach the main road, the scent of pine needles wafting in through the air-conditioning.

Zoe watches Will, sees the furrow between his eyebrows deepen as Claire's shrieks of laughter get louder. She can smell the distinctive scent of his Drakkar Noir aftershave and shakes away the memory from last night of his face leaning over hers, his hand on her cheek.

She must be imagining it. Muddling it up with memories from their house in Birmingham. He hasn't really looked at her properly since they arrived, and he's been avoiding her today. Sitting on a teak lounger on the terrace as far as possible away from her and getting out of the pool as soon as she got in.

The driver drops them in Deià, a few miles down the coast, where the views over the valley below take Zoe's breath away. She is still amazed that the heat of the day lasts this long into the evening, that she can be out in a sleeveless top and skirt and still be warm. The small town is nothing like the tacky nightclubs she'd imagined from photos of Magaluf. This place screams intimacy and sophistication. A cobbled road winds its way up the side of the Teix mountain, lit up by the shops, restaurants and bars, all built in the same style, with traditional beige stone walls and terracotta-tiled roofs. Their thick wooden doors are propped open, the sound of conversations spilling out on to the street.

'The locals call it Es Puig,' Nina says as Zoe looks around her. 'It means "it goes up" in Catalan.'

'It's beautiful,' Zoe says as Nina hands a fistful of notes through the window of the van, walking off before the man can give her the change. 'Is there somewhere I can cash some traveller's cheques?'

She'd changed quite a lot of money at the airport, but it isn't going to be nearly enough. Her throat had tightened earlier when Nina suggested the amount they should contribute to a kitty. More than her mum spent on food for a month at home.

Nina shrugs.

'I don't know, but we can ask in the pharmacy. I need to get some antihistamine cream anyway. We've got none in the villa and my legs got bitten to shit last night.'

Zoe stares at Nina's bronzed skin as they walk up the road. She can't see any tell-tale red lumps. Whenever Zoe gets bitten, she swells up like a balloon. Just the thought of it makes her skin itch. They stop outside one of the arched doorways and she sees Nina whisper something to Seb. He smiles as he takes his arm away from where it was encircling her waist.

'You guys wait here,' Nina says. 'We won't be a minute.'

She gestures for Zoe to go in ahead of her, and Claire follows. The pharmacist lifts up the wooden flap in the counter when he sees Nina come in and walks forward with a huge smile, his arms raised.

'Nina! *Cómo estás?*

He kisses her on both cheeks as the two of them proceed to have a conversation in Spanish. Nina sounds fluent. Another thing Zoe didn't know about her. Nina follows him to the back of the shop, where she ducks under the raised wooden flap, bends down in front of a woman in a wheelchair who is watching television and hugs her, squeezing her eyes shut with the effort. It's the most emotional Zoe can ever remember seeing her. Nina doesn't do displays of affection.

'My wife, Juliana,' the man says, smiling. Zoe looks at her and thinks of her mother at home, wonders what the carer will have made for her lunch, whether she's been outside today. The man looks at Zoe, misinterpreting why she is staring. 'She had an accident,' he says.

'I'm so sorry.'

Zoe's words come out too loudly in the small shop, and her face flushes. She wants him to know she's not being insincere, that she really is sorry, that she knows what it must be like trying to manoeuvre that chair around the narrow aisles in here, but can't find the right words.

Claire picks up a packet of paracetamol and takes it to the counter, fiddles in her purse to find the right coins. Zoe knows she doesn't need them – Claire has got every tablet she could ever want back at the villa – but she's grateful for the distraction; perhaps it will encourage Nina to hurry up so they can get out of here.

Nina says something in Spanish and the man answers as he puts a tube of antihistamine cream into a brown paper bag.

'Antonio says you can cash traveller's cheques at the

bank just up the road,' she says. 'But you'll have to wait until tomorrow. It's not open now.'

Zoe hopes she's got enough cash on her to last the evening.

'Antonio has known me since my parents bought the villa,' Nina says as they get outside. 'He's such a darling. Knows all the right people to get things at short notice. My mother said he was invaluable when they first came out here.'

'What happened to his wife?' Claire asks.

Nina hesitates. 'I think she was hit by a car. Now spends most of her time stuck in front of the TV. Tragic.'

Zoe thinks of the photos of her sister on the mantelpiece at home, a five-year-old girl with red bows in her bunches who would never get any older thanks to the man who decided to drive home after downing four pints.

Will turns away from her and looks in a shop window as Nina points further up the road to where groups of people are sitting outside on an upstairs veranda, hundreds of lights suspended from the ceiling at different heights, illuminating four bartenders who are throwing around cocktail shakers.

'That's where I've made a reservation,' Nina says. 'Shall we go?'

They are shown straight to a table, order drinks with fancy names that arrive in frosted glasses, rims dusted in salt and sugar. Zoe sips hers slowly, conscious of her earlier hangover as well as the prices scrawled on the menu. The place is buzzing. A woman smiles at her, glassy-eyed. She bets if she went to the toilets, she could run her finger across the cistern and find traces of white powder. No wonder Nina likes this place.

By 2 a.m., they are all downing shots of flaming sambuca, apart from Will, who is still sipping the same pint of lager he ordered after the first round of cocktails. Zoe can't remember ever seeing him drunk – or not properly drunk, like the rest of them. She has to stop herself from touching his head – there is something both unfamiliar and attractive about the roughness of his stubble since he shaved it. She wonders why he did it. Whether it was a way to put what had happened last term behind him. He had been as worried as she was; he just hadn't wanted to admit it.

She wishes she could do that, but the guilt sits inside her stomach, swilling around every time she thinks about it, alleviated only by alcohol.

Seb is chatting up some girl in a green silk dress at the side of the dance floor; she has her mouth pressed up against his ear and Zoe can see he's smiling, his eyes flickering away from hers every now and again towards her chest. His hand is around her waist, her dark hair falling in a sleek wave down her back.

Zoe slides off her seat, pulls on Will's arm, but he shakes his head as she stumbles on to the dance floor to join the others. She can see him watching her, which makes her laugh harder when Aiden says something, even though she can't hear him. She wants Will to think she's having the time of her life – which part of her feels like she is, the part that's full of cocktails and sambuca, but beneath that there is another part: a layer of emptiness.

And as her skin glistens with sweat and she looks back at him, she's sure he knows this, that he feels something similar. *But what does she know?* Just before he dumped her, she'd thought things had been going so well. If she hadn't already paid for the flights and if Nina hadn't been so insistent, she's not sure whether she would have even come here. She has a feeling Claire would rather she hadn't.

Seb comes on to the dance floor, hand in hand with the girl with dark hair.

'This is Gaby,' he shouts above the music. The girl smiles, and Zoe watches Nina run her eyes over her, up and down, the fixed expression on her face pronouncing judgement. She knows Nina too well. She might not want Seb for herself, but that doesn't mean he's allowed to show interest in someone else.

'Gaby says there's a beach party in one of the coves down the coast tomorrow night,' Seb says. 'To celebrate that thing you talked about . . . the fire –'

'Correfoc.' Nina and Gaby say the word at the same time, and Nina's eyes narrow.

'Yeah. That.' Seb laughs. 'We should go. All of us.'

Zoe watches as Nina smiles at him, her thoughts impossible to read.

'Maybe. I'll think about it.'

The DJ puts on Madonna's 'Like a Prayer', and Zoe links hands with Aiden as the guitar-riff intro played by Prince kicks in, presses the palms of their hands together, looking for a connection she knows she won't find. She glances back at Will, but he's talking to some girl who flicks her hair as she leans over the table. Over him.

Nina follows her as she leaves the dance floor and heads into the Ladies. She stands in front of one of the sinks and wipes away black streaks of mascara from beneath her eyes. Nina runs the cold tap, sticks a paper towel underneath it and tells Zoe to hold up her hair as she presses it on the back of her neck. Zoe wants to dissolve into the coolness, like she did in the pool earlier, submerging herself below the surface.

'I'm not surprised you feel like shit,' Nina says. 'Sambucas and cocktails on top of what you had last night.'

'I didn't drink that much,' Zoe says.

She tries thinking back to last night but she still can't remember much, nothing to explain the pounding headache and nausea she'd woken up with this morning.

'I'm not talking about the drink,' Nina says. 'I'm talking about the pills.'

Zoe twists round, pushes Nina's hand off her.

'What pills?'

Had she taken something? She might smoke the odd joint now and again, but she doesn't take pills. Not after that night out in Birmingham. She tries not to think about the way her foot had slipped on the canal bank, how one minute she'd been on the path and the next underwater, unable to breathe. She swallows.

Nina smiles, her bubble-gum-pink lipstick still immaculate.

'The ones you and Claire took.'

'But Claire knows I don't take Es.'

Nina shrugs as she dumps the paper towel in the bin and opens the door back to the bar, the draught of cool air making Zoe shiver.

'Maybe I've got it wrong,' she says. 'Forget I said anything.'

Chapter 11

July – 1989

The man moves in a way that mesmerizes Aiden. Beads of sweat cling to his neck, his lips opening to reveal bright white teeth as he raises his arms above his head in time with the music. Strobes highlight different parts of his body in slow motion and Aiden gets flashes of a shoulder, a cheekbone, fingers; shapes that stir something familiar in him, something he pushes back into the dark as he pretends not to stare.

Claire puts her hands on his shoulders, moving her hips closer to his, and it's all he can do to stop himself shoving her away. She smiles at him and he smiles back, fixing it on his face, keeping his eyes on the man as much as possible without it being obvious; quick glances where he captures the images, storing them away for later.

Claire reaches in her pocket for some gum and offers Aiden a piece. He takes it, biting his thoughts into tiny pieces alongside it, swallowing them so they disappear into what feels like a bath of hydrochloric acid that's bubbling in his stomach. Strong enough to dissolve most things. Even bones and teeth.

Will joins them in the heat and stickiness, drapes his arms around Claire so the two of them are dancing together to the thumping beat, blocking Aiden's view, and the man gets lost in the crowd. Aiden balls up his fists, a wave of frustration sweeping down the length of his spine.

'Where's Seb?' Claire shouts in Will's ear.

He points over to the table where they were sitting. Seb is kissing the girl with dark hair, his hands moving over her dress, making patterns like rippling water on the green silk.

'Where else?' Will asks.

Claire grins, but Will doesn't smile back. Aiden is too preoccupied to notice, searching the crowd, unable to find what he's looking for. Claire reaches for his hand, but he breaks away from the group and walks towards the toilets.

Will goes to follow him, but Claire grabs hold of his hand and doesn't let go, keeping him on the dance floor. He frowns as Aiden vanishes among the horde of people. Something isn't right. He can tell by the way Aiden won't keep still. Fiddling with his Swatch, picking at the skin around his fingernails. The others haven't noticed, but he has; he knows him better than they do and he also knows what Aiden is likely to do when he gets like this. Something stupid. Like getting into a fight. He'll give him five minutes, and if he isn't back by then he'll go after him. Whether Claire has let go of his hand or not.

The urinals either side of Aiden are empty as he stands and looks at his face in the mirror.

'C–c–c–coward.' His reflection stares back at him, eyes widening at the sound of the stutter he thought he'd got rid of years ago. He takes a step back and punches the wall beside the glass. The door opens behind him and Seb walks in. Aiden lowers his head and covers his grazed knuckles with his other hand, anger bubbling under his skin.

He had hoped Seb was someone else, but what would be the point? He wouldn't say anything, do anything, even if it had been. He shuts his eyes briefly, blocking out what he can see in the mirror, something invisible to everyone except him.

'All right?' Seb asks.

Aiden nods, unsure whether the words in his head are going to get stuck again when he tries to say them.

'Nina wants to make a move,' Seb says. 'Do you want to stay a bit longer?' For a fleeting moment Aiden thinks he's been given a second chance, and an hour that will never happen unrolls in his imagination, snapshots of flesh and sweat and sunburned skin. Then he remembers the uniform that's waiting for him, the same one worn by his father and his father before that, and for a second, he can't breathe, the shock as brutal as when he'd shut his hand in a car door when he was younger.

'We should probably make a move,' he says, watching his lips move in the mirror as the words tumble out without hesitation. 'Go back to the villa for shots?'

Seb grins.

'I'm up for that, Buckley,' Seb says. 'Gaby's going to come back with us too. Should be a good night.'

Seeing Seb now, Aiden can almost forget how angry he was after what happened in that final term. *Almost, but not completely*. He can still remember Will having to physically restrain Seb after they saw what was hidden in his wardrobe, can remember hearing Seb rant to Nina, pacing up and down in her room. They'd agreed to an uneasy truce so as to focus on their finals, and the horror had dulled a little under the intensity of exams. But if it hadn't been for the fact they all knew it had been Nina's idea in the first place, he's not sure whether he'd be here now.

Seb zips up his chinos and slaps Aiden on the back as he walks out. Aiden looks at his reflection again and licks the graze on his knuckles, allows himself to imagine it's the man's skin under his tongue instead, and wonders what the others would say if he didn't come back with them to the villa.

Chapter 12

July – 1989

Zoe loses Aiden somewhere in the crowd as she leaves the bar. She waves at the others to go on and they grab one of the local taxis queuing up outside. Will hangs back, waiting for her. Part of her wishes he hadn't; she's too tired to face any awkwardness on the journey home, but the other part feels a bubble of excitement that he's chosen to stay. Aiden finally reappears and they jump into a cab.

The six of them invariably seem to divide up in this way; Nina and Seb never not together, Claire always following Nina. They are like creases on a piece of paper; once made, they now fold in exactly the same place over and over again.

Zoe can see the taxi Nina and the others are in ahead of them, its number plate lit up intermittently in their headlights as it weaves along the bends of the coastal road. The heat settles around her, softer at this time of night. She wants to confront Claire, to ask her face to face about what Nina had said in the toilets at the bar. She thinks of the security guard by the scanner at the airport, of what could have happened if he'd picked Claire's rucksack up off the conveyor belt, of what she herself might have swallowed last night, and shivers.

Aiden puts his arm around her.

'You OK?'

She nods. Will leans forward in his seat and turns to look at her.

'You sure?'

'Yes.' The word comes out more sharply than she'd intended. 'Was I totally out of it last night?' She stares at Will as she asks the question, knowing Aiden will reply with something reassuring no matter what state she was in. Despite what they've said to each other in the past, she hopes Will can be honest with her, but then she remembers his face, leaning over hers while she lay sprawled on her four-poster bed in the villa, and wonders whether he is the right person to be asking at all.

'Yes,' he says. 'But everyone was,' he adds, his cheeks flushed. 'As you'd expect after that many shots.'

'You weren't,' she snaps back.

He doesn't reply.

'Did I do something stupid?' she asks.

''Course you didn't.' Aiden pulls her closer to him, but she continues to look at Will, watching something unfamiliar flicker over his face, disguised by the shadows from the cars that pass them in the opposite direction. She holds her breath, waiting for his judgement.

'No,' he says finally.

She sits back and stares out of the window at the ocean, unconvinced. The lights further down the coast elongate and blur into odd shapes as her eyes well up.

The truth seems to have twisted into something unrecognizable that slips further out of her grasp every time she reaches for it.

*

Nina is floating on a lilo in the pool when they get back, still dressed in her bright pink polka-dot ra-ra skirt and off-the-shoulder top, the water glowing an iridescent blue beneath her. Zoe can see the dolphin mosaic on the bottom lit up by the underwater spotlights. Claire hangs on to the edge of the inflatable; her dress has turned see-through, her underwear now visible, her wet hair forming ringlets in the water as she calls out to Aiden and Will to get in and join them.

The scent of night-blooming jasmine wafts across the terrace, and Zoe can hear cicadas in every direction, their chirping filling her head.

She goes inside to get a bottle of water from the fridge, wanting something to dilute the alcohol that's swilling around in her stomach after the taxi ride, and hears Claire shriek as Seb cannonballs into the pool, tips Nina off the lilo and splashes both girls with water. The noise grates against her still-fragile brain. She slips off her shoes and goes upstairs, listening to their voices that drift in through the open windows.

Claire's bedroom is next to hers, and she presses down on the wrought-iron handle on the door, bracing herself for it to squeak, but it opens silently. She steps inside, leaving it ajar so the light from the landing spills into the room. Claire's rucksack is slung over the back of a chair and she walks over to it, unclips the fastening and reaches into the pockets. A packet of Durex, some chewing gum, Body Shop kiwi fruit lip balm, Marlboro Lights and several cassettes with mix-tapes recorded on them. No pills. She fastens the bag back up and hangs it on the chair.

Claire's window overlooks the pool, and Zoe peers out

through the white muslin curtains identical to the ones in her room. The airy fabric shifts in the slight breeze. She watches Seb shake himself off as he gets out of the water, stick his T-shirt back on and walk back inside the villa, where she can hear Will, Claire and Aiden prising off beer caps in the kitchen.

'I think my dad looks after your pool,' she hears Gaby say to Nina from where she's sitting on the outdoor sofa. 'I remember coming here with him when he was working, years ago. I was only about seven or eight. Your mum gave me a glass of orange juice and we played with the hose.'

Nina trails one hand lazily in the water, making ripples as the lilo glides across the surface. 'Small world,' Nina says. 'I don't remember you being here, sorry. My parents had people traipsing in and out all the time. They needed work doing on the villa and it was cheaper to get it done locally rather than flying people out from home. The language barrier was a bit of an issue, of course, but my mother loves teaching English. *Mi casa es tu casa*, as she always used to say.' She smiles at Gaby, as if she's now remembering. 'Which still applies, of course.'

The others reappear on the terrace. Seb hands Gaby a beer and she curls up beside him, her arm around his waist. Will flops down opposite them, picks a deck of cards up from the table and deals them out. Zoe can see that Aiden isn't paying attention; he keeps glancing around the patio rather than looking at his cards.

There's a short pause before she hears Gaby ask, 'So will you come to the beach party tomorrow night?'

'I'm up for it,' Seb replies. 'Do you guys fancy it?'

'Where?' Aiden says.

'Just down the coast,' Gaby says. 'You'll come, Nina, won't you? It's going to be a great night. One to remember. Please?'

Nina looks over from where she's still stretched out on the lilo. Zoe sees her mouth twitch when Gaby says, 'please,' in a strong Spanish accent. If Nina doesn't go, the rest of them won't either. And perhaps because Gaby acknowledges this, Nina slides silently into the water, swims to the side of the pool to get out, wraps herself in a towel and takes a swig of the beer Seb is holding before perching on the seat next to her.

'Seeing as you've asked so nicely, we'll come,' Nina says. 'It'll be good for these guys to experience a traditional festival. Tick that culture box.'

Zoe can see Nina is smiling and wonders what's in it for her. *You're being unfair. She helped you pick up the pieces after Will dumped you. Persuaded you to still come out here.* Zoe crosses her arms. Maybe she's jealous. Just because she can't imagine being able to afford this villa doesn't mean she has to think the worst of someone who can. Maybe it is as simple as Nina wanting them all to have a good time.

She steps away from the muslin curtains, trying to ignore the memory of the mask pressed up against the window of the Jeep that flashes into her head.

She searches through Claire's washbag. Nothing. She should just ask her instead of poking around in her things. But does she trust her not to lie? She remembers the way she'd acted when they went through security at Manchester airport as if there had been nothing to worry about – until the dog had appeared. *No*, she thinks, *I don't*. She sits down on the edge of the bed, her cheeks flushed.

'You fucking lucky bastard,' she hears Seb shout.

Will laughs. 'It's skill, mate. Not luck. Don't play if you can't stand losing.'

Seb mutters something in reply, and Zoe looks out of the window again, sees him and Gaby go inside the villa. She walks towards Claire's door and is about to step out on to the landing when she hears footsteps coming up the stairs. She freezes, her heart pounding, and runs through excuses to justify being in here, dismissing them one by one. The footsteps go silent. She strains to hear the voices from downstairs, trying to work out who is up here with her, and waits, not daring to breathe.

Then as the footsteps go back downstairs, she notices something sticking out from beneath Claire's pillow. She pulls out a small brown bottle, clicks and unscrews the lid, tips it upside down, and a couple of tablets fall out into the palm of her hand, smiley faces and tiny hands indented into the surface of each one.

Nina had been telling her the truth. Claire *had* brought them out here with her. Why had she risked doing something so stupid? Did she realize what would have happened if she'd been caught? To Zoe, as well as her? Her hands shake with anger as she tips the pills back into the bottle, screws on the lid and puts it back under Claire's pillow. She needs to talk to her, find out if she'd given her one of these last night.

As she walks out of the room, she notices Nina's bedroom door is firmly shut. The same way hers should be; just as she left it before they went into town and how it had been when she let herself into Claire's room.

Except hers isn't. It's wide open, and when she peers inside she can see Claire sitting on her bed, Aiden's Walkman beside her.

Zoe stares at her. 'What are you doing in my room?'

'I could ask you the same thing.'

Zoe's cheeks burn. *She knows.*

'Did you put something in my drink last night?'

Claire looks at her, her expression unreadable. 'Like what?'

'Like an E.'

'Of course not,' Claire says.

Zoe hesitates, trying to work out how to ask the questions she has about the airport without telling Claire she's been poking around in her things, but can't find a way to do it.

She points at the Walkman in the awkward silence that follows.

'Aiden's been looking for that. Why didn't you tell him you had it?'

'I needed to borrow it, but I didn't want anyone to know.'

'Why?'

Claire lowers her voice until it's almost a whisper. 'Do you think Nina always tells the truth?'

Zoe frowns. 'What do you mean?'

'Like last night, for example. What she said when the three of us were playing Truth or Dare.'

Zoe tries to think back to last night, but everything is a still a jumble of images and noise. Will's eyes on hers.

What is Claire talking about?

'You don't remember, do you?' Claire asks.

Zoe hesitates, and Claire runs her hand over the duvet cover, smoothing it out as she stands up.

'Forget it. It doesn't matter. I didn't get what I needed anyway. The recording was fuzzy when I played it back and you can't hear it properly.'

She walks out, leaving Zoe with a sense that she has uncovered one thing, only to find out there is something worse lurking underneath.

Chapter 13

July – 1989

Will lies awake in the dark, his heartbeat thrumming in his chest in time with the ceiling fan circling above him. He can hear Claire's voice through the wall, muffled, like his ears are full of cotton wool. She's been talking to Nina for ages. Or it feels like she has. Time is doing that funny slippage thing when it bends in on itself in the dark, folding over and over until he can't be sure how long he's been listening.

What's she saying? Maybe he doesn't want to know?

It sounds like Nina is trying to reassure her about something, but he wishes Claire would just fuck off back to her own room or go and annoy Seb further down the corridor so he can go to sleep.

He'd thought Nina and Seb were a couple when he first met them. Everyone did. They were always together. A perfect match. Like models out of the pages of the Next directory. Both blond. Both with attitude and razor-sharp cheekbones. But then he'd stood next to Nina and watched Seb snogging some girl on a dance floor on a university night out and realized they weren't actually *together*. Not like that. But he'd never seen two people so close who weren't shagging each other. Nina spent evenings curled up on Seb's lap in front of the TV at their house while he played with her hair, looping it in and out of his fingers. Like brother and sister – or how you'd imagine a close sibling relationship to be. Andy is eight years older than him and they've only spoken a handful of times in the last few years. Seen each other even less.

He turns on to his side, trying to find a cool spot on his pillow. His sheet lies in a bundle at the bottom of the bed where he's kicked it off, too hot to bear anything touching his skin, even the crisp white freshly laundered cotton. The fan pushes the heat around the room, buffeting him in waves. The sound of Claire and Nina's voices through the wall drills into his head, the noise stopping and starting, too inconsistent a pattern to allow him to drift off.

He gives up trying, gets out of bed and walks past Nina's room, pauses at the top of the stairs to look out of the window. The pool glows like a giant blue lamp in the darkness, the surface of the water unnaturally still, as if it's waiting for something. The sky stretches out to the horizon, sprinkled with stars, and he can't tell where it meets the sea; they merge together somewhere in the blackness.

He remembers his mum holding him up at his bedroom window at home when he was little, his brother kneeling on a chair beside them, wiping off the condensation that ran down the single-glazed panes with a towel they kept on the sill, pointing out the various constellations. They were allowed to make one wish each, and he'd listened to his mother's, whispered under her breath. He'd never asked Andy what his was. He doesn't even know if he made one. He wonders whether Andy gets the chance to look at the sky now. If he can, Will knows it'll only be a tiny section of the vast expanse, one small piece of a jigsaw that means nothing when you can't see the whole picture.

He goes silently down the staircase, the marble flooring cool on his bare feet, and walks into the kitchen, opens the door of the fridge, takes out a bottle of water and pulls off the blue plastic top with his teeth, swigging gulps of the cold liquid without bothering to get a glass. He catches a movement out of the corner of his eye and turns around to find Zoe sitting on one of the wooden chairs by the table, staring at him.

'Sorry,' he says. 'I didn't realize you were down here.'

She shrugs. 'You've as much right to be here as I have.'

'I couldn't sleep,' he says finally.

'Me neither,' Zoe says. 'Too hot.'

'Yeah. That and Nina and Claire chatting away next door. I think Claire is fluthered.'

Zoe smiles, and Will knows what she's thinking. That word. *Fluthered.* Something only he would say. The kind of thing he used to come out with every now and again when they were together. He'd once said to her that he'd picked up phrases like that from his dad, who grew up in Dublin, but had then changed the subject – just as he always did when she asked anything about his family.

He stares at her, as if he's reading her thoughts.

'Look,' he says. 'I'm sorry about . . . you know . . . before we left . . .' He trails off as he realizes how green her eyes are. He notices it each time he looks at her – really looks at her – and then never quite believes it until he sees them again.

She blinks. 'You shouldn't wind Seb up like that,' she says, changing the subject.

69

Will can feel the water he's swallowed sitting heavy in his stomach and reaches for the chair beside her.

'I didn't.'

'Yes, you did. It's like you have to prove something to him. You don't have to make it quite so obvious that you get on better with Aiden.'

Will doesn't answer. He can't explain why Seb annoys him sometimes; how he doesn't realize how lucky he is, with his dad being the CEO of some firm in the City and a job waiting for him when they get back from this holiday. He has no idea what it's like to live with uncertainty, to have responsibilities you never signed up for. Wanting to beat him at cards is petty, but he can't help himself.

Sometimes he feels she knows him better than he knows himself. Her green eyes stare at him and he feels his fingers tremble as he grips the bottle of water.

'Zoe, there's something . . .'

She turns her head away to look out of the patio doors, and the opportunity to speak disappears with her movement.

'Did you hear that?' she whispers.

'What?' The silence roars in Will's ears, as if he's underwater. Zoe pushes back her chair, walks over to the glass and stares out over the pool.

'It sounded like someone coming up the steps.'

Will gets up and stands next to her, their arms almost touching, the smallest gap between them. So easy to lean across. The surface of the turquoise water in the pool is as smooth and motionless as it had been when he'd looked out of the window upstairs.

'I can't see anything,' he says.

'There was something. A rustling noise.'

Will puts his hands on the glass and stares out into the darkness. He remembers the shadow by the bushes Zoe saw when they first got here and something crawls across the back of his neck. Nina's gardener? The thought that someone had been watching them when they arrived was one of the reasons he hadn't got as hammered as the rest of them on the first night. He hadn't wanted his reflexes slowed, his speech slurred, his reaction times impaired. He's only too aware of the consequences of drinking too much. But it hadn't stopped what had happened last night, and he doesn't think Zoe can even remember.

Thank God.

'There's nothing out there now.' He wonders if she really had heard something, or whether it was an excuse so she didn't have to listen to what he was going to say. They'd drawn lines, visible only to each other, silently agreeing not to cross them in order to get through this holiday. He wants things to be back the way they were before.

You only have yourself to blame for that.

He wonders if he should tell her about the conversation he'd had with his mum at Gatwick, try to explain. His mind jumps to a prison cell; to being in a tiny space for twenty-three hours a day, four steps from one wall to the other, memories of having to leave his belongings in a locker, of hard plastic seats, of the distinctive smell of unwashed male bodies. He runs his hand over the stubble of his buzz cut. She wouldn't understand.

There's a sudden noise from outside, one that he hears as clearly as Zoe this time, and all the lights on the patio, including those in the pool, go out. Zoe puts her hand over her mouth and Will hears the catch in her breath. He wants to do something to protect her but can't bring himself to move.

He thinks of this moment afterwards; the missed opportunity; the small gaps between them that he could have erased by just reaching out. How differently he'd do things if he could go back and start all over again.

A figure appears at the glass in the patio door. Will steps backwards, away from the window, his fists clenched. Zoe's eyes widen as the handle turns on the patio door and Aiden limps into the living room.

Chapter 14

'Aiden! What the hell are you doing?' Zoe hisses, taking her hand away from her mouth. 'You're soaking!'

He is naked apart from his boxer shorts and stares at them, small pools of water gathering on the floor around his feet.

'I went for a swim,' he says. His cheeks are flushed as he slicks his wet hair back from his face. Will has a sudden flashback to him walking through the door of their house in Birmingham with a similar wild-eyed look on his face, and his stomach tightens in fear.

'But you weren't in the pool,' Will says.

He glances through the patio doors, expecting to see ripples in the surface of the water, but from what he can make out it's still as flat as glass. Something catches his eye, a movement in the shadows, but when he looks more closely, it's gone.

'Sorry about the lights. I think I tripped over a wire or something,' Aiden says.

Will walks over to the kitchen counter, grabs a towel off the folded pile of laundry and throws it at Aiden, who wraps it round himself. He flicks the light switches on and off, a clicking noise that echoes in the silence, but the patio outside remains in darkness.

'Where did you swim?' Zoe asks. Her words come out like an interrogation, and Aiden shivers, the flesh on his arms standing up in goosebumps.

He hesitates. 'Off the jetty,' he says finally.

Zoe frowns. 'You went all the way down there in the dark?'

'There are lights by the steps,' Aiden says. 'I couldn't sleep.' He stares at Will with such intensity that Will wonders for a moment if Aiden saw him looking out of the window before he came downstairs, whether he can read his thoughts.

'Why didn't you just get in the pool?' Will asks.

'I didn't want to wake anyone.' Aiden glances out of the patio doors into the darkness, as if he's looking for something.

'You scared the shit out of us,' Zoe says. Aiden winces, and Will notices his leg is bleeding; a red stripe appears on the towel when he dries himself off.

'I scraped it on the jetty when I got out,' he says.

Zoe goes over to the counter, rips off a couple of pieces of kitchen roll and bends down beside Aiden, pressing them against the cut. Will feels his skin tingle in false anticipation.

'Don't fucking go down there again without telling someone, Aide,' she says. 'You could have drowned.'

He nods but continues to look at the terrace, his hands trembling.

Will thinks Aiden must be cold, that swimming at night in the sea hadn't been as easy as he'd thought it would be, even for someone as fit as him. It isn't until after he has walked past Seb's door on the way back to his room, ignoring the moans of pleasure he can hear coming from inside, and is lying back in his own bed that he realizes it wasn't cold he'd seen in Aiden's body language at all. It was desire.

'Pass me one, will you?' Claire sits up on her sunbed, leaving a damp indent in the fabric cushion and squinting as she holds out her hands for a Marlboro Light. Nina throws her the packet, followed by her Zippo lighter. 'Anyone else?' Claire's words come out slurred as she tries to speak and light up at the same time.

Will shakes his head as Aiden appears at the patio doors carrying a plastic bag.

'I've left the Jeep keys in the bowl in the hall by the front door,' Aiden shouts.

'Great,' Nina replies. 'Did you drop Gaby back into Deià OK?'

He nods. 'She said her dad won't be happy she stayed out.' He looks over at Seb, who is lying on a sunbed with his straw hat tipped over his face. 'You know she's only seventeen, right?'

'And?' Seb mumbles. 'I didn't force her to stay.'

'Never a good idea to get too close to the locals, Seb,' Nina says. 'They can get rather attached. My dad said he had problems getting rid of a couple of the guys they got in to build the steps down to the jetty here. Thought they'd been hired permanently when he only needed them for a few weeks. It all got very messy.'

Aiden walks over to Nina's sunbed and holds open the plastic bag. 'Look what I got,' he says. 'Fireworks! For tonight.'

Nina rummages through the dozens of packets. 'Think you got enough?'

'We can always save some to have here later,' Aiden says. 'I went for a walk around Deià. All the way down to the beach, where there was this beautiful cove. Crystal-clear water. You can see straight to the bottom. It was like swimming in an aquarium. And did you know Robert Graves is buried here? I saw his tombstone.'

Nina looks at him blankly.

'The poet,' he says.

She shrugs. 'Never heard of him.' Claire flips open the lid of the packet and offers Aiden a Marlboro Light.

He shakes his head. Running is Aiden's drug. Hours and hours spent pounding the pavements when they were living together at university; up before dawn and back before most of the house had even woken up. Will doesn't understand how he doesn't find it boring but presumes he's expected to do that kind of thing if he's going to join the army after qualifying as a solicitor. Aiden had told him how much he wants to follow in his father's footsteps. Make it to Colonel. Will had noticed the way he lifted his chin and moved his shoulders back when he talked about it and felt a squeeze of envy. He doesn't know where his dad is, let alone if he has a job.

He jumps up suddenly and grabs the side of Seb's sun-bed, lifting it up in an attempt to tip him into the pool. There's a moment when it looks like Seb might be able to cling on and save himself; the chair hesitates in its arc of motion, wobbling on two legs, trying to decide whether it's going over or will fall back the same way it went up, but momentum wins out and Seb falls into the water, reappearing a couple of seconds later, his sodden T-shirt clinging to his skin.

'You total fucker, Lawson,' he says, wiping his eyes.

Will stands grinning on the side of the pool while everyone else laughs. Seb wades over to the steps and climbs out, leaning over to fish out his wet straw hat from where it's floating in the water.

'You wait,' Seb says. 'There will be retribution when you're least expecting it.' He's smiling, but there's an edge to his voice.

'Chill out, mate. It's only water,' Will says.

Seb flips his sunbed back over the right way and sticks the soaking-wet cushion on the ground to dry, hesitating before he pulls his T-shirt off over his head. He lies down on the wooden slats, but not before Will has noticed the four small red circular marks lined up next to one another in a neat row across the top of his back, almost as if someone has pressed their fingertips into his skin.

Will swallows, his laughter dissolving in his throat. He's never seen those marks before. He flicks back through his memories but can't think of a single one where Seb wasn't wearing a top. Even coming out of the bathroom in their house, he'd always had a towel slung round his neck. Seb stares at him and raises one hand up by his forehead to shade his eyes from the sun.

'I mean it, Lawson,' Seb says. 'It's your turn next.'

Chapter 15

July – 1989

Zoe watches Claire mirror Nina's movements through half-closed eyes from her position on a sun-lounger; the way Nina holds her cigarette, the way she blows out the smoke when she exhales. She knows Claire would like to *be* Nina if only she had the chance. She buys the same make-up, listens to the same music, claims to fancy Rob Lowe.

Zoe knows how exhausting it is to try and live inside someone else's skin. To feel their life is so much better than yours. She's spent the last three years playing various characters in drama productions, almost believing she was them for a while, hoping she might end up forgetting who she was in the first place. But now all that's over. Now she's moving back home and there's an emptiness inside her when she thinks about living with her mum and working in the local supermarket, a fear that this is now her life.

Claire laughs at something Nina says, and Zoe allows her eyes to fully shut and pretends she's asleep, the brightness of the sun making patterns on the inside of her eyelids.

It's as if their chat on her bed last night never happened.

She's tempted to sit up and confront her, to demand to know exactly what was said in that game of Truth or Dare, to ask whether Claire had dropped one of her

78

ecstasy tablets in her drink. *Why can't she remember?* But she knows that Claire will deny it, Nina will take Claire's side, as always, and it'll ruin the beach party tonight. They're only here for two weeks. Maybe she should just let it go. Focus on having a good time, not give Claire another reason to make her the odd one out.

Zoe taps on Nina's bedroom door, a bottle of vodka in one hand, her make-up bag in the other. She can hear Nina and Claire inside and 'Girls Just Wanna Have Fun' playing at full volume.

'I just need to *know*, you know?' Claire says.

'Uh huh.' Zoe can picture Nina pouting in the mirror as she outlines her lips with her favourite Max Factor pencil, a couple of shades darker than her lipstick.

'I thought once finals were done . . .'

Nina's voice. 'Just ask. You're never going to get a better opportunity.'

Zoe knocks harder on the door, a couple of loud raps, and then turns the handle.

'Can I come in?' she asks. 'I brought vodka.'

'You star.' Nina takes the bottle and kisses her on the cheek. Zoe thinks she sees a flash of annoyance in Claire's eyes as Nina unscrews the cap and swallows a mouthful, but she doesn't care. This evening she wants to forget about whatever Claire has done and focus on having fun. Deal with it tomorrow. 'Going to get ready with us in here?' Nina asks. Zoe nods. Nina unzips her make-up bag and tips it out on to the bed.

'Help yourself,' she says. Zoe picks out a couple of lipsticks, layering frosty pink on top of shimmering purple, pressing her lips down on to a piece of toilet paper between each application. She leaves her own make-up bag with its inch-long stub of black eyeliner pencil and cheap Cover Girl foundation unopened on the side of Nina's dressing table and rubs at her cheek, trying to get rid of the lipstick mark Nina has left on her skin.

Claire turns up the stereo even louder. Nina sings into the bottle of vodka like it's a microphone, then passes it to Zoe, who delivers the song's chorus pitch-perfectly before Claire grabs the bottle back off her and Nina covers her ears.

'You're screeching!' Nina shouts over the music, and rolls her eyes at Zoe. Claire shrugs, pretending she doesn't care before turning her head upside down and spraying her hair liberally with Elnett, filling the room with the distinctive smell. Nina wrinkles her nose as she fastens the backs on to a pair of black lightning-bolt earrings.

She takes another swig of vodka and pushes the bottle back into Zoe's hands, but the song is ending and Zoe shakes her head when Nina tells her to sing again, knowing the moment has passed, leaving behind a dizzy feeling, as if she's stood up too fast. She doesn't even care when she sees that her make-up bag has been opened and one of her lipsticks is lying on its side without its case, the sharp red point squashed down to a squat stump.

Zoe half wishes they didn't have to go out at all. She's breathless from laughing, her stomach bubbling with happiness. Her mother's face has shrunk again, disappearing to the back of her brain, so far away she can almost pretend she doesn't exist at all.

'I'm so glad we're here,' Claire says. She looks at Zoe. 'I told you it would be OK, didn't I?'

Zoe knows exactly what she's talking about. Remembers the jolt of horror when Aiden had opened his wardrobe, but it doesn't seem important now. They're in the most stunning villa in Mallorca and her life at home is hundreds of miles away.

There is something fierce among the three of them this evening, the intimacy that exists only between girls, the personality traits that sometimes dig into each other like sharp needles smoothed out by the vodka. Nina envelops both Zoe and Claire in a hug before they leave the room and for a moment Zoe thinks she sees her eyes well up.

Nina's bed is strewn with discarded tops and bikinis that didn't make the grade, eyeshadow palettes, bottles of Lou Lou, Opium and Poison. Zoe hesitates in the doorway, knowing she doesn't have many more nights like this, that the holiday won't last for ever. Claire puts her hand on the small of Zoe's back, a sudden coolness against her skin, and ushers her out of the room, shutting the door behind them. Nina is waiting for them at the top of the stairs. She reminds Zoe of a figure in a stained-glass window, her blonde hair lit up by a shaft of evening sunlight.

Zoe will think back to this moment afterwards, will imagine what could have happened if they'd stayed in, dancing around Nina's bedroom, and will wish more than anything in the world that they had never left.

Chapter 16

July – 1989

'No fucking way, Lawson.' Seb throws his cards down on the coffee table in the living room as Will laughs, the noise mingling with the humming of the cicadas that he can hear through the open patio doors as the sun starts to set. Will picks up the pile of pesetas Seb has put down as a bet.

'You snooze, you lose, Seb. What can I say?'

He slides the coins into his wallet as Seb watches him, a tight smile fixed on his lips.

'What does that make the total so far this holiday?' Will asks. 'Fourteen to one?'

'Fourteen to two,' Seb says. 'I beat you on the plane on the way out.'

'Well, as you don't seem to be having a lot of luck, I'll let you have that one. We won't mention the fact you cheated by looking at my cards.'

Seb's smile slides off his face. 'I didn't cheat. And winning streaks always end at some point.' He leans over the table and lowers his voice. 'Make the most of it while it lasts, eh?' He puts his hand on Will's shoulder, squeezes it tightly.

'Shall we go, people?' Nina asks. She sweeps down the stairs, Claire and Zoe following behind. Seb stands up, holds out his arm for her to take in one of his typically overly dramatic gestures. Will sees Aiden grin nervously and fiddle with the strap of his Swatch, clearly relieved something has distracted Seb from the game of cards.

He knows Aiden doesn't like it when there's tension between the two of them; for someone who says he wants to join the army, it's ironic that he steers clear of conflict.

The heat is less intense as the sun touches the horizon, a yellow ball that looks as if it could set the surface of the ocean ablaze at any second. Nina locks the doors, and the six of them head across the patio, past the motionless surface of the pool, past one of the lemon trees with its glossy green leaves in a terracotta pot at the top of the steps. Will breathes in the heavy smell of jasmine that mingles with the girls' perfume in the air.

Seb carries the boombox he's brought out of the living room, the lascivious lyrics of Salt-N-Pepa's 'Push It' being shouted by the girls as the song blasts out of the speakers. Will can see the tops of the two bottles of Absolut vodka Nina has taken out of the freezer poking out of the raffia beach bag she's slung over one shoulder, the glass misted up and slippery, covered in beads of condensation. Claire had insisted two wouldn't be enough and is carrying another, Will has the beach towels and Aiden's got the fireworks he bought earlier, packets of sparklers and a few Roman candles. The firecrackers have been left behind at the villa for later. Will sees the carrier bag full of cans bump against Zoe's calf as she walks and watches Nina grip the rope handrail tightly all the way down the steps, not letting go until she reaches the jetty.

The boat is around ten metres long, a white fibreglass

hull that's shaped like a bullet cut in half lengthways, pointed at one end. He had been expecting something with a sail, but this is engine-powered. A speedboat. Very flash. He can't imagine how much it must have cost. There's space for two people at the front beneath the windscreen that tilts backwards at an angle and white leather seats at the back of the boat form three sides of a rectangle for everyone else to lounge on. A red-and-blue painted stripe encircles the entire hull which has 'Sunseeker' written in capital letters on one side, 'Nina' in large black italics below it.

The cassette tape in the boombox comes to a sudden stop as they stand on the wooden planks of the jetty and stare at the boat.

'Fucking hell,' Will says.

Nina looks at him.

'Haven't you seen a boat before, Will?'

'Not one like this.'

'My parents got it last year,' Nina says, 'but they hardly ever use it. They usually keep it out of the water on the jetty, but I asked Luis to get it ready for us. He's always asking for extra work.' She climbs on board and presses the blower switch. Will follows, dumps his pile of towels on one of the seats. He stares at the instruments in front of him, a panel covered in switches and dials.

'Come on, Lawson,' Seb says, standing behind him and looking over his shoulder. 'You said you'd driven one of these things before.'

'I have,' he says. 'But it was ages ago. And it wasn't this big.'

'If you've lost your nerve,' Seb says, 'I'll do it.' He

nudges him out of the way and steps in front of the controls as he looks at Nina. 'I told you he'd bottle it,' he says.

Will tries to move back in front of the steering wheel, but Seb blocks him.

'What was it you just said to me after that game? You snooze, you lose? My turn now, Lawson.' There's an edge to Seb's voice, and Will steps back, holds up his hands. He turns to Nina.

'Are you sure your parents won't mind if we take it out?'

Nina stares at him from behind her dark sunglasses.

'It's got my name on it, hasn't it?' she says, running her hand over one of the metal rails attached to the side of the boat. The deck rocks slightly and Zoe sits down, her legs unsteady. 'Untie that last line, will you, Claire?' Nina makes a tutting sound. 'I thought you'd be more up for this, Will.'

He stares at her, then runs his hand over the sharp ends of the stubble on his head and sits down on the seat at the back of the boat. Sometimes it's better to walk away. A lesson he'd only finally learned after bitter experience.

Chapter 17

Zoe watches Nina throw the ignition keys to Seb and he catches them. Claire steps on to the boat, holding the docking rope, and Nina takes it, loops it through her hands and knots it over the handrail, then sits down on one of the cushions, stretching out like a cat, her legs already a deep nut-brown. Zoe wishes hers would tan like that. She'd had to cover herself in factor fifty just so as not to burn and hers are still bright white. There's a vivid pink line just below the bottom of her bikini top where she's missed a bit which feels like a hot wire against her skin.

Seb grins as he turns the key and the boat starts with a roar, the water bubbling out from beneath the propeller as he shifts one lever into gear and pushes the other forward. The boat accelerates away from the jetty as Claire shrieks in excitement. Zoe watches Will's fingers curve round the edge of the seat, digging into the cushion. She has a sudden flashback to that first night, of his thumb pressing into her skin in the same way. She blinks, trying to remember what he was doing, where she was, but everything from that evening is still a blur.

Nina takes one of the bottles of vodka out of her bag

and unscrews the cap, has a swig and passes it to Claire then walks up to the front of the boat and stands behind Seb, her arms round his waist, her hair blowing around her face. Claire hands the bottle to Will, who gives it straight to Aiden without taking a mouthful. The boat skims over the water, bouncing when it hits the odd choppy patch of ocean, but generally the water is calm and Seb keeps the edge of the coast in sight as he follows the curves around towards the lights they can see ahead of them in the distance, the beach party a glow against the darkening sky.

Zoe counts at least twenty boats anchored in the small bay, and Seb edges between them as far into shore as he can until Nina tells him to stop. He drops anchor and Zoe can see the dark silhouettes of dozens of people gathered on the beach at the bottom of steep cliffs about a hundred metres ahead. Some are dancing around small bonfires on the sand; a few are holding long poles, waterfalls of white sparks shooting out of the ends, horned masks covering their faces. She can hear the music, can feel the faint vibrations of the bass through the deck.

She shivers as she looks down at the water, an inky black below the hull of the boat. She hadn't thought this through. She has always hated deep water, knowing she can't tell what is below her, but since she fell into the canal it has become a phobia, something to be avoided at all costs. *Breathe*. Her mind is capable of conjuring up all manner of horrors reaching up to grab her legs.

'How deep is it?' she asks.

'Not as deep as it looks,' Nina replies, pulling her dress over her head.

Zoe swallows. *There won't be weeds. Nothing slimy that wraps itself around your feet.*

Nina stares at her. 'You're OK to swim, aren't you? It's not far. You can see the beach, and you'll be able to stand up after a minute or so. Chuck your stuff over to Seb if you don't want it to get wet – he'll stick it in a bin bag with the vodka and swim with it.'

Zoe's teeth start to chatter despite the heat as she takes off her skirt, and fights to keep her jaw clamped shut.

'The Med is a lot warmer than a canal, Zoe!' Claire yells as she jumps into the sea, disappearing with a splash.

Zoe can hardly bear to look as the dark water closes over Claire's head and then separates again as she reappears.

'And it's not like there are sharks or anything,' Claire shouts. 'You can almost see the bottom. Nina and I will meet you on the beach.' She turns over, floats on her back and starts paddling towards the shore.

Zoe takes a deep breath and passes her skirt to Seb. She knows she's being stupid. *This isn't Birmingham. You're not off your face. You can swim.*

Will reaches for her hand, his palm warm against hers, and she thinks she might cry. She wants to ask him not to go, to stay on the boat here with her, where it's safe. *He won't be able to save her twice.* But she knows he wants to party with the others. She can see Aiden in the water below, looking up at her.

'It's fine, Zo. Honest. It's not even that cold. I'll swim beside you if you want.'

'Ready?' Will asks.

Zoe nods, tears pricking at the back of her eyes. She

looks behind her to where Seb is still staring at the bonfires on the beach and tries not to think of the face of the
man in his mask with no mouth pressed up against the
Jeep window, his eyes locked on hers, horns pointing at
the sky. She lets go of Will's hand, closes her eyes, holds
her breath and jumps off the side of the boat.

Chapter 18

July – 1989

Seb pushes Nina and Claire's dresses and Zoe's mini-skirt into the bottom of a black bin bag and rolls it up. Jam jars with candles in them are dotted along the beach, and he watches the small flames flickering on the sand.

'Come on, Seb.' He can hear Will splashing below him, already in the water. 'Get a move on, mate.'

Will's voice echoes in the murky blackness, the same words his father used to say. *Hurry up, Seb. Stop lagging at the back. Get your arse into gear.* His brother had always done things quicker and faster than he had, and he'd trailed behind in his wake. No one had been more astounded than he was when he got a scholarship into the sixth form at Daltings Abbey boarding school, where he'd met Nina. He'd always wondered whether his father had said something to the governors to get him a place.

His father had little patience with him when he came home in the school holidays; it had been like treading on eggshells, always one step away from being shouted at, or worse. He looks at the flames in the distance, his skin prickling, and swallows the bile that rises up from his stomach.

'Fuck you, Lawson,' he says under his breath. 'I'll come when I'm ready.'

He sticks two bottles of vodka into the bin bag together with the clothes, ties a knot in the bag to fasten it and pushes everything else the others have left on the deck into the small cupboard under the seat cushion. They might want more to drink when they come back. He fastens the padlock, then sticks both sets of keys in the box by the driver's seat.

Claire and Nina are standing up in the shallows and wading towards the shore when he looks over the side of the boat, the other three swimming behind them, Will out in front. Of course he is. Will is determined to win, even when it isn't a race. Aiden's way fitter; he could beat him hands down if he wanted to.

Seb looks ahead at the beach, at the man in the horned mask whirling a pole, sparks flying out of the fireworks attached to the end and falling on to the sand like rain.

Still gripping the bin bag, he reaches over his right shoulder with his left hand and feels the grooves in his skin – perfect circles with tiny, ridged whorls inside them – spreading out his fingers so he can touch all four. He tries to focus on the figures in the water, make his legs move towards the side of the boat and follow the others into the sea, but they seem to be frozen.

He remembers holding the brown envelope as he got into the passenger seat of their red Lotus Esprit, the envy of all his friends, wishing he could swap places with any of them, or with his brother, who had been told to get in the back. He'd read out his O-level results as they drove down the road – six As, three Bs and one C – his father looking straight ahead through the windscreen, his fingers tightening on the wheel every time an A wasn't mentioned.

Seb had expected him to shout when he pulled over at the side of the road next to their local park, but he said nothing, pressing the button for the cigarette lighter by the gearstick that glowed red, indicating that it was heating up. He'd waited for his father to reach inside his jacket pocket and pull out one of his Cuban cigars, the ones Seb was told never to touch, even though he didn't want to – the smoke made him cough and his eyes sting – but instead his father had told him he should have done better. The cigarette lighter reached the right temperature and popped out with a click.

Then his father had moved, not to reach inside his jacket pocket, as Seb had expected, but to pull the lighter out of its holder and press it against Seb's school shirt, where it burned straight through the thin material and into his skin. The metal had been so hot that for a fraction of a second he had thought it was actually cold. He hadn't felt anything after his father had done it the first time. His head had been so full of pain there hadn't been room for anything else.

His brother had turned his head away, his gaze fixed on the grass outside his window until his father told him to look at Seb, to remember that the men in the Hughes family should never be satisfied with anything less than the best.

Seb never made the same mistake again. He understood that his purpose was to win at any cost. He takes a deep breath, dives into the water and swims after Will.

*

Seb holds the black bin bag out of the water as he wades the last few yards. Nina grabs it and throws her arms around his neck.

'You superstar,' she says.

She takes out her dress and wriggles into it, pulling it over her bikini, drops of water trickling down her legs on to the sand. She opens the bottle of vodka, takes a gulp and then hands it back to Seb, watching his Adam's apple bob up and down as he swallows mouthful after mouthful.

'Jeez, Seb. Leave some for the rest of us, why don't you.'

She snatches the bottle away from him as a group of people walk towards them. Seb smiles as he sees Gaby, her dark hair loose around her shoulders.

'I hoped you'd be here,' he says. 'Did you get home OK after Aiden dropped you off?'

She nods. 'My dad wasn't happy,' she says.

'Did you tell him where you'd been?' Seb combs his fingers through his wet hair, slicking it back.

'I just said I went back with you guys to your villa for a party,' she says. 'He threatened to come and keep an eye on me this evening, but I left without telling him.' She looks at Seb. 'You don't have to worry. I didn't say anything about us.'

Nina leans her head on Seb's shoulder.

'I didn't know there was an *us*, Seb?'

She smirks at Gaby before taking another swig of vodka then walks back across the beach to where Aiden and Zoe are talking to Claire.

Seb can't see Will anywhere. He'd jumped off the boat

before him. And before Zoe. So where is he? He watches Claire grab hold of Aiden's shoulder and point at something. In the flickering lights he can just make out a shape in the water a short distance away from the beach. His legs are rooted to the spot as he watches Aiden break away from the others and sprint across the sand, the waves splashing around his ankles as he charges into the sea shouting Will's name.

Chapter 19

July – 1989

Zoe reaches Will first, closely followed by Aiden. The sea is still shallow enough for her to stand up – the water only reaches to just above her waist. Will is floating on his back, his arms spread out in a T-shape either side of him.

Zoe grabs hold of his wrist, and he turns his head towards her.

'What?' he asks.

'What the hell are you doing?' Zoe shrieks. 'We thought you'd drowned or something.' Her hands are trembling, despite the heat.

'You fucker, Will. You had me worried there for a minute.'

Aiden pushes him under the water and starts to walk to the beach. Will disappears below the surface then comes up and wipes his face with his hands.

Zoe stares at him.

'You scared me.' She hates herself for admitting it, but the words come out before she can stop herself, leaving a rawness behind as if she's stripped off a piece of her skin. Will takes a step forward and she moves back, not wanting to give him the chance to get any closer.

'I'm sorry, Zoe. I just wanted to float for a minute, you know? Have you even looked up there?' He points up to

95

the sky, an inky blue that seems to curve above them, covered in a million pinpricks of light, tightly clustered together in some places, sprinkled more lightly in others. 'I didn't mean to scare you.'

Zoe doesn't answer. The beach looks further away than ever and she can feel her heart begin to race, her breath coming in shallow gasps. She focuses on Will's face. Even before she fell into the canal, she'd hated being out of her depth. She hadn't learned to swim until she was thirteen; her mother's illness had made getting to the local leisure centre tricky. Give her a pool over this black, bottomless ocean any day; clear water where she can touch the bottom.

It was your own fault. If you hadn't been so out of it, you wouldn't have slipped.

She realizes Will has his hand on her arm.

'I've got you,' he says.

She leans back into the blackness, swallowing her fear of what lies beneath her in the dark, focusing on the sky instead. It's so beautiful it almost hurts to look at it. A vast space that stretches for infinity, filled with tiny lights. She's relieved Will can't see that her legs are shaking, aware of the irony that the sea is literally holding her up. She thinks of her mother, tells herself that one day she'll bring her to see this, that – somehow – she'll manage the logistics.

Will links his fingers with hers and lies in the water beside her. She holds on, not wanting to let go. Time and place slip in her head and for a moment she's not sure if she's in Mallorca, Birmingham or somewhere else.

'I'm sorry for all that stuff I said before we left uni,' he says. 'It's not that I don't want . . . things are just really complicated at the moment.'

Zoe doesn't answer, concentrates on the feeling of being weightless. The stars look like they're moving and she realizes that nothing in nature is ever completely still, that sometimes you just have to grab a moment when you see it, before it transforms into something else and is gone for ever.

She can hear Will breathing beside her as he stands up, then he leans down and kisses her, blocking out the stars, which still burn brightly in her head.

There is a fizzing in her stomach when she finally pulls away. She dips her head below the surface of the water then re-emerges, her pale skin slick; a creature that belongs in the sea. She runs her hands over her red hair and squeezes it out. The liquid pools on her sun cream in small droplets, miniature hemispheres whose surfaces reflect the light from the dozens of candles on the beach.

Will is already walking back through the water towards the beach. She strides after him, trying to catch up.

'Will! Can you just wait a minute?'

He turns around.

'I'm sorry.'

'Don't fucking apologize. What's the matter with you? You've practically ignored me on this holiday, and now you kiss me?'

He stares at her, biting at the cuticle on his thumb.

'Is it because of what happened with Aiden?' she asks.

He doesn't respond.

'I know you didn't want me to go to the chancellor, and I'm sorry we argued about it, but what we did was wrong and I just wanted to try and put it right.'

'How would that have worked, Zoe? It was too late by then. We'd already lied. You'd have got us all kicked out.'

'But it didn't even come to that, did it?' Zoe says. 'I did what everyone wanted. I kept quiet.'

Will runs his hand over his buzz cut.

'It's not even about that, Zoe. There's just stuff I need to deal with.'

'What?'

'Just stuff, all right?'

He turns away, but not before Zoe has heard his raised tone of voice, has seen the look on his face, one that she's familiar with. The one he had whenever she'd asked about his past. About his family. The one that tells her he's lying.

Chapter 20

July – 1989

Claire reaches for Nina's hand as they join a crowd of people dancing to the loud beat, some wearing masks like the one the man outside the Jeep window had on. A DJ has set himself up on one side of the cove, a couple of generators beside his decks. She smiles as she feels the sand vibrate beneath her feet.

'Isn't this wicked?'

Nina shouts to be heard above the sound of the music.

'I'm going to say something to Aiden,' Claire mumbles. She knows she's slurring the ends of her words and that Nina can tell, but she doesn't care. Nina takes the Marlboro Light from between her fingers and takes a drag.

'Do you think I should?' Claire stares at her, her pupils large in the darkness. Nina ignores her, looking instead at the figures she can see in the sea.

'Let's go find Seb,' Nina says.

'But do you think I should say something?'

Nina holds up her hands.

'I don't know, Claire. I don't have all the fucking answers. I just want to enjoy this party. Chill out. Have a good time. Is that too much to ask?'

Claire shakes her head, swallows the feeling of rejection.

'Good,' Nina says, flashing her a smile. 'So, let's party. Did you bring anything with you?'

Claire looks over to where Seb is snogging that girl from the bar. Sometimes she thinks she might as well be invisible. It's the same when she's at home. Her dad always away and her mum spending most of her time in her bedroom. She felt that Nina was her soulmate. They'd done everything together at university, Claire had made sure of that, but now it's finished and there is a lump in her throat at the thought everything is going to end.

Why isn't anyone looking for her? Fuck him. Fuck Nina. Fuck everything.

'No,' she says to Nina, her voice clear. 'No, I didn't bring anything.'

Nina stares at her for a moment then squeezes her shoulder before walking over to Seb and Gaby, dodging the people in masks who step in front of her, whirling poles and fireworks around their heads. Claire watches her go, an emptiness in her chest at the lie she's just told, followed by a flash of anger. *Fuck her.* Let her miss out on something for once. She wishes Nina weren't here at all. She hopes Seb ignores her and that she has a shit time at this crappy beach party.

She staggers across the sand, the soles of her feet rubbed raw from dancing. She has been looking for Aiden for what feels like hours. It probably isn't that long; she knows the feeling of time being distorted is just one of the many side effects of the tablet she swallowed before jumping off the boat. The one she'd brought for Nina is still stuffed into her packet of cigarettes, carried on to the beach in Seb's bag. A thrill of pleasure expands in her chest at the thought she didn't give it to her. *Why should Nina always get everything she wants?*

Nina has no idea how hard Claire tries to be the kind of person Nina wants to be friends with. How much *effort* it takes just to keep up with her. To not irritate her. And every time she thinks she's within touching distance, Nina seems to move further away.

She hasn't seen her, or any of the others, for ages. Not since Gaby had asked that guy to take photos of them all with her camera, Seb moving position so he didn't have to stand next to Will, who was smoking a spliff someone had given him, Nina pretending not to pose beside Gaby's friends, the whole group huddled together in front of one of the beach fires, their hands stretched up in the air above the flames.

The DJ, an Oakenfold wannabe, announces that it's three minutes to midnight. Everyone around her is stripping off, leaving T-shirts and skirts on the sand, ready to run into the sea. The guy she'd tapped on the back earlier, thinking he was Aiden until he'd turned around, had told her it's a tradition. She thinks it's a fucking stupid thing to do. Just a way of conning tourists into believing they're experiencing an authentic part of local culture when in fact it's just a load of desperate twenty-something-year-olds getting trashed as a way of not having to think about what the fuck they are going to do with the rest of their lives. She remembers what Nina said on the way to the villa, that crap about it being the one night you can dance with the devil.

She brushes past another girl, who is swaying backwards and forwards in front of one of the bonfires, and feels the hairs on her arm stand on end as their skin touches. The girl holds out her hands, invites Claire to join her, but she carries on walking, desperate to find Aiden.

There are so many people. He could be anywhere. She needs to tell him how she feels. How she's felt for weeks. That the odd snog isn't enough. He'd said he needed to concentrate on his finals, and she'd been happy to wait, and then finals came and went and he's still avoiding her, pushing her away whenever they get too close. She wonders whether he doesn't want to commit because he knows he's joining the army, but she doesn't care, she just wants to be with him.

The DJ starts a countdown and everyone joins in. It swells to a roar of sound when they reach zero and they run towards the sea, shrieking as they get wet. Claire runs with the rest of them, falling into the water, welcoming its cool embrace. She's hugged by a stranger and hugs them back, imagining it's Aiden's strong arms that are wrapped around her.

Is that him? She squints through the crowd of people milling around in the shallows. It looks like him. He stands up, the water only up to just above his knees, and he's laughing, and in that moment she is so happy to see him she feels as if she might burst.

She wades towards him and, as she gets closer, she can see that the guy standing next to him is laughing too. Aiden's talking to him. Staring at him. And then her stomach turns over with a violent jolt as he reaches out and touches the stranger's face. Everything suddenly clicks into place and her insides shrivel up as she realizes the two of them are holding hands.

She sinks down in the water, knowing it's too late, that he must have seen her. She can see him staring in her direction, trying to work out if it is actually her. She turns around and backs away, out of the sea and on to the beach, a bitterness running through her veins like poison.

Chapter 21

July – 1989

Gaby matches Seb's pace all the way from the beach to the boat, making smooth strokes that cut through the dark water. He swims to the stern, where the metal steps are, climbs up, turns around and holds out his hand to help her. Nina's boat is one of the only ones still moored; most of the others have already slid away into the darkness. They have the small cove to themselves, along with the last few remaining people sitting around the fires on the beach. The DJ has finished his set and a stillness hangs in the air, broken only by the waves splashing against the hull of the boat.

'You're a good swimmer.' Seb dries himself off and puts his T-shirt back on.

'I started young,' Gaby says. 'It's mad not to, living on the coast here. My father never learned, but he insisted I should. He worries about me too much. *Padres*, eh?' She smiles.

Seb looks at her. She has no idea.

'Yes,' he says. 'Fucking screwed up.'

He takes the key out of the boat's lockbox and fiddles with the padlock on the small cupboard underneath the seat cushion, cursing when he can't get it to open.

'Want me to have a go?' Gaby asks.

He nods, and she bends down, takes the key out and

puts it in the lock again, turning it slowly. It pops open and Seb unhooks it, fishes around inside. He pushes the packets of sparklers to one side, pulls out the last bottle of vodka, two plastic tumblers and a can of Coke.

'You drink a lot,' she says.

'Do I?' He knows she's right. His head is buzzing, the memories he dredged up earlier still too vivid. He rubs the back of his shoulder as he hears his father's voice saying, 'Get a bloody move on.'

'Is this Nina's?' Gaby balances a tumbler beside the metal guard rail on the side of the boat and pours in a large measure of vodka, tops it up with Coke and downs it in one go.

For a moment, Seb thinks how easy it would be to pretend it's his, but he nods.

'Nina's parents'. Same as the villa.'

'My father calls them *guiri*,' Gaby says, sitting down beside him. 'Like all the others that come out here from your country. He despises them, but he needs the work. Did you know Nina's villa used to be owned by my grandfather?'

Seb shakes his head.

'He sold it because he couldn't afford the upkeep. And Nina's parents bought it cheap. They only come out here a couple of times a year, just like all the others that are buying up our houses. It means there is less and less work for people like my father.' Gaby pours herself another drink. Then another.

Seb relishes the fact that his head is beginning to spin; thoughts of his father, of Will, of everything, dissolve into the blackness.

'Where did you meet her?' Gaby asks.

'Nina?'

Gaby nods.

'We shared a house at university,' Seb says. 'In Birmingham. But we knew each other before that.'

'Was she your girlfriend?' Gaby asks.

'No. She's . . . she's . . .' He holds up his hands. 'It's difficult to explain.'

'Just a friend?'

He hesitates before he answers, the things he and Nina have done falling through his head like shooting stars, leaving a burning trail behind them.

'Yes, kind of,' he says finally. 'We went to boarding school together. It's complicated.' Gaby nods. Seb knows she doesn't understand. How can she? He doesn't have the words to describe his relationship with Nina. His best friend and worst enemy all rolled into one; the only person who knows what he has done.

He leans towards Gaby, feels her breath on his face as their lips touch, but flinches away when she puts her arms around him. She looks at him, a question in her eyes as he moves her hands so they are around his waist, away from the four circles he can't bear anyone to touch.

There's a noise from the back of the boat, and Seb looks up. For a second, he sees his father's face and smells cigar smoke before realizing it's only Will clambering on board.

'All right?' Will smiles, but Seb doesn't reply. He wants to tell him he's ruining things, that he needs to leave, but swallows his words as the others appear behind him: Nina, followed by Claire, then Zoe and finally Aiden.

Gaby looks at Nina. 'You have a lovely boat,' she says. Seb notices her lean to one side slightly in her seat before she sits upright again, as if she's moving in sync with the motion of the boat.

Nina nods. 'I know. I hope Seb is making you feel at home?' She looks at him. 'Thanks for taking the bin bag back with you, by the way; Aiden had to nick one off someone on the beach to put our stuff in.'

He winces at her sarcastic tone as he takes another mouthful from the bottle beside him. He can see the looks Nina is giving Gaby, like sharp needles designed to prick her skin.

'Seb was just telling me what good friends you are,' Gaby says. She holds out the bottle of vodka, and Zoe drinks some before offering it to Will, who shakes his head.

Nina hesitates.

'He would say that. Just doesn't want me giving away any of his dark secrets. Isn't that right, Seb?'

There is an edge to her voice that would make Seb uneasy if he hadn't drunk so much, but the vodka has numbed his awareness and he raises one of the tumblers towards Nina in a toast instead. She looks at Gaby.

'He's right, though. We're best friends. I would never let anything come between us.'

Claire hides her face in a towel. Gaby flushes, and Seb notices the sheen of perspiration that has appeared on her forehead.

'I should go,' Gaby says. 'My friends are waiting.' She stands up, but then sits down again.

'Are you not coming back to the villa with us?' Seb asks.

She shakes her head. 'Not tonight. I have to work in the morning.' She gets up and clasps the metal handrail to steady herself.

The corners of Nina's mouth twitch.

'I thought you were a student?'

'I work on Saturdays when I'm not at college,' Gaby replies. 'In the supermarket.'

Nina raises her eyebrows.

'How about I get a photo of you both before you go?' Nina says. 'Come on, Seb. You can't pass up the opportunity for a souvenir to remember a holiday romance.'

'Sure,' Gaby says easily. 'Take it with my camera.'

The word 'camera' comes out slurred and Seb can't tell if she's speaking Spanish or English. She sits on Seb's lap, one arm draped around his neck, and smiles. He keeps very still, trying to resist the urge to shrug her off, his father's voice filling his head in a giant roar.

Can't you get anything right?

He picks up the bottle of vodka, takes another slug.

Nina hands Gaby back the camera and she shoves it into the bottom of a bag, rolling it up ready to take with her.

'See you soon?' Gaby says.

Seb grins.

'Definitely. Tomorrow night? Same bar in Deià as before?'

He doesn't look at Nina, doesn't want to hear her mimic Gaby's accent as she repeats, 'In the supermarket,' something he knows she's going to do for the rest of the holiday.

Gaby takes a deep breath and dives off the side of the

boat. Seb watches her cut through the water again, more slowly this time, a small, pale shape in the dark ocean. He waits until she disappears out of sight, until all he can see is the glow from the flickering candles on the beach.

Will looks at the bottle of vodka, and then at Seb.

'Are you going to be OK to drive us back?' he asks.

Seb stares at him, the buzzing in his head reaching a crescendo.

'Who the fuck are you to ask me that, Lawson?' He lies back on one of the seats and looks up at the sky. *You're too stupid to be a son of mine.* Nina leans over and whispers something in his ear, but he pushes her away.

'You ruin everything,' he says. 'You can't stand me being happy.'

Will frowns. 'Listen, mate, I . . .'

Aiden puts his hand on Will's arm.

'Leave it, Will.'

Will shakes him off.

'Don't tell me what to do, Aiden. You're in no position to lecture me. First you nearly get us kicked out of uni, and then you go and scare us shitless by creeping around in the middle of the night.'

Nina frowns.

Aiden swallows. 'I only went for a swim.'

'Off the fucking jetty at three o'clock in the morning!' Will says. 'Without telling anyone. You were lucky you didn't drown.'

'You can talk, Lawson,' Seb says, taking another mouthful of vodka. 'You're hiding just as many secrets as Aiden here.'

Will shakes his head. 'You're drunk, Seb.'

Seb holds up the bottle. 'I might well be. But that doesn't mean I'm not telling the truth. You were the one who brought it up in the first place.'

Will frowns, a sinking feeling in his stomach when he thinks of the conversation they'd had while smoking spliffs on the beach. He remembers lying on his back on the sand, looking at the sky. Seb telling him to stop talking shit.

Had he said something he shouldn't have?

Seb stares at him before putting his forefinger against his lips.

'Don't worry, Lawson. You keep my secrets, and I'll keep yours.'

Chapter 22

July – 1989

Zoe looks at Will, her forehead creasing in confusion as he runs his hand over his buzz cut.

'Shut up, Seb,' Nina says. 'You're hammered.' She gets up, walks to the front of the boat, gets the ignition keys out of the lockbox and throws them to Will.

'You drive,' she says, pulling up the anchor.

'I . . . I don't know if I can,' Will replies.

'Just give it a fucking go,' she says. 'It's not that hard.'

He starts the engine, shifts one of the sticks into reverse and moves the other forwards, edging the boat around so they're facing out to sea. He pushes the accelerator and Zoe feels the boat cut through the water. Nina switches on the boombox and turns the volume up as high as it will go, singing along out of tune to the Human League's 'Don't You Want Me'.

'The party's not over, people,' she says, her wet feet slipping as she steps up on to the white cushions and motions for Claire and Zoe to get up beside her. Zoe can see Claire's pupils, her brown iris a narrow sliver of colour.

'I thought you said you didn't bring anything with you?' Nina shouts over the music.

Claire smiles and shakes her head, but Zoe can tell she's lying.

Another track kicks in and Claire pulls Nina towards her and kisses her on the lips. Nina pushes her away and reaches down for the bottle of vodka on the table. Zoe sees Claire's face fall as she looks across to where Aiden is sitting and realizes he has turned around and is staring out over the water, drumming his fingers on his knees.

Zoe walks towards Will, who is squinting at the dials on the red dashboard. The sound of the engine roars in her ears and she stumbles as the boat moves. She can feel the wind pushing her hair back off her face, cool enough to make her shiver in her T-shirt and wet bikini. The boat bounces more than it did on the way out, the waves choppier. She isn't sure if they are still heading out to sea; the coastline is difficult to make out in the darkness. She can still see the candles and bonfires on the beach behind them, but the flames have merged into a single pinprick of light that seems to be moving up and down in the distance. Her head swirls with a wave of giddiness.

'What was Seb talking about?' she asks, shouting the words in Will's ear.

He shrugs, keeping his eyes fixed straight ahead.

'About your brother?'

He glances at her. 'It's nothing.'

'It must be something. What did he mean?'

Will bites his lip. 'I don't want to talk about it.'

'You never want to talk about it,' she says. All the time they were together, he'd change the subject if she started asking questions about him growing up. Every now and again a piece of information would slip out, like a bubble escaping from a pocket of air underwater; it would rise to the surface and she'd get a glimpse of his past before he clammed up again. 'If not now, then when?' she asks.

'Stop grilling me, Zoe.'

The infinite possibilities she saw earlier in the stars shrink into blackness, something small and hard settling in her stomach. She turns away and staggers back to where Nina and Claire are dancing on the seats. Their movements blur into one another, and she narrows her eyes, trying to separate them.

She grabs the bottle of vodka Gaby was drinking from the table and takes a few gulps, attempts to join in with the beat of the music, which now seems to be one step ahead of her. She waves her hands in the air, a smile fixed mawkishly on her face.

Aiden examines the contents of the bag he's brought with him as Seb sits up beside him.

'Whatcha doing?'

Aiden holds the bag open so Seb can see.

'We didn't get to let them off on the beach,' he says.

'Let's do it now, then.' Seb goes to stand up, then staggers as the boat hits another wave, and sits down again.

'We should wait until we're back at the villa,' Aiden says.

Seb ignores him, grabs the bag and pulls out a packet of sparklers. Aiden reaches for them, but Seb pushes him and Aiden falls on to the seat, landing on his wrist.

'Seb, the others won't be happy. You can't just –'

'I thought you didn't care what others thought, Buckley? Or am I wrong about that?'

Aiden doesn't answer. Seb fishes around in Nina's bag to find Claire's Zippo, flicks the lid open and turns the wheel. At first, the flint doesn't spark, but as Aiden leans forward it catches, lighting the fluid that covers the wick, and a flame rises up in the dark.

Nina and Zoe stop dancing and jump off the seat.

'Put those down, Seb.' Nina points at the sparklers.

'Don't you want one?' Seb asks, waving them in front of him. 'Aiden bought two packets. Four for each of us.' He holds one out to Nina. 'I don't think Lawson's going to need his. Even he can't drive and hold one of these at the same time.' Nina pushes away what Seb is offering her and grabs the unopened packet.

'Stop being stupid,' she says. 'Give me the lighter.'

Zoe glances towards the front of the boat, where she can see Will turning around to see what they're doing. Aiden is rubbing his wrist, but her vision blurs and she keeps having to blink to focus.

She looks at Claire, still dancing, and feels an urge to shout at her to get down and quit messing around. Nina turns off the boombox and the music cuts out abruptly, leaving just the roar of the boat engine, but Claire doesn't stop, moving to a beat inside her head that only she can hear.

'Give me the lighter, Seb.' Nina holds out her hand.

Seb ignores her, holds two sparklers in the flame, which catch fire, throwing out white sparks, too bright to look at. He shoves the Zippo in his pocket, moves one of the sparklers into his other hand, then holds out both his arms and draws huge circles in the dark. Nina and Zoe take a step back.

'Come on, you lot, don't be such boring fuckers,' Seb says. 'We're here to have fun, aren't we?'

'Put them down, Seb.' Aiden's voice is gobbled up and

carried away by the wind. Seb whirls the sparklers in front of him, white streaks of light falling by their feet.

Zoe can see Will staring at them from the front of the boat. His mouth is moving but she can't make out what he's saying. Claire sinks down on to her knees on the seat, the upper half of her body still swaying to a silent beat.

One sparkler gives out and the white lights disappear to leave an orange ring in the darkness as Seb continues to whirl it in a circle. Zoe closes her eyes and can still see it, the image burned on to the back of her eyelids. The other sparkler gives out as well, and they are suddenly in darkness. Seb frowns at the twisted pieces of wire as if he can't quite understand what has happened. He lets them fall on to the leather seat and there is a horrible smell of burning hair.

The last thing she remembers is catching Will's eye as he turns around at the front of the boat to look at her, his slight smile making something inside her chest flutter, despite herself, as if she can trust him to make everything right.

The roar seems to come from inside her, so loud that it fills every millimetre of space in her body until there is no more room and it bursts out of her mouth, pushes her off her feet and sends her tumbling through the air. She sees her mother's face, feels her arms tight around her as she falls backwards softly into an infinity of stars and everything turns black.

Chapter 23

Now

Did you really think you were going to get away with it? After thirty-three years, perhaps you had assumed that you would, but everyone knows your past always catches up with you in the end.

I bet you thought you'd buried it deep enough. Pushed it down beneath your skin, invisible to anyone looking in from the outside, but what you did still pulses like blood through your veins. And if I cut you open, those secrets will spill out, pooling in crimson puddles on the floor, just like back then.

Have you told anyone else what you did? Your nearest and dearest? A whispered hint in an unguarded moment prompted by the desire to unburden? I doubt it. You wouldn't want anyone else to know. They'd realize you weren't the person they thought you were at all. How could you be, if you were capable of doing that? *You're not a monster.*

Instead, you stuck it in a box like an old toy you don't play with any more, sealed the edges, put it up in the loft and tried to forget all about it. But it's still there. It might be covered in dust and cobwebs, but when I make you open it back up, everyone else will see what you've tried to conceal for so long.

You've pasted a shiny new life over your past, like strips of wallpaper. But it won't take much to rip them off. That's the problem with trying to hide things. It's something I've learned too. It only takes the sound of someone's voice, a glimpse of a certain shade of blue or the smell of jasmine to inadvertently generate a spark of recognition that turns into a flame and spreads to everything in your brain before you can stop it.

The horror of what you did lives and grows in the dark. I hope whenever you think about it, it fills you with guilt and shame. The only way to cope with it is to pretend it never happened. That you weren't there. That you weren't involved. But you were. And it might have taken me a while to find you, but now you're going to pay.

Chapter 24

July – 1989

There is something hard beneath Will's fingertips. This is the only thought he manages to form amid the pain that feels like nails are scraping across the inside of his head. He waits, knowing there is no point in trying to do anything else until it lets up enough for him to breathe.

A few minutes pass. Or is it a few hours? He's not sure. The agony recedes for a moment, as if taking a breath before deciding where to go next. *Where's Zoe?* Will wishes he could shut his eyes and go to sleep, but then he thinks his eyes might be shut, and perhaps he is asleep already.

He moves his fingers backwards and forwards, reassures himself that something is *there*, beneath them. He can feel it. Smooth and hard. *Why is it so dark? Need to find Zoe.*

He thinks of his mum, of how she'd cope with losing him as well as Andy. She'd liked Zoe when she'd met her briefly. Had told him he deserved to be happy. And he'd known how much it had meant for her to say that. After Andy had gone and his dad had left, they'd clung to each other and hadn't let anyone else in. And now he's fucked it all up.

Maybe he's gone blind. *Was there an explosion?* He remembers there being a bright light. One that burned into the back of his eyeballs. He shouldn't have looked at it. Like Andy used to tell him not to look directly at the sun when they were younger. He hadn't realized how much he missed him until he'd stood in front of his bathroom mirror the night before he'd come away and had seen his brother looking back at him.

He'd squeezed his eyes shut, had wondered whether if he wished hard enough, Andy would come back. And then the next thing he'd been aware of had been his mother standing beside him, crying as she'd taken away the pair of scissors he was holding. She'd turned on the tap to rinse the tufts of his dark hair lying in the sink down the plughole. He didn't remember cutting them off and he hadn't managed to make himself look anything like his brother. His mum had ushered him downstairs and trimmed off what was left with an old pair of clippers.

He shouldn't have come on this holiday at all; he should have turned around and gone home after that phone call at Gatwick.

As he tries to move his head the pain returns, jumping out of the shadows like a surprise game of Hide and Seek. It digs its claws into his brain and wipes out all coherent thoughts as he surrenders to it.

Chapter 25

July – 1989

Claire thinks Nina is bleeding. At least, it might be blood; it's difficult to be sure. It's black, but that could be because the entire boat is enveloped in shadows, the only light coming from the moon and a single white bulb on the stern of the boat. The one on the prow seems to have disappeared. They are still moving; she can hear the sound of the engine, feel the boat going through the water, but doesn't understand why, as Will is slumped on the floor by the helm.

She slides herself across the deck, closer to Nina, who is lying by the side of the seat that now has two large scorch marks in the white leather, deep gashes where the filling is visible, the smell of singed hair still pungent. *Please, please, be OK.* She looks at the damage and wonders for a moment what they will tell Nina's parents but is then struck by how ridiculous this is and laughs, the sound echoing in the darkness.

Where are Seb, Aiden and Zoe?

She needs Nina to wake up.

She puts her hand on Nina's face, ignores the blood she can see on her leg (*and it is blood, it's wet and sticky on her fingers when she touches it, thicker than seawater, but she won't think about that*). This is her fault. She'd wished Nina wasn't here. She hadn't meant it. Nina knows how much she means to her. She swallows, her throat tight.

Nina's skin is warm and she thinks this is a good sign. Claire's mum's was hot and clammy when she had to call an ambulance for her after she'd taken too many of the tablets she kept in the bathroom cabinet. Her chubby ten-year-old's fingers had fumbled over the buttons when she dialled 999. She hadn't been able to find a pulse; her heart-beat had been hammering too loudly to hear what the person on the other end of the phone was saying. She'd been terrified that by the time the ambulance arrived her mother would be dead, that maybe she already was. But she'd pulled through. Just as she had again, a few years later.

'Just as you will,' she whispers to Nina.

Claire would give absolutely anything at this moment for Nina to open her eyes, because otherwise she is going to be stuck out here *alone*. Will isn't going to help her.

He's not moving.

She covers her ears, trying to ignore the noise she can hear above the hum of the engine – a knocking, as if something heavy is hitting the side of the boat.

Chapter 26

July – 1989

The water is cold. So much colder than it felt on the beach. Seb can't stop his teeth chattering. The soft, fuzzy feeling that he'd been wrapped in – his giant coat of vodka – has been ripped off and has disappeared somewhere among the waves.

There is nothing apart from black water on every side of him that stretches away as far as he can see. The lights along the coast, tiny dots in the distance, are only visible every now and again when his face rises above the waves. *Don't panic.* He clings to the words like a lifebuoy, repeating them silently in his head, over and over.

What the fuck just happened? He remembers lighting the sparklers and then a crunching noise so loud it sent a shooting pain through his eardrums, and then he'd found himself underwater, salt stinging his nostrils, frantically kicking his legs to get up to the surface.

He must have fallen over the side of the boat. *Don't panic.* They'll turn around and come straight back. It's only been . . . Seb's not sure how long it's been, his thoughts swim away as quickly as he tries to grab hold of them, but he tells himself Will is going to come back. It'll just take a few minutes. There's something wrong with his ears – the sound of the sea, of everything, is muffled. He tries waving his arms, but it's hard to stay above the surface when he does that and he needs to save his energy.

Don't panic.

He tries to remember the swimming lessons he had at school, the ones when he'd put on his pyjamas and dived down to the bottom of the pool to retrieve a brick before carrying it up to the surface and putting it on the side. He'd managed to do it. Had got his bronze award. Something his dad had been proud of him for. He'd kept the badge in the pocket of his school bag for years.

He turns on his back now, spreads himself out like a star, attempts to ignore the waves that splash against his face, tells himself to breathe, *don't panic*, and tries not to scream.

The ringing in his ears suddenly stops. Above the sound of the waves, he hears the familiar hum of an engine and sees the boat heading straight towards him.

Chapter 27

July – 1989

Nina can feel drops of rain on her face. She forgot to pack her umbrella and now her hair is going to get wet and stick to her head. Which means her ears will show. Another chance for the girls at school to pick on her. They hadn't let up since she'd started in primary school, names like Dumbo and Mr Spock whispered behind her back, accompanied by fits of giggles.

She'd stopped wearing headbands, had made her mother book a hairdresser's appointment and had got her almost waist-length hair chopped into a bob. It covered her ears, but it hadn't made any difference. If anything, the taunts had got worse. She has a tingling feeling in her bladder, a sign she's going to lose control unless she goes right now. She'd done that when they'd locked her out of the school toilets yesterday, a hot rush flooding down her leg and making a puddle on the floor.

She can hear a voice. Claire is calling her. Nina feels her body slump in relief. She's not at school any more. 'Course she's not. She'd left years ago; had refused to eat until her mother had let her have otoplasty, then moved to Daltings Abbey and on to university.

Friends had been something she'd chosen very carefully, gathering a select few who would prove useful. Her mother had always told her the worst thing in life was to be alone, had forgiven her father for his many 'indiscretions', and Nina was determined that would never happen to her.

Claire's voice is right by her ear and her face floats into view. She's crying.

'Nina, thank God.'

Nina runs her tongue over her teeth; they feel loose. She swallows the metallic taste in her mouth.

'What happened?'

'I don't know.' Claire's eyes shine with panic. 'You fell. I think you must have landed on one of the bottles of vodka or something and hurt your leg. But it's OK, it's not bleeding that much.'

Nina sits up, winces.

'The boat,' she says. 'I meant, what happened with the boat?'

Claire glances at the seat where Will should be sitting.

'I think . . . I think we hit something.'

'Who's driving?' Nina says. 'Where are the others?'

'Will's on the . . . but he's not . . . I'm not sure if he's . . . I don't know about the others . . .'

Nina holds on to the burnt seat to pull herself up and looks at the helm, where the crumpled shape of Will's body is lying on the floor.

'Fuck.' She staggers towards him and pulls back the throttle to stop the boat. It slows down, finally stopping its continuous circling. She cuts the engine and kneels down on the floor next to him, puts her fingers on his wrist.

'I can't feel anything,' she says, looking at Claire. 'You're a fucking medic – you need to do something.' She hobbles from one side of the boat to the other, trying to ignore the stabbing pain in her leg as she looks over the edge.

'You know I'm not a medic,' Claire says. 'I switched to Law after a term, and I don't –'

She breaks off when she realizes Nina isn't listening.

'Seb?' Nina screams his name into the darkness, but there's no reply. 'How long since the accident?' she shouts. 'How long have I been unconscious?'

'I don't know!' Claire has her hand on Will's wrist as she starts to cry. 'A couple of minutes? Don't yell at me!'

You wanted her to come back.

Nina turns her head as she hears a knocking sound from the back of the boat. She stumbles across to the stern and leans out over the sea, holding on to the top of the metal steps.

'What is it?' Claire shouts. 'Is it Seb?'

Nina bends down to reach something in the water, then turns around slowly, holding out an oar that drips water over the deck.

'No,' she says. 'It's not Seb. I think we hit another boat.'

Chapter 28

July – 1989

Aiden wonders if being thrown out of the boat is a form of retribution. The kind of thing his parents think should happen to people like him. Drowned. Suffocated. Stabbed. Just like the enemy on a battlefield. They would never say it to Aiden's face, of course; their opinons sit like shadows in their heads, hidden from view. But just like blood, they are still there, running through their veins.

Aiden had heard his father talking to one of their local councillors last year, offering his support for the introduction of Section 28. The man whom he had looked up to all his life, whom he had idolized for as long as he could remember, had visibly shrunk in front of him, and Aiden wishes more than anything that he'd never overheard the conversation. His parents pretend that Aiden's particular sexual preferences don't exist – especially not in the armed forces. And Aiden knows if he wants a career in the military, he needs to pretend they don't exist either.

His parents have no idea what they'd find beneath their son's skin if they peeled away the layers. And now they'll never know. At least Aiden has spared them that. He wonders how long it will take for his body to wash up, the tide returning it to one of the beaches beneath the lights he can make out in the distance when he isn't shutting his eyes against the waves.

Aiden thinks he remembers seeing another boat before the crash. A split-second glimpse, when he'd turned away from Seb and the smell of burnt hair. A sudden flash of something solid illuminated by the light on the prow; shades of red, yellow, brown, followed by that awful noise that seemed to explode in his head before he found himself in the water.

There are no colours visible now – everything is just a different shade of black, even the pieces of broken wood floating on the surface of the ocean. He's too terrified to move from where he's treading water, watches their boat circle around him like a shark.

He wishes Luis was here. The thought of him is the only thing that stops his teeth chattering. They'd talked that first morning at the villa when Aiden had got up early; just the two of them outside by the pool. He'd reached out to shake Luis's hand, an overwhelming desire to make contact with his skin. Luis had told him about the beach party, had said that he was going, and Aiden hadn't known what to say, had been unsure whether he was being offered an invitation or whether it was something more than that, a tentative step over an invisible line that he wanted to take further but didn't know how, so had run down to the jetty instead, his body tingling with anticipation.

And then he'd bumped into him in the bar, had hung back while Luis had asked to meet him later that night on the jetty, his mouth so close to Aiden's ear he could feel his breath. He'd hesitated, then remembered the cowardice he'd seen in his own eyes in the Gents, had thought of how he would lie in bed later, alone, and had said yes. An acceptance that was a semi-vowel – a trigger sound, according to his speech therapist. His nerves forced the word out as a stutter. He'd expected to see a familiar shadow of disappointment pass across Luis's face, the same one he'd seen wipe out any notion of attraction in others so many times before, but Luis had reached out and put his hand on Aiden's cheek, setting his skin on fire, holding it there for a fraction longer than necessary. And yet it wasn't long enough.

The boat circles him once again, following the same loop it has completed at least ten times already, and Aiden turns around on the spot, tracking it as it moves. He scans the surface of the water, searching for one of the others, for anyone, his hopes raised briefly when he thinks he sees a flash of something amid the waves, shapes that stay solid for more than just a second in the swell. But then they vanish again and disappointment pulls at his ankles, threatening to drag him under. He forces himself to focus on the boat. Just the boat.

He remembers the warmth of Luis's skin pressed against his, the feel of the smooth wooden boards of the jetty against his hands and his desire, so strong it was almost a physical pain; like someone cutting him open. Of how they'd been kissing less than an hour ago and how he hadn't wanted to stop. He can still taste the salt on his lips.

Something moves on the deck of the boat. The possibility that someone else is alive temporarily stops the panic he's been frantically swallowing, along with mouthfuls of seawater. Please let them see him. He squints but can't make out who it is.

Is it Claire?

His stomach lurches when he remembers the look she gave him on the beach, and for a moment he wonders whether she would help him, even if she could. The thought is so terrifying that his body freezes; he forgets to kick his legs and disappears under the surface, spluttering as he comes back up, fighting to catch his breath.

He thinks of Luis, and then of his future, and sends a prayer to a god he doesn't believe in, offers his soul in return for getting him out of here. *He will change. He will not give in to temptation. He will be a better man. One like his father.* And in that instant, he hears the boat engine stop, watches the nightmare circling come to a halt.

He begins to swim, shouting when his mouth isn't full of seawater, putting one hand in front of the other. He pushes away the pieces of wood that float across his path, diverts to avoid the larger ones, focusing on the boat, only the boat. It doesn't seem to be getting any closer.

Twenty more strokes. He can do this. He's fit; he runs every single day. Literally follows in his father's footsteps. He counts in his head and forces himself to push his body through the water, but it's difficult to catch his breath with the waves hitting his face. Is the swell getting worse? His legs scream with tiredness.

He pauses, rests for a moment and lets his legs sink underneath him, looks for the boat. It should be in front of him. But it's not there.

Chapter 29

Seb – Now

Seb stands behind the memorial to the Royal Air Force Eagle Squadrons in Grosvenor Square Gardens. It reminds him of Aiden, of the letters he'd received from him before Seb was sent to prison. Keeping up any kind of regular communication had become so much more difficult after that. He has no idea where those letters are now. Probably buried somewhere in landfill, along with most of his other possessions. His whole life had disappeared when he went inside.

On the top of the fifteen-foot-high obelisk of pale sandstone sits a bronze sculpture of an eagle. Not a vulture, but close enough. He wonders whether Nina knows it's here. What she thinks about when she walks past.

This dawn stroll while the rest of the city is still asleep could become his next addiction, a new desire to replace the old. It had only taken him an hour through the leafy streets of Primrose Hill and Regent's Park, but it feels like a different world compared to his flat on the seventeenth floor of the Chalcots Estate.

His left knee creaks as he sits down on one of the park benches. He tells himself being in prison for so long has made him unfit, but he knows, deep down, this isn't the only reason. He looks at his digital watch; he'd taken it off his cellmate in a bet that he couldn't win twenty games of blackjack in a row. It's over ten years old now, worthless, the once transparent plastic face scratched and almost opaque, but he's grown attached to it. A reminder of the person he once was. Someone who didn't always lose.

The apartments that surround the square are all worth well over a million. Many over ten, some over forty. He can see inside one of them through a gap in the curtains, catches a glimpse of an Eichholtz pendant light, a huge piece of art hung above a stone fireplace. His studio flat has paper-thin walls and a patch of damp that expands by a few centimetres on a daily basis. The entire place isn't much bigger than his cell.

At least he doesn't have to share a toilet.

When he goes back, he'll be forced to listen to the continual noise of drilling from the contractors who are on site twelve hours a day, replacing the cladding and fire doors considered to be ineffective after the Grenfell disaster.

His next-door neighbour had told him the day after he'd moved in that they'd been there for years and no one has any idea when the work will finish. And when the workmen go home, the parties start. Footsteps thumping on his ceiling. Music coming through the floor from the flat downstairs. People coming and going all hours of the night. Arguments outside his window in the hallway. The noise never stops. In prison, after lights out, so long as his cellmate wasn't snoring, it was quiet.

He'd asked his probation officer if he could be rehoused but had been told he was lucky to have been given this place, considering he'd failed to pay his rent last time he'd been sent down, which apparently meant he'd made himself intentionally homeless.

He pulls his fleece a bit more tightly around him as he stares at the luxury flats on the square. He was supposed to have had this life. Everything the residents do around here is intended to be noticed – the designer clothes, the flash cars, the expensive jewellery. His lack of wealth makes him invisible, a magician's trick unintentionally pulled off with an outfit from a charity shop and the lack of a decent haircut.

He inserts one of the earbuds on the pair of headphones Aiden gave him, leaving the other one dangling. Bitter experience has taught him that it's best to be vigilant at all times, even somewhere like here. He feels for the button to turn on the tiny portable radio in his pocket, the tinny sound of Belinda Carlisle's normally husky voice filling his ear. 'Heaven is a Place on Earth'. He can't help silently mouthing the words to the chorus as he sinks back thirty-three years and remembers the woman he is unable to let go of after all this time – Nina, dancing with him in the sticky heat of a club, her eyes fixed on his.

He senses her coming before he sees her; a tingling across his skin as the hairs rise up in anticipation. She emerges through the front door of her apartment block. Designer suit, a blonde, shoulder-length, blunt bob. Cheekbones as sharp as ever. Instantly recognizable, unlike him. But then he's relying on that.

She shivers as she encounters the early-morning chill in the air, and he watches her pull her grey throw (cashmere, no doubt) a fraction tighter around herself. His heartbeat quickens, but he ignores it, focuses instead on the small details, mentally storing away the images for later to add to his existing collection, her Mulberry handbag in one hand, the latest iPhone in the other.

He listens to the click of her heels as she walks down the stone steps and across the pavement towards the car that sits waiting for her. Something flash. A Tesla. He takes a photo of her on his phone before the vehicle pulls away silently and emerges from behind the memorial, watches as it drives away down the street. His knee aches as he walks quickly along the path to the edge of Grosvenor Square Gardens, but he ignores it and puts out his hand to hail a cab.

He wonders if she ever thinks of him, of what they did. Whether it haunts her, swirls around at the bottom of her stomach, as it still does in his, even thirty-three years later, like he's swallowed something rancid that might be violently ejected at any moment. She'll be able to tell him now that he's found her again. She shouldn't have underestimated him. No one can disappear for ever, not even her.

Chapter 30

July – 1989

It can't have just vanished. Aiden's breath comes in shallow, uneven gasps. It was here before he started those last twenty strokes. It *has* to still be here. He kicks his legs, tries to raise himself above the surface of the water. As a wave lifts him up, he spots it again. Further away than before. *How the fuck is that even possible?* It was just in front of him. He shouts out, but his words are swept away by the sea.

Swim and focus on the boat. He forces himself to start again: seven strokes, then check on the boat, seven strokes, then check on the boat. It seems closer. A bubble of hope rises up in his stomach, helping to keep him afloat. Another seven and he can see Nina staring out over the stern. She's looking in his direction.

Surely she can see him?

Another seven. He's crying now – he can't help it – but seven more strokes and he reaches the metal steps. He clings to them, his feet too numb to get a grip.

Nina helps pull him on to the deck. He sinks to the floor and she takes off his T-shirt, wraps the towel she had pressed against her leg around his shoulders. He tries to ignore the blood on the white material, streaks of horror in the dark. She looks at him, and he knows she hasn't forgotten. *He owes her. Now his debt is even larger than before.* He

135

can't stop shivering as he looks at Claire leaning over Will at the front of the boat.

'Where are Zoe and Seb?' he asks. He wishes the towel wasn't so wet.

'I don't know,' Nina says. He can hear the panic in her voice. 'They must be in the water.'

'Why aren't you looking for them?'

'I am,' Nina says, raising her voice. 'But it's hard to see anything with so many pieces of wood in the way. If we turn the engine on, we won't be able to hear them, and if we move the boat, I'm worried we'll hit them by mistake.' She glances at him. 'The propeller will cut them to shreds.'

She wraps her arms around herself, and Aiden can see that she's shaking almost as much as he is. She scans the water, her entire body vibrating with the cold, or fear. Probably both. *Fuck.* He watches her crouch down next to Claire, who is holding Will's hand.

'Is he conscious?' Nina asks.

'He keeps opening his eyes,' Claire says, 'but I don't think it means anything. He could have concussion, a haematoma, haemorrhage, a skull fracture . . .' She hesitates. 'I just know he's got a massive bump on his head. He needs to get to a hospital.'

Aiden stares at them.

They're floundering in the dark.

'We need to find the others,' Nina says. As she stares over the side of the boat, Aiden glances at Claire, but she turns away and he realizes she hasn't said a word to him.

Chapter 31

July – 1989

Seb floats on his back. He's managed it for so much longer than he thought he would be able to, but his legs are beginning to feel like pieces of lead, pulling him towards the bottom.

He'd held his breath and dived down in the water as deep as he could when the boat came towards him, told himself it was no different from picking up a brick from the bottom of a swimming pool, but he had surfaced into a nightmare. Broken planks, a fender, a pole with material still attached to it; horrors that were once part of something whole now chewed up and torn into unrecognizable pieces.

He focuses on the brightest star he can see and blocks out all thoughts of anything other than staying afloat. Survive at all costs. *The Hughes never lose.* He can hear his father saying the words, his family motto.

He is concentrating so hard that it takes him a while to realize that the boat's engine has cut out and someone is calling his name. He asks his father for permission to look, desperate for a higher authority to give some order to this chaos. His father hesitates, then agrees, and Seb starts to swim towards the voice as the engine starts up again.

Chapter 32

July – 1989

'Go slower!' Aiden shouts.

Nina's hand trembles as she pulls back the throttle. Aiden has never seen Nina scared. He grips the metal rail on the side of the boat, her fear heightening his own. He wants to curl up on the deck, pretend this isn't happening. He isn't like his father at all; he will always be a coward. He blinks away tears as he searches the water.

'I can see something!' he shouts. 'Turn the engine off.'

The boat goes silent apart from the knocking sound of pieces of wreckage hitting the sides, and Aiden leans over the stern, holds out his hand as Seb grabs hold of the rail on the steps. Aiden helps pull him over the side; Seb's legs give way before he is on board and he collapses. Aiden hugs him; he's a hysterical mess that he barely recognizes as Seb at all, his fear flooding out of him like a wave.

'I thought you weren't going to come back' – Seb coughs – 'I tried to keep afloat, but it was too hard . . . I did try . . . I didn't want to . . . I didn't have a choice, Aiden. He was . . . I honestly didn't have a choice.'

Aiden can't follow what he is saying, can only feel how tightly Seb is gripping his arm. He peels away his fingers.

'Are you hurt?' Aiden asks.

Seb looks at him.

'I don't know. I can't feel anything.' His whole body is shaking.

'We've got one towel,' Aiden says, handing it to him, 'but it's soaking wet. Wring out your T-shirt and use it to dry yourself off.'

Seb grips Aiden's arm again.

'Don't leave me,' he whispers.

Aiden stares at him. 'I won't leave you. I'm right here. But we need to find Zoe.' He nods at Nina, who restarts the engine, and the boat moves slowly forwards.

Aiden watches Seb shuffle over to the seat, water still dripping off his T-shirt as he sits down on the burnt leather. He curls his legs up to his chest and stares over the side, clinging to the metal rail, shivering uncontrollably.

Aiden turns away and shouts Zoe's name over and over into the darkness.

Chapter 33

July – 1989

'Get up.' Will's brother's voice is insistent, but Will wants to sleep. He'd worshipped Andy while they were growing up, had done whatever he'd asked, bragged about him at school, covered up for him when he started drinking, agreed to hide the cans of lager in his wardrobe behind his school blazer.

He'd been in the middle of revising for his maths O-level when the police turned up, had been unable to reconcile the equation he was working on with the two men standing on his doorstep. None of them had seen it coming, least of all the woman Andy had mown down on the zebra crossing the night before, her body landing on the pavement in the dark. Andy had carried on driving a further nine miles to his friend's house, as they found out later, reporting his car stolen, leaving four empty cans of Foster's in the footwell.

The doctors said Neve Morgan might have survived if she'd received medical help more quickly, if Andy had stopped, called someone. But she wasn't found until two hundred and eight minutes later, a fact the prosecution barrister continually emphasized at the trial, so instead her life had ebbed away at the side of the road in the dark. A painful, lonely, unnecessary death.

'Get up,' Andy says again.

Will had promised to visit him in prison, but after that first time he hadn't gone back. Hadn't wanted to sit on the metal chairs screwed to the floor in that grey room that smelled of cigarettes and unwashed clothes. Hadn't wanted to hear about the new 'mates' Andy had made inside, how they'd promised to look after him when he got out and had already taught him to do things that made Will flinch.

And now the authorities had moved him a hundred and fifty miles further away. An overcrowding problem, apparently. Five years into his twelve-year sentence. His mum hadn't known how she was going to manage the journey when he'd spoken to her at Gatwick, and her voice had had that nasal tone that he knew meant she'd been crying.

And somehow Seb has found out about it, even though Will hadn't told anyone. Not even Zoe. Especially not Zoe.

Had he told Seb? When they were sharing one of their many spliffs on the beach? *He can't remember.*

'Get up.' Will opens his eyes and squints through the pain, feels the reinforced plastic deck beneath his fingers.

The realization of what has just happened hits him like a wave. The other boat, the look of surprise on the man's face as he opened his mouth to say something just before they'd collided and his own silent reply that it was already too late.

He watches Aiden turn around at the back of the boat and shout to Nina, 'Cut the engine and get over here. I can see something in the water.'

Chapter 34

July – 1989

The object floats into view under the light at the stern of the boat.

A body. Nina's stomach contracts. A man with a beard wearing a red T-shirt, his dark hair splayed out around his head like seaweed.

About the same age as her dad.

'Is it Zoe?' Will asks, his voice cracking.

'No,' Nina says quickly. 'It's not Zoe.'

Will staggers, and Claire catches hold of him as he slumps to his knees, one hand on his head, tells him to sit down.

They watch Aiden use the wooden oar to manoeuvre the body towards the boat. He leans down, grabs hold of the man's arm and, with Nina's help, pulls him on to the deck. Nina puts her fingers on his neck and feels for a pulse. She lifts up his eyelids then feels his wrist then looks at the others and shakes her head.

'Nothing,' she says.

Aiden drops the oar and crouches down next to the man's body. Seb makes a groaning noise and hugs his knees tighter into his chest. Nina wonders if he's going to be sick.

This can't be happening.

She goes to put her hand on Seb's wet T-shirt, but he flinches away from her.

'What should we do?' Aiden asks. 'Do we try and lift him on to one of the seats?'

Nina doesn't answer.

'Nina?' Aiden twists around to look at her. Her hands are trembling and her head twitches each time a wave slaps against the side of the boat.

'*Nina!*' Aiden says. Her face has turned a horrible grey colour. 'What do you want me to do?'

She swallows.

'There's nothing we *can* do.'

She can't comprehend how she has managed to find herself in this position, when less than an hour ago she was on a beach, dancing by a bonfire, her feet covered in soft white sand. She clenches and unclenches her fists, her pulse racing.

'Move out of the way, Aiden.'

She picks up the oar and prods the man's body so it slides off the boat and back into the water. The light on the stern sends ripples over his face as he floats a few feet away, defying the waves that should be taking him further from the boat.

'What the fuck was he doing out here in the middle of the night, anyway?' Nina's voice is bitter. 'I can't imagine someone his age going to a beach party.'

Aiden takes the oar away from her and throws it into the sea.

'Let's just concentrate on finding Zoe.'

She walks to the front of the boat and starts the engine. Aiden and Will shout Zoe's name as they look over the side. Pieces of debris morph into familiar shapes, an arm, a head, a hand. Nina blinks to clear her vision.

'There!' Will points at something. Nina cuts the engine. Her stomach sinks as she watches Aiden take a deep breath and dive off the side of the boat into the water.

Chapter 35

Claire – Now

'Come on now, time for your shower.'

The nurse repeats her request for the third time, but Claire holds the thin sheet over her head, her fingers the only part of her still visible. The nurse fishes around on the bed for the remote control and turns off *This Morning*, Holly and Phil at full volume now muted on the television fixed to the wall.

'Do you not want to have a wash? You've got some new shower gel. It's that nice smell you like. Jasmine and honeysuckle.' The nurse tugs gently on the sheet, but Claire clasps it tightly, her blunt, varnish-free fingernails turning white with the effort.

The nurse slides the tray table on wheels with the half-eaten bowl of cornflakes on it away from the bed and makes a mental note that Claire hasn't drunk anything this morning.

'You've been here over two years and you're still my most tricky patient when it comes to using the bathroom, do you know that?'

Claire mutters something and the nurse smooths down her plastic disposable apron.

'What did you say? I can't hear you if you try and talk

with that sheet over your head. Put it down and we can have a proper conversation.'

The nurse waits, familiar with this routine, feels a stab of pity for the woman in front of her who is trying to hide in her bed. Most of the patients with dementia she looks after in this private facility are in their seventies, but Claire only turned fifty-four last year. They'd had a party for her. Silver helium balloons, party hats and a cake without candles to comply with the fire regulations. Not that Claire would remember.

A large picture in a silver frame of Claire's husband and son sits on her dressing table. Smaller photos have been Blu-tacked on the wall next to the bed, but the nurse has never seen her look at them. The husband seems like a nice bloke. Always calls in at the nurses' station to say hello when he comes to visit her – once a week, which is more than many of them get in here. Most relatives can't bear to see their loved ones deteriorate, some faster than others, and rarely come in person, relying on the staff to provide meaningful interactions and on their health insurance to settle any outstanding bills.

Claire lowers her hands so her head is poking out above the sheet but doesn't loosen her grip. She looks at the nurse.

'I'm not getting in the shower.'

The nurse shrugs. 'OK, I'm not going to make you do anything you don't want to. We can have a bed bath instead. Would that be better?'

Claire nods.

'What is it about showers that you hate so much?' the nurse asks.

Claire stares at her blankly and doesn't reply.

'Is it because the bathroom's too cold? I can always ask them to turn up the heating if it's . . .'

The nurse breaks off as she sees a tear roll down Claire's cheek. She perches on the edge of the bed and pats her shoulder, the brushed-cotton sleeve of the new pyjamas her husband brought in last week soft under her hand.

'Hey, there's no need to get upset. We can have a wash here, OK?'

The nurse disappears into the bathroom and re-appears carrying a bowl of warm water. She sets it down on the melamine tray table, together with a toothbrush and toothpaste.

Claire lets go of the sheet and beckons to her. The nurse leans over the bed.

'I need to tell you something,' Claire says, her mouth next to the nurse's ear.

'What's that, then?'

'I need to tell you about the man.'

'What man?' the nurse asks.

'The one from the villa. He's in my shower.'

Chapter 36

July – 1989

Zoe is floating face down. Aiden turns her over, puts his hand under her chin and drags her to the bottom of the metal steps where Nina and Will reach down and pull her on to the deck. Her left arm has been sliced open by the propeller; Will can see three gashes, one underneath the other, parallel lines that have dug deep into her flesh. They gape open as Will moves her body, her humerus shiny white amid the blood.

'Fuck,' Nina says. 'Did our boat do that?'

Aiden shakes himself to get the water off.

'I don't know. Maybe it happened when she fell overboard. Pass me that towel, Seb.'

Aiden pushes the wet material against Zoe's wounds, trying to stop the blood that mingles with the water on the deck, swirling in dark puddles around their feet. Claire kneels down beside Zoe's body and feels for a pulse. Will watches as she puts her mouth over Zoe's and gives two breaths then starts chest compressions.

'I don't know if I'm doing this right,' Claire says.

Will can hear the panic in her voice. He sinks down on his knees as Claire pumps her hands up and down on Zoe's chest, her palms covered in dark stains that come off on his T-shirt as she pushes him away.

He has the sense that his life is twisting and that nothing will ever be the same again. His head fills with the thoughts of everything he hasn't said, hasn't done, of the things he always imagined there would be time to say. He holds his breath, hoping he can somehow transfer his oxygen to Zoe as she lies on the deck.

Claire stops for a second and Zoe suddenly convulses, water spilling out of her mouth.

'I can feel a pulse.'

Will puts his fingers on Zoe's neck, hesitates, then nods. Claire buries her face in her hands and starts to sob as they watch Zoe's chest rise up and down on its own. Her eyes open and then close again as Will prays that the faint beat under her skin doesn't stop.

'Zoe?' He isn't sure whether she can see them.

She murmurs something he doesn't understand.

'We need to get her back to the villa.'

Seb stares over the side of the boat. Will hopes the man's body has disappeared and they can pretend he never existed.

'I'll drive,' Will says.

Claire looks at him. 'I don't know if you're –'

'I'm fine.'

'You've got concussion, you've been smoking dope and you just hit another boat,' Nina says.

There's a silence.

'It was an accident,' Will says quietly. He remembers the same words coming out of Andy's mouth and how hollow they sounded back then. 'I only turned around for a second to look at Seb, because of the sparklers . . .'

'Don't fucking blame me, Lawson,' Seb growls. 'You were the one driving. You should have seen it.'

'It didn't have any fucking lights on,' Will says. 'How was I supposed to see it?'

'Didn't it? Really?' Seb says, his eyebrows raised. 'Are you sure?'

'I don't . . .' Will looks at Zoe. She has her eyes open and is staring at him. Time skips backwards to when he was standing beside her on the canal bank in Birmingham. He sees her shallow breathing, the way she keeps tightening her jaw.

Is she high?

She wouldn't have taken anything. Especially not when she knew she had to swim back to the boat.

He bends down beside her as she leans forward and vomits over the deck. She grabs his arm and pulls him towards her so her mouth is next to his ear.

'Claire did this, Will. You have to help me.'

Chapter 37

July – 1989

Aiden helps peel Zoe's fingers off Will's arm.

'What did she just say?' Nina asks sharply.

Will shakes his head, bewildered.

'She's not making any sense,' Aiden says. 'I don't know if she's taken something or if it's the pain, but we need to get her back to the villa.'

'I'm sober.' Will swallows. 'I'm in a better state than any of you lot. I can drive, but if one of you would rather do it, that's fine with me.'

Will looks at Claire, trying to block out what Zoe just said.

Claire wouldn't hurt her.

'You drive, and Nina can sit up at the front with you,' Aiden says. 'But what do we do about the guy in the water?'

'He's dead,' Nina says, after a silence.

'We can't just leave him,' Aiden says. 'Not without reporting it.' He points at another piece of wood as it floats past. 'Someone is going to see all this.'

'What do you suggest?' Nina asks.

Aiden raises his hands. 'I don't know. Shouldn't we call someone? There's a radio on the boat, isn't there?'

Nina nods but makes no attempt to pick it up.

'There must be some kind of emergency number we can use to contact the coastguard or the police?'

Aiden looks over the side of the boat and squints into the darkness, thinks he can see something among the waves. A flash of yellow. He points at it.

'What's that?'

Nina peers into the blackness.

'Where?' she says. 'I can't see anything.'

'I thought I saw something.' Aiden looks again, but whatever it was has gone, merged with the waves. 'We should go and look,' he adds. 'What if someone else is out there?'

No one moves.

'We could be looking all night,' Nina says. 'We're all freezing. Zoe's in a really bad way. We need to get her back to the villa.'

'But shouldn't we check?' Aiden asks. 'Or call for help on the radio?'

Nina and Seb exchange glances and Claire puts her hand on Aiden's arm.

'Aiden,' she says. 'No one knows we're out here. If we call someone, we're going to have to explain what happened. We've been drinking. We killed someone. We need to leave. Now.'

'We could just circle round a couple of times,' he says. 'Just to be sure –'

'It's easy to think you've seen something when you haven't,' Claire interrupts, tightening her grip. 'Especially when stuff is moving around in the water. Things change shape in the dark.' She squeezes so hard he knows he's going to wake up tomorrow with bruises where her fingers are. 'I've made that mistake before, Aiden. We just need to get back to the villa. Before anyone else gets hurt.'

He realizes she's talking about what she saw on the beach. A threat she's prepared to hold over him if he doesn't do what she wants. No possibility of a military career. No chance to prove himself. His parents' *disappointment*, which would almost be worse than their outright disapproval.

Aiden looks out over the waves, the water blacker than ever, and thinks of them, of how they'd feel if they knew who their son really was.

'OK,' he says eventually. 'You're right. Let's go.'

Claire smiles and releases her grip. His skin burns with shame.

Will starts the engine and eases the boat forwards. Nina stands beside him, her arms wrapped around herself, her fingers tapping to an inaudible beat. Seb curls up beside Aiden, who presses the sodden towel against Zoe's arm as she drifts in and out of consciousness.

Chapter 38

The jetty comes into view ahead of the boat. The steps up the cliff are lit up in the darkness and Aiden can make out the shape of the villa at the top, illuminated like a beacon of refuge against the night sky. Glancing at Claire, he wishes they were already inside, that they'd never left. There is a bitter taste in his mouth when he thinks about what she saw on the beach. A secret she's going to keep hold of, like a small bird, its heartbeat racing, ready to fly away the second she opens her hand.

Maybe he's being paranoid. Maybe what she said about making mistakes hadn't been about him at all. Maybe she'd just been trying to do the right thing. Getting Zoe back to the villa was more important than spending time searching for whatever he'd seen in the water. And she's right – it could have been anything, or nothing. *A hand.* Probably just another piece of boat wreckage.

It's the man he can't get out of his head. The man they left behind, his eyes staring blankly at the sky like a dead fish when Nina opened them. The image is imprinted on the inside of Aiden's eyelids, accusing him every time he blinks.

What if he wasn't dead?

He pushes the thought out of his head. Of course he

was dead. He was floating face down. And Nina checked his pulse. Twice. She's right. There's nothing they could have done for him. *You could have tried harder.* His teeth begin to chatter as the jetty lights get close enough to highlight the carnage they have created on the deck of the boat.

Will cuts the engine. Aiden can smell diesel as they bob silently in the water, the grey cliff face towering above them. The six of them look at one another. Aiden's eyes are drawn to the insects fluttering around the glaring bulbs, sending out tiny shadows that flicker across the wooden boards of the jetty. He barely recognizes the people who left here a few hours earlier. Zoe lies across the seat, her head in his lap.

'Someone needs to help me carry Zoe up to the villa and then I'll call an ambulance,' Will says. 'Or I can take her to hospital in the Jeep.'

Nina glances at Seb.

'Let's all just get inside first. Drop the anchor, Will. Claire, take this.'

She throws over the docking line and Claire climbs off the boat, ties it around a post on the jetty. Nina clambers off after her, holding on to Seb's hand, her wet feet slipping on the wooden slats.

Aiden and Will hold Zoe between them, her undamaged arm draped around Will's neck, the other dangling by her side. Aiden presses the already sodden towel against her deep gashes, the material changing from black to dark red beneath the lights.

So much blood.

He swallows, tries not to think about it; they just need to

get her up the steps and inside. Her face is so pale he wonders if she's about to pass out again. There are smears of blood on every surface as he climbs out of the boat – across the seats, on the deck, on the railings. His stomach turns over and he tries to keep his eyes fixed on the cliff, something firm and solid.

The three of them make their way slowly towards the steps up to the villa. The air is still warm, but Aiden can see that Will is shivering and wonders if he's going into shock.

'We'll be OK when we get inside,' Aiden says.

He's lying, but he needs to say something to distract Will from the horror. He knows his best friend well enough to see he's about to lose it and, if Will disintegrates, he thinks he might too.

'We're nearly there, Will.'

Please don't fall apart now.

Will's teeth start to chatter and his grip on Zoe slips. She lets out a small gasp. Her skin is wet, slick with blood.

Aiden looks at the steps carved into the rock and his stomach sinks. They move slowly, stopping after every few for Zoe to catch her breath. Her arm is starting to bleed more now, and he presses the towel harder.

He looks at the red droplets they are leaving on the ground behind them. He'll need to come back and clean up once they get Zoe inside. What if Luis sees them? What if he comes here after he leaves the beach party?

He can hear Claire talking to Nina and Seb below on the jetty, their voices too quiet for him to make out exactly what they're saying. He doesn't know why they're still down there; they should be up here, all sticking together.

He flinches, the noise when they hit the other boat replaying in his head. A crunching sound that reaches down into the roots of his teeth and twists them around in their sockets. A wave of nausea sweeps over him. As soon as anyone sees Nina's boat, his life is going to fall apart. Everything he's worked so hard for. He has a sudden flashback to when he felt that hand on his shoulder. He'd thought everything was over then, too. But Nina had saved him. And now she's going to have to come up with another plan.

'You all right?' Will is staring at him. His friend who had stuck by him, despite everything. Hadn't given him a hard time, even though he deserved it. Had helped him revise when the others were ignoring him.

Aiden nods. 'Can we stop for a sec?'

He looks at Zoe, who has her eyes shut. 'Zoe? Are you OK?'

Stupid question.

She murmurs something indecipherable. The skin on her face is almost translucent.

'We need to get her to hospital,' Will says. 'Can you carry her?'

Aiden nods. 'You're going to have to take the towel and press it on it, then. Try and stop the bleeding.'

He picks Zoe up, cradling her in front of him like a small child, and continues up the steps, glancing back at the others, who are looking up at him from the jetty below.

Chapter 39

July – 1989

Claire squats down beside Nina and peers at the front of the boat. The white prow is covered all the way down to the waterline in a series of deep scratches, and streaks of blue paint flake off when she scrapes at them with her nail. The fibreglass hull is dented, a small hole below the word 'Nina'. There's no way they can hide the damage, but at the same time it doesn't seem devastating enough to reflect the horror of what has just happened. What they've just done. *Killed a man.* She shuts her eyes briefly to block out the thought. *It was an accident.* She mutters the words to herself, feeling their familiarity spread out in her mouth, then looks up and sees Seb pull on Nina's hand.

'You OK?' he asks.

Nina nods. She walks back down the jetty with him. Claire pretends to examine the boat while eavesdropping on their conversation.

'We've been through worse than this before, haven't we?' Nina says.

Seb doesn't answer, glancing to where Will, Aiden and Zoe are making their way up the steps.

'We can't have Will taking her to hospital,' Nina says.

'He's not going to agree to that,' Seb mutters.

'We need to make him realize we don't have a choice. You know that, don't you?'

Claire sees something pass between them, a look that makes her start shivering again.

'You trust me to do what's best for us?' Nina adds.

Seb swallows, then nods.

Claire examines the bow of the boat again, the hole below Nina's name staring back at her like the pupil of a giant eye. She wonders how long it will be before someone reports the other boat missing. How long they've got to work out what they're going to do. What Nina is capable of. She thinks back to what Aiden said he saw over the side of the boat between the waves. That flash of yellow. She should have admitted she'd seen it too.

A man's torso.

She shakes her head to clear away the image before she walks down the jetty to join Nina and Seb. As they start up the steps she tells herself it was nothing, just another piece of painted yellow wood that had sunk beneath the surface of the ocean.

'If Will insists, though,' Seb says as he follows Nina up, 'and Aiden takes his side, I don't think there's much we can do to stop him.'

'Aiden won't take his side,' Nina says. 'He still owes me.'

Claire rubs at the mark that has appeared on the back of her hand, but the red streak doesn't budge. It doesn't hurt, so she knows she hasn't cut herself, but the thought that it isn't her blood, that it belongs to someone else, makes her rub harder, bruising her skin.

'Aiden will go along with whatever we suggest,' she says.

'Will he?' Seb asks.

Claire looks at him as she licks the tip of her finger and wipes it over the back of her hand, the red streak finally dissolving in the wetness. She doesn't stop rubbing even when it's gone.

'Yes,' she says. 'I'll talk to him.'

'He might not –'

Claire interrupts Seb before he can finish. 'Just trust me, Seb. He will.'

Chapter 40

Droplets of Zoe's blood fall off the towel into the pool, spreading out below the surface like miniature swirls of smoke and creating small ripples in the otherwise motionless water. Will hovers next to the patio doors as Nina runs up the last few steps, her fingers shaking as she puts the key in the lock.

'Wait there a second,' she says. Aiden stands by the door with Zoe still in his arms. 'I don't want to trash the living room as well as the boat,' she adds. 'I've got too much to try and explain to my parents already.'

She disappears into the hall and reappears a few seconds later with an armful of towels, which she spreads out over the sofa. Will is desperate to get rid of the one he's holding and goes into the kitchen, throws it into the dustbin. It lands in the bottom with a heavy thump, like a piece of raw meat. He turns on the tap and washes his hands four times, scrubbing them furiously with soap until the scent of lavender disguises the metallic smell in his nostrils that he can taste when he swallows.

This is what his brother did. But Will had never understood why Andy had washed himself as well as the car. Now he does. He'd just wanted to feel clean again.

Aiden lowers Zoe carefully on to the sofa. She groans as he moves her. Nina perches beside her and presses a clean towel against her arm. Will puts his hand on Zoe's forehead and flinches at the coolness of her skin.

'We need to get her to hospital,' he says. 'She's lost so much blood. Should we call an ambulance? Or would it be quicker if I just took her in the Jeep?'

Nina adjusts the towel to hide the patch of redness that is already beginning to seep through it, and Zoe briefly opens her eyes. Will notices she still can't seem to focus properly.

'I think we need to wait,' Nina says after a pause. 'Discuss what we're going to do. We should get our story straight before you go driving off to the hospital in the middle of the night.'

'What do you mean, wait?' Will's voice echoes in the large room. 'We can't wait. Do you realize how serious her injuries are? She needs urgent medical attention.'

Nina stares at him before replying, her voice cold.

'I'm not saying Zoe doesn't need medical attention. I'm just saying we need to work out what we're going to tell people first.'

Will opens his mouth to protest, but Nina holds up her hand.

'Listen to me, Will. It won't be long before someone reports the man we killed as missing. We have to assume he told someone where he was going. Once they start looking for his boat, I don't think it will take them long to find it. There were pieces of debris floating all over the

162

place. If we take Zoe to hospital, the doctors are going to realize her injuries are from a propeller. They'll start asking questions if she appears at the same time a boat accident is reported. The police will come here and, if they do, they'll see the damage to the hull of our boat. We don't have a licence. Or insurance. You'll be charged with manslaughter. We could all go to prison. You can kiss goodbye to your career, to seeing your family for the next ten years, to everything you've worked for.'

There's a long silence.

'You don't have a licence or insurance?' Will asks eventually.

Nina flushes, then shakes her head.

'The other boat didn't have any lights on,' Will says. 'It wasn't our fault we didn't see it.'

'*You* didn't see it,' Seb says. '*You* were the one driving.'

'It was an accident!' Will's voice is shrill. He watches Zoe fumble to move the towel away from her arm, her face creased in pain, but Nina pushes it back into place.

'*We* know it was an accident,' Nina says, 'but that doesn't change the fact that you killed someone. I couldn't swear whether that other boat had its lights on or not. It all happened too fast.'

'I thought I saw something . . .' Seb mumbles.

'You can't remember what you saw,' Aiden snaps. 'You were too busy lighting fucking sparklers.'

Will silently mouths 'thank you'. At least he has one person's support.

'Even if the boat *didn't* have any lights on,' Nina continues, 'we still hit it and drove away, leaving' – she pauses – 'leaving someone dead.'

Will hesitates. 'We don't have to tell anyone about the man we saw in the water. We could just say we think we might have hit something, Zoe fell overboard, got injured by the propeller and we drove straight back here to report it.'

'Don't be fucking stupid, Lawson,' Seb says. 'They'll ask why we didn't radio it in at the time. It's like driving a car – you can't just leave the scene of an accident. And once they find that guy dead, they're going to come straight here and arrest us. In fact,' he adds, 'it won't be *us* they'll arrest as, technically, we didn't kill him. It'll be *you*.'

Chapter 41

July – 1989

Will shivers as Seb glares at him.

What exactly had he said at the beach party?

Fragments of their conversation flicker in his head.

'What if they find out we were there?' Seb continues. 'People saw us drinking. We'll all be done for that as well.'

'I wasn't drinking,' Will retorts.

'Smoking dope, then,' Nina snaps. 'What if they give you a drug test? How long does it stay in your system?'

'A few days.' Will pauses. 'Maybe longer. It depends how much you've had.'

How much had he had? Too much to be driving a boat.

Nina looks at Zoe lying on the sofa.

'We need to try and stop the bleeding on Zoe's arm, clean ourselves up and work out exactly what we're going to tell people. If Zoe gets any worse, we'll take her to hospital.'

'We could just say she fell off a boat yesterday and we didn't realize how serious it was until now,' Will says.

'Think about everyone who saw us at the party, Will,' Nina replies. 'All those people know Zoe was fine then.' She walks into the kitchen, fishes about in a drawer and brings out a roll of duct tape. 'I'll cut off a piece of towel to put over the wound and we can bind it up with this for now.'

Will shakes his head. 'She needs a doctor.'

He looks at his friends, one face at a time; searching for help, but no one speaks.

'Aiden?' he says finally. 'What do you think?'

Aiden opens his mouth as if he's about to reply, but no sound comes out.

'He agrees with the rest of us,' Claire says. 'We need to get our story straight before we do anything.'

'Can't Aiden speak for himself?' Will asks.

'Perhaps we should wait,' Aiden says eventually. 'Nina's right. No one should be driving the Jeep right now. I think we should get our story straight and take Zoe to hospital tomorrow.'

Will throws up his arms in frustration.

'It doesn't look like I have a choice, does it? Fine. We'll wait.'

He drags the coffee table from between the sofas and over to the other side of the room, then pulls the empty sofa into the space, closer to Zoe.

'I'll stay down here with her,' he says. 'We need to at least try and clean her arm. Antiseptic. Have you got any?'

'There's an old tube of Germolene in one of the bathroom cabinets, I think,' Nina replies.

Will shakes his head. 'That's no good. Get me some scissors.'

He unwinds a piece of tape from the roll and takes one of the towels out of Nina's pile, cuts off a large piece and folds it over a few times.

'Zoe?' She doesn't open her eyes, but she nods, a tiny movement he wouldn't have seen unless he was looking for it. 'I'm going to put something on your arm. Take that towel away, Nina.'

She puts it on the floor, streaks of blood zig-zagging across the white material, and Will is hit by a wave of nausea. Three deep gashes run across the top of Zoe's arm. He thinks he can see bone at the bottom of one of them, bright white, as if someone has scrubbed it clean. He presses the folded piece of towel down on top of the horror and fastens it in place with the duct tape, wrapping it around Zoe's arm and pulling it tight to try and bring the edges of the wounds together.

Zoe opens her eyes and watches him while he does it. After he's finished, she reaches for his hand with her uninjured arm and holds it against her face. Will takes a deep breath, knowing what they are doing is wrong, that they should be taking her to hospital. He looks at the four people standing watching.

'Happy now?' he asks. 'What are you waiting for? Go and clean yourselves up and then come back down so we can discuss what we're going to do.' He glances at the streaks of blood covering his clothes. 'And can you get me another pair of shorts and a T-shirt so I can change out of these.'

They slope off, like wolves in a pack, Aiden last. He pauses briefly at the bottom of the stairs and looks at Will as if he's going to say something, then turns away, puts his hand on the banister and follows the others up.

Chapter 42

Seb – Now

Nina's car is almost out of sight by the time Seb manages to hail a cab on Grosvenor Square. He tells the driver to follow the Tesla as he checks the cash in his pocket; small amounts saved over weeks from his Jobseeker's Allowance. He hopes they reach their destination before it runs out.

The cab passes through Mayfair, where he stares out of the taxi window at a dog-walker, the company name emblazoned on the back of their sweatshirt; another service quietly outsourced here, people working away in the background on minimum wage to keep everything running smoothly.

They continue through Chinatown, along Shaftesbury Avenue and High Holborn, the pavements beginning to fill with a smattering of commuters as he gets closer to the City. By lunchtime, they'll be overflowing. Buildings become sleeker, taller, larger. Intricate cornices, carved stone doorways, ornate details that once took time and skill to create, transform into a landscape of glass and polished concrete.

After his first conviction, Nina disappeared. She'd cut off the last contact number he'd had for her and moved out of her flat. When he got out after that first stretch, he had tried visiting her parents, but they'd refused to give him any information and had told him not to come back. And then his life had disintegrated and he had more pressing things to do than look for Nina, like finding something to eat and somewhere to live.

But despite her lack of presence on social media and a change of name after a wedding that had cost more than he'd earned in a year, legally and otherwise, when he got out of prison this time, he'd found her. It had been her husband who had given her away. Seb had found an announcement of their wedding in an old edition of the *Telegraph* in the local library and had looked him up. Hugo Thornton. A barrister at Connaught Chambers. He'd been quoted in an article complaining about a proposed basement extension to an apartment block in Grosvenor Square. Seb knew people like that didn't complain unless it affected them directly, so he had made a note of the address and knew, if he turned up early enough and waited, Nina would have to come out eventually.

She didn't appear to have any children, but that didn't surprise him. He couldn't imagine Nina ever having kids, not even before everything happened. People change, but not that much. Her world had always revolved around her, no one else, and he was certain she'd taken every precaution to ensure it stayed that way. The photos of Hugo, on the other hand, had squeezed something in his chest, making it difficult to breathe. Blond hair, slicked back. It was what he'd imagined he'd see in the mirror if he stripped away the last thirty or so years and was allowed to start over again.

He unfolds the free copy of the *Metro* that he'd picked up outside Baker Street tube station and flicks through it slowly, savouring the words, trying to distract himself from the numbers ticking over too fast on the meter in the front of the taxi. The sports page with details of the results from the weekend has the news of Saturday's nil–nil draw against Italy in the UEFA Nations League. Another squandered opportunity. Someone should have explained to them why planning is so important. In prison, he'd spent as much time as he could in the library, reading anything he could get his hands on, when the methadone allowed. It was where he'd come up with this plan in the first place. A kernel of an idea that had jumped into his imagination several years ago and had grown over the years into something bigger. He just needs to double-check a few final details.

The Tesla pulls up next to a building and Seb watches Nina open the door as he asks his cab driver to stop. He gets out, pays with a few five-pound notes, still unused to the feel of the polymer, not taking his eyes off her. She has to walk past him to join the dozens of other employees that are funnelling in through the doors of the vast building. He stands motionless on the kerb, pretending he's about to cross the road, so close to her that he inhales her perfume as she sweeps past, oblivious to his presence. *Not the one she used to wear.*

She disappears inside, and he watches her go, adrenaline still coursing around his body. He rubs his beard, his jaw sore from where he has been clenching it. What happened on that holiday hasn't touched her. She's buried it, just like she's buried so many other things in her life and walked away, leaving the rest of them to suffer.

Not any more. He takes a photo of the sign on the

outside of the building and glances at the email he received late last night, looks again at the sender's address: beachparty89@me.com. He opens it and reads the contents again, a chill passing over his skin.

Nina isn't the only one who needs to worry about someone finding them.

Chapter 43

July – 1989

Will wakes up early the following morning. He's sprawled on the sofa in the pair of shorts and T-shirt Seb had brought down for him last night; the ones he was wearing on the boat are in the kitchen bin. The knot in his stomach tells him something is wrong even before he's fully conscious.

Zoe is lying motionless under the blanket on the sofa opposite. For one horrific moment, he thinks she's dead. He stares at her in the dim light, not daring to move until he sees the slight movement of her chest, up and down, and experiences a rush of light-headedness.

He must have fallen asleep while the others were talking. A circular conversation in which no one could agree what to do. He leans over and puts his hand on Zoe's wrist. Her pulse is racing. He counts in his head. Well over a hundred and twenty beats per minute. This is madness. She needs to go to hospital.

He creeps out of the living room into the hallway and looks in the copper bowl where Nina leaves the keys for the Jeep. His chest tightens when he sees it's empty. He peers out of the window by the front door. Nina's gardener is raking the grass and raises his hand when he sees Will staring at him, but Will doesn't respond.

He's focused on what he can see at the bottom of the driveway: the metal gates are open and the Jeep is gone.

Chapter 44

July – 1989

Claire grips the grab handle above the passenger window in the Jeep as Nina goes around a bend. She went to bed in the early hours after Will fell asleep, but lay awake, debating whether to call home.

During all the years she'd been at university she'd never once felt that urge. Her dad would probably have been away on business and she only phoned her mum out of duty, keeping the call to under five minutes each time – the words between them stilted: exchanges of perfunctory information. But today she wishes she could hear either of their voices, even if her mother's is blurred from her medication; anyone in a position of authority who could tell her what to do.

Nina puts her foot down to overtake another car and Claire clenches her teeth together so tightly that her jaw starts to ache. She can tell Nina is scared; can see it in the way the tendons stand out in her neck, and this terrifies her even more than thinking about what they've done. She wants to ask her to slow down but is worried it might make her go even faster.

'We need to buy these things and then go straight back to the villa,' Nina says, glancing across at her. 'I don't like leaving Seb there on his own.'

'He's not on his own,' Claire replies, but she knows what Nina means. She wonders if the split between the six of them is fixed and, if it is, whether she has picked the right side.

You aren't Nina's best friend. Seb is.

She stares straight ahead, trying not to think of how Zoe had looked before they left – a shrunken figure lying on the sofa, her face so pale it almost disappeared among the cream cushions.

Nina stops the Jeep, looks in the rear-view mirror and scrapes her hair back with her nails into a ponytail. Her eyes are a steel-grey colour as Claire watches her rub her cheeks and practise smiling; trying to look more natural, with less of a grimace.

'Shall we get this over with?' Nina doesn't make any attempt to move, and Claire is unsure whether she is waiting for an answer or whether it's a rhetorical question. 'Antiseptic, Elastoplast tape, bandages and paracetamol.' Nina repeats the list of items they've come for, counting them on her fingers. 'Do we need anything else?'

'How am I supposed to know, Nina?' Claire feels the connection between them loosen, like a rope slackening. She doesn't want the responsibility of having to try to make Zoe better. It's like dealing with her mother all over again. 'I only studied medicine for one term,' she adds. '*One*. I know nothing about dealing with serious wounds.'

Nina stares at her, her bottom lip sticking out in a pout.

'What the fuck is the matter with you, Claire? You know more than me, Seb or Aiden. And Zoe is depending on you.'

The nausea that has been washing around the bottom of Claire's stomach rises up in a wave. Nina opens the driver's door, gets out and slams it behind her, the noise echoing in the silence. Claire shakes the image of her mother's face out of her head and follows after her.

'Nina! *Cómo estás?*' Antonio grins as they walk into the pharmacy. Claire feels like a lifetime has passed since they were last here. She glances down at her hands, halting mid-step as she sees a red smear across her skin which disappears when she blinks.

'*Estoy bien, gracias,*' Nina says.

Claire thinks Nina's voice sounds more high-pitched than usual. A slight hesitancy in her fluency that wasn't there before. She looks at the pharmacist. His expression says he's noticed it too. Nina grabs three packets of Elastoplast tape and a couple of packets of paracetamol off the shelves, nodding as Antonio continues to talk to her.

Claire can see his wife sitting in her wheelchair watching the news on the television in the same place as when they came in before. She smiles at Nina and raises her hand in a wave. Antonio lifts up the wooden flap as Nina walks over to the counter and beckons for her to come through.

Nina holds out the Elastoplast and paracetamol.

'I'm sorry, I can't stop to chat today.'

The smile on Juliana's face falls. Claire thinks of the man floating in the water at the back of the boat and rubs her hand again. She looks at Antonio.

'We're in a bit of a rush. Do you have any antiseptic or bandages?'

Antonio's hand hovers on the wooden flap, unsure whether to shut it or leave it open. Claire can see a line of perspiration on Nina's forehead.

'*Tiene algún antiséptico o vendajes?*'

Nina hesitantly repeats Claire's request in Spanish. Antonio reaches for a small bottle of liquid and a cardboard packet then puts them down in front of her as he closes the wooden flap. The bottle is tiny. Not nearly enough for what they need. Nina swallows.

'*Más?*' she says. The pharmacist's eyes narrow, but he reaches up to get another bottle off the shelf and puts it next to the first.

'*Estás herida?*' his wife asks, turning away from the screen.

Nina shakes her head. 'No,' she replies. Claire watches her smile and hopes her shorts don't ride up to reveal the cuts on her leg. 'I'm not injured. I'm fine. It's our friend.'

Juliana looks at Claire, and she nods in agreement.

'He's back at the villa,' she says. 'He scraped his leg getting out of the pool. A nasty cut. Quite big.'

She holds out her hands a small distance apart to try and demonstrate, increasing the gap between them. Antonio stares at her. Nina frowns and Claire lowers her hands, entwining her fingers together.

'*Necesita un doctor?*' Antonio asks as he puts down another packet of bandages.

They both shake their heads.

'No, I'm sure he'll be fine,' Nina says. She slides several notes across the counter, her fingers shaking.

Claire holds out her hand for the brown paper bag Antonio is putting everything into.

'*Gracias,*' she says confidently. One of the few words in Spanish she knows. She feels a warmth spread across her chest as she realizes Seb might be Nina's best friend, but he isn't here and, at this moment, she is the person who Nina is relying on. She smiles at her, but Nina's gaze is fixed on Juliana's television screen.

Her eyes widen as she realizes what Nina is looking at. There is a photo of Gaby on the screen beside the news-reader, 'DESAPARECIDA' written in large red letters below it.

'One of my customers told me about that this morn-ing,' Antonio says. 'Apparently there was an accident last night.'

Claire watches the colour drain out of Nina's face. Her heart thuds beneath her ribs and she can taste salt in her mouth.

'Was there?' Nina's voice sounds unnaturally loud.

Antonio nods, studying her over the top of his glasses. 'At the correfoc beach party. A girl drowned. Were you there?'

Claire stares at the blood that seems to be dripping off her hand on to the floor.

It's not real. It's not real.

She remembers Gaby diving off the side of the boat into the water to swim back to the beach. The contrast of her white bikini against her tanned skin. She thinks she might be sick.

'We went for a bit,' Nina says. 'But we left early. I'm so sorry to hear about the girl.' She turns to Claire and holds out her hand. 'We really need to go.'

'*Espero que tu amigo esté bien,*' Juliana says as they head towards the door.

Nina swallows. 'I'm sure they will be. I just need to get these things back to them.'

Claire looks at Nina's face as she says the words, convinced that everyone in the pharmacy, including Nina herself, knows she is lying. She leans against the wall when they get outside.

'Whatever happens,' Nina says, 'when we get back to the villa, we do not mention this to Seb. OK?'

Claire nods. She has no desire to tell Seb, or anyone else, about this. Secrets on top of secrets. The weight is beginning to suffocate her.

Chapter 45

July – 1989

Aiden shuts his eyes and pretends to be asleep when Seb pushes open his bedroom door in the morning. He's been awake since five, too scared to move, hoping somehow if he stays exactly where he is the events of the night won't have happened, that he'll go downstairs to find the living room in a mess, the kitchen table covered in empty bottles, the tang of tequila hanging in the air, Nina, Zoe and Claire sunbathing by the pool and Will and Seb playing blackjack.

A small voice in his head tells him this isn't going to happen, that he can't pretend he hadn't heard Nina whispering to Claire as they'd passed outside his bedroom on their way downstairs, followed by the sound of the Jeep starting up. If he listens to what it is telling him, it means he'll have to get up and face what is lying on the sofa downstairs. And despite his dissertation on law and morality, despite telling his father he would be prepared to sacrifice himself for his country, he knows what lies at the very heart of him is a coward.

'Buckley,' Seb says again, shaking his shoulder, 'you need to get up. Nina's gardener is here. You need to get rid of him.'

Aiden doesn't answer.

'Buckley!' Seb repeats. 'If that guy looks through the patio doors and sees Zoe on the sofa, we're in all kinds of trouble. Fucking get up. Now.'

Aiden opens his eyes.

'Wh–wh–wh–what do you want me to do?'

Seb frowns. Will is the only one in their group who has heard him stutter.

'You speak Spanish better than I do,' Seb says. 'Just tell him Nina doesn't need him to come in today.' He throws the duvet back and pulls at Aiden's arm. 'Come on. Now.'

'Just gi–gi–give me a sec.'

'Are you all right?' Seb stares at him, and Aiden nods, not trusting himself to speak. He takes a deep breath, looks at his Swatch and imagines the space in his mouth.

Don't say yes. Don't start your reply with a semi-vowel.

'I'm fine.' His voice is almost a whisper.

'Just get a fucking move on, then,' Seb says.

Aiden catches the way Seb looks at him. The same way everyone looked at him while he was growing up, potential friends keeping a distance once they heard him speak. In the end, his parents had shelled out money they couldn't afford in a desperate attempt to get rid of the excruciating silences that permeated every conversation, tired of waiting and smiling politely while he fought to get a word out. He thought he'd fixed it, but it looks like he hasn't even won that battle properly.

He goes downstairs and walks on to the lawn by the driveway as Seb watches from the front door. Luis smiles as he sees him approaching and Aiden feels something inside him break, as if part of him is falling away. It hurts so much he can barely breathe. He swallows, the word he'd stammered in the urinals at the bar burning in his head.

I am a coward. I deserve this.

'We don't need you today,' he mumbles. Luis stares at him, then glances at Seb, who's still standing by the front door.

'*Tus amigos no saben,*' Luis says quietly.

'No,' Aiden shakes his head. 'My friends don't know.' He looks directly at Luis. 'But that's because there is nothing to know.'

Luis's forehead creases. Aiden wants to throw his arms around him, tell him about Zoe lying on the sofa, beg him for help, but then remembers the feeling of almost drowning, and the promise he'd made in exchange for his life. He thinks of his parents, of how he doesn't want to let them down, of the Royal Artillery Regiment, which he is planning to join. He thinks of what he owes Nina.

I will reform.

'Nina doesn't need you today,' Aiden says again slowly. '*Quiero que te vayas.* You need to go.' He flaps his hand in a shooing motion, and Luis shakes his head.

'*Pero anoche —*' he starts to say.

'That night was a mistake,' Aiden replies flatly. His insides feel as if someone has scooped them out, leaving nothing behind.

Luis hesitates, then slowly puts his shears down on to the grass. '*Mi error,*' he says, holding up his hands. Aiden allows himself to remember what happened on the jetty: their bodies entwined together, the feeling of Luis's skin against his, the different shades of colour — his paleness against Luis's tan, stained brown by the sun. He will not allow himself to think about this again. He cannot.

He has blocked out what he did at university in the same way. It had been Nina's idea to steal a book from the library. A dare to see who could get away with it. But after he'd done it once, he hadn't wanted to stop. One book had turned into several, textbooks stuffed into his backpack each time he'd left the building. He still doesn't know why he did it – he'd made a few extra quid on top of his grant by selling them to other students, but it was never about the money. He'd savoured the kick he got from getting away with it.

And then one evening he'd given his usual wave to the librarian on reception and felt the security guard's hand on his shoulder, followed by a request to open his bag.

He'd begun to stutter an admission of guilt, but Nina had intervened, taken control of the situation, calmly informing the guard that the books had been sold to Aiden by another undergraduate, James Harding. Everyone had heard the rumours circulating round the student union that he was on a final warning, having been caught smoking dope in the toilets.

The others had backed up Nina's story, even after Seb's furious explosion when he got home and saw how many books were stuffed into Aiden's wardrobe. Nina had been the one who came up with a plan. She'd taken a couple of books out of the pile and told Zoe to put them into James Harding's bag during a lecture the following morning. Except Zoe had lost her nerve at the last minute and Claire had been left to finish the job, dropping them into his rucksack while he was eating lunch.

The security guard had followed James across campus later that afternoon. The six of them had watched out of one of the library windows as the guard caught up with him just as he reached the clock tower, disappearing beneath one of the arches at the foot of the hundred-metre-tall structure. The guard had pulled James's rucksack off his shoulder and opened it, waved the stolen books in front of his face.

Aiden had watched the expressions on James's face morph from surprise to anger and finally fear. Nina's lips had twitched as James sank to the ground, his head bowed. Aiden had clasped his hands together and started to step away from the window, ready to walk outside and confess, but Nina had grabbed his arm, told him to stay where he was.

He'd heard later that week that despite vehemently protesting his innocence James Harding had been kicked off his degree course with only a few weeks left until graduation.

Aiden remembers how Nina had bought sambuca and Baileys on the way back to their house, already planning to make Slippery Nipples to celebrate. As if they hadn't just destroyed somebody's life. Even the smell of them now makes him nauseous.

Luis stares at him before he walks up the driveway and out through the gates. Aiden watches him, his feet rooted to the spot, blinks back the tears that threaten to fall down his cheeks. His heart shrivels and he wonders if it will stop beating completely. *Don't let him leave.*

'Aiden!' There's a shout, and he turns around to see Will with Seb by the front door, their faces white. 'You need to see this. Get in here now.'

Chapter 46

July – 1989

Aiden runs across the lawn towards the villa, feeling the grass prick the soles of his feet with each step. Every atom in his body screams at him to go after Luis, to call him back and apologize, but then he thinks of Zoe lying on the sofa and the stains on the steps to the jetty and keeps moving towards the front door.

The Jeep pulls into the driveway and Claire gets out of the passenger side holding a brown paper bag.

'What is it?' she asks.

'You need to see this!' Seb shouts.

Claire follows him into the living room. Aiden glances at her and, for a second, he catches a glimpse of the friendship they had before the beach party, remembers their easy banter. Then she blinks and her expression hardens. He feels the flutter of wings in his chest.

This is all your fault.

Zoe is still lying on the sofa, her face paler than ever. Will's DIY bandage has held together; Aiden can see the black duct tape encircling her arm. The others are all staring at the television on the other side of the room, the volume turned up so loud it makes him want to cover his ears.

The newsreader is speaking in a stream of Spanish, too

fast for him to understand. Video footage is playing, taken from the deck of a boat, and the camera pans around to show numerous pieces of debris floating in the sea. There aren't as many as when he was in the water last night; some have disappeared, presumably sunk to the bottom or carried away by the current. He sees Will swallow as the close-up shot focuses in on one particular piece, a plank almost as long as him, blue and yellow paint clearly visible on the wood.

'What are they saying?' he asks.

Nina continues to look at the screen, her face white. 'Fuck.'

'What –' he starts to say, but Nina holds up her hand to silence him. He can feel her thoughts stab into him, over and over, like a knife.

You owe me. You owe me. You owe me.

The news anchor continues to talk, and the video pans away to a wider shot of the ocean, where they can see several boats with uniformed officials retrieving pieces of wreckage from the water.

'Christ.' Will puts his hand over his mouth as if it will somehow silence the newsreader.

A photo appears on the screen showing a man with dark, curly hair, smiling through his beard. Aiden puts his head in his hands. He tries to tell himself this isn't the man they hit but can see from everyone else's faces that it is. Another photo appears on the screen – the same man, this time holding a little girl in a pink sundress, his arm around a woman's waist. All three of them are laughing, standing in front of a wooden fishing boat, the hull of which is painted in blue, yellow and brown.

The photo has been taken on the stone jetty of a small port in the sunshine; in the background, traditional stone houses form a splash of yellow and blue along the front of the quay. Aiden notices a metal frame shaped like an 'n' clipped on to either side of the hull. Attached to the horizontal bar is a large light, clearly visible. The man's name appears on the screen beneath the photo: Señor Lopez.

He can't bring himself to say it out loud, knows it would come out as a stammer. He looks at Will, whose face has turned a horrible grey colour, and knows exactly how he feels. He has the same tingling in his chest, the same rock-hard ball in the pit of his stomach as he felt when the security guard confronted him in the library. There was a light, he mouths to himself, silently.

There was a light. We just didn't see it.

Chapter 47

Now

*What do you think would be a fitting punishment for what you did?
Life in prison? Death? I used to fantasize about that for you – an
eye for an eye, a tooth for a tooth – but I think in your case dying
would mean things were over with too quickly. I want you to suffer
first. To experience the pain you put me through.*

*Do you ever regret it? Are there times when you're out enjoying
yourself, laughing with friends, when you suddenly remember? A
split second when it feels like your skin has been sliced open with a
knife? A sharp sting that makes you catch your breath and sours the
moment, all pleasure ripped away. I hope so. I hope you feel a fear
that twists your insides when you think someone is going to find out
what you did. I hope it's so painful it makes you double over in
agony.*

*But even if it does, I can tell you that it's nothing compared to
what you put me through. You shattered my life into thousands of
tiny pieces, impossible to put back together again. Every day since
has been tainted by your actions. I don't have a single moment when
I can forget about it, not even for a second. It's there, all the time,
hovering in the background, a dark cloud that smothers everything I
do. You'll know how that feels once I've finished with you.*

*You thought you'd covered your tracks. Destroyed all the evidence.
Come up with a plausible explanation. Created an alibi. And it
was almost perfect. Almost. But you forgot something. And I've*

found it. It's been sitting here all this time – I like to think it was waiting for me. I did wonder back then; thoughts that floated around inside my head in the small spaces between the grief. I didn't want to believe you were capable of that. I couldn't prove it, so it was easier to believe what everyone else was saying.

But now I can. And I'm coming for every single one of you.

Chapter 48

July – 1989

Will feels as if he's swallowed something greasy that coats his stomach in a thick layer of guilt. Everyone stares at him as the news switches to another topic.

'He had a family.' The words come out of his mouth, but he doesn't recognize his own voice. Up until now, the man's body has been detached from reality, an object floating in the ocean, something to be covered up at all costs. But now he has a name and seems to be reaching out, like the tendrils of a plant, attaching himself to their lives. A daughter, a wife. People he's left behind who are still here.

Nina puts her hand on his shoulder.

'Don't think about it,' she says.

'How can we not think about it?' Will replies. 'A man is dead. He had a family . . .' He breaks off, his voice trembling, thinking of Neve Morgan and the grief etched on her mother's face when she looked at Andy in the dock in court. 'And why didn't you tell me you were going into town? I woke up and you'd gone.'

'We didn't want to disturb you,' Nina says. 'Seb knew where we were.' She glances at Zoe lying on the sofa and lowers her voice. 'We needed to get her some things from the pharmacy.'

'We need to take her to a doctor,' Will snaps back.

'The bandage stayed on OK,' Nina says, almost as if he hasn't spoken.

'She needs to go to hospital,' he says.

'Were you just watching the same news report we were, Will?'

Nina holds out her hand for the paper bag Claire still has in her grasp. 'They know about the boat we hit. They are showing photos of a man *you* killed. Do you want to try and explain Zoe's injuries to someone at the moment?'

Will opens his mouth to reply but then shuts it again. Nina is right. His mother has already lost one son. He can't put her through the same thing again. She won't cope.

He walks over to Zoe and puts his hand over hers.

'Zoe? Are you OK if we try and treat you here?' he says. 'Nina has got some antiseptic and proper bandages to put on your' – he thinks but doesn't say, *horrifically deep gashes that really need stitches* – 'arm.'

Zoe runs her tongue over her cracked lips. 'I know if you take me to hospital they might find out about the accident,' she says. 'I don't want to get anyone into trouble. I won't tell them about the boat.'

Nina bends down beside Will.

'We're going to make sure you're looked after,' she says.

Zoe opens her eyes briefly, looks at Nina.

'Do you think you can fix it here? It really hurts.'

Nina squeezes Zoe's uninjured hand. ''Course we can. You're going to be fine.'

Will waits for one of the others to say something, but no one does. Every atom in the room vibrates with dishonesty, their unspoken lies gathering into something heavy and solid that he fears will stop Zoe breathing altogether. If he was a good person, he wouldn't be doing this. But it turns out he's much more like his brother than he has wanted to believe. He stares out through the patio doors at the pool and the motionless surface of the water. It feels as if he's suffocating and he wants to be outside, anywhere other than in this room.

'Have you got any painkillers?' Zoe croaks.

'I'll get you some,' Nina says as she turns to the others. 'I think it's best to try and treat Zoe here, for now. Are we all happy to do that?'

She addresses the question directly to Aiden, who hesitates briefly, then nods. Claire does the same, followed by Seb. Will swallows.

'I'll go along with it for now,' he says. 'But if she's not any better by tomorrow, we need to agree we'll take her to hospital.'

'Let's just see how things go,' Nina says. 'Seb, can you help carry Zoe upstairs. I think she'll be more comfortable in bed, and –'

'I think it would be better to keep her down here where we can keep an eye on her,' Will says. 'Where would you rather be, Zoe?'

Zoe's eyes are cloudy with pain. He has failed her again. He was right to break up with her when he did. He's not good enough for her. 'I don't care,' she says.

Nina disappears into the kitchen and comes back with a glass and two tablets.

'They're co-codamol,' she says. 'Should be more effective than paracetamol. You take these and we'll give them fifteen minutes to work and then Seb can lift you upstairs. You'll be more comfortable in bed than on a sofa.' She turns to Will. 'Then we all need to sit down and work out what to do next.'

Will looks at her. 'All of us apart from Zoe, you mean.'

Nina ignores him and adjusts Zoe's blanket, pulling it up over her arm so it covers the duct tape. The towels she has put down move at the same time and Will can see that Zoe's blood has already soaked through them, leaving dark red stains on the cream sofa.

Chapter 49

Nina pretends not to notice Zoe whimper as Seb lifts her off the sofa. She picks up the blanket and follows him upstairs as he carries her into her bedroom and lays her down on the bed. He plumps up the pillows, adding an extra one from the top shelf of the wardrobe.

'I'm cold.' Zoe's teeth chatter as Nina tucks the duvet in around her. She pats the blanket Nina is arranging over it. 'Can I get another one of these?'

Nina nods as she turns off the fan that is circling above their heads, moving the hot air around the room. *It must be ninety degrees in here.* 'I'll get you one.' She hesitates. 'We need to put some antiseptic on your cuts to make sure they're clean. OK? I'll get Claire to help. She knows what she's doing. She had medical training at uni, remember? Back in a sec.'

Nina ushers Seb out and pulls the bedroom door shut behind them.

'She really needs a doctor,' he says.

Nina runs her hand through her hair, finding grains of sand from the beach under her fingernails. 'You know we can't take her to a hospital.'

Seb looks at her. 'The police might believe it was an accident. And anyway, Will was driving the boat. Not us.'

194

'Do you remember anything you learned in your law degree?' Nina hisses back at him. 'It's not just about Will. We could all face charges. None of us has a boat licence, we'd all been drinking or taking drugs. We were grossly negligent, Seb. And if it came down to it, Will could argue that you distracted him by lighting those fucking sparklers. Think what your father will do if you're arrested. We can't risk it.'

Seb swallows. 'I'm sure they'll . . .' he begins, but Nina grabs his arm and digs her nails into his skin.

'We are not taking Zoe to hospital, do you understand? You need to trust me on this. We both know what can happen when you don't listen to me, don't we?'

Seb's face flushes. *How could he forget? The steep stone steps, the headmaster's interrogation. The ambulance outside the school gates.*

'I'm just trying to keep us both out of trouble,' Nina continues. 'This could ruin everyone's entire future. There are five of us to think about. Zoe stays here. At least for now.'

Seb twists his signet ring round on his finger as he nods.

'Can you ask Claire to come up and give me a hand?' Nina says.

She walks across the landing to her room and then reappears holding a blanket. Seb is still standing where she left him.

'What?' she says.

'I'm supposed to meet Gaby in Deià tonight,' he says. Nina stares at him.

'You're not seriously suggesting you go, are you?'

He flushes. 'If I don't turn up, she'll wonder where I

am.' He hesitates. 'And I could find out if anyone saw anything.'

'You can't,' Nina says.

'I'll take the Jeep. I won't stay long. I'll make some excuse and leave early.'

Nina swallows.

'You can't go, and you can't repeat what I'm going to tell you to the others. I don't want them to know. We've got enough to deal with here.'

Seb frowns. 'What are you talking about?'

'Keep your voice down,' Nina says. 'It's about Gaby. When Claire and I went to the pharmacy, Gaby's photo was on the news. Antonio said one of his customers told him she'd drowned after the correfoc party.'

The colour drains out of Seb's face. Nina puts her hand on his arm but he shakes her off.

'After she dived off the boat, Seb, did you actually see her reach the beach?'

He stares at her, then slowly shakes his head.

Chapter 50

July – 1989

In the living room Will sits opposite Seb and Aiden in silence, listening to Nina and Claire's footsteps echo on the marble floor above their heads. There is a loud shriek, then a moaning noise, followed by sobs. He hears Nina telling Zoe to shush and Claire repeating that it will be all right, her voice growing increasingly high-pitched.

Seb gets up, throws open the patio door and disappears outside. Will watches him walk past the pool and rub his eyes as he looks out over the wall.

Zoe moans again.

'She needs a hospital,' Will says.

Aiden stares at him. 'I know.'

'If she's not any better tomorrow and I say I'm taking her, will you back me up?'

Aiden puts his head in his hands and doesn't answer. Another cry comes from upstairs, one that reaches out and twists Will's intestines.

'Aiden, I need you to . . .'

Aiden gets up and goes into the kitchen, fetches a mop from the cleaning cupboard and runs it under the tap. He looks at Will as he steps outside.

'I can't just sit here and do nothing.'

Will watches him go down the steps, wiping the surface

of the pale grey rock as he goes. He walks out of the living room into the hallway, trying to block out the sound of Nina's platitudes, now being delivered into an eerie silence, as he passes the bottom of the stairs and looks out of the window at where the Jeep is sitting in the driveway.

He could take it and get out of here. He thinks of Andy and how it must feel to sit in a tiny cell looking at the same four walls day after day. Then he thinks of Zoe upstairs, how pale she looked. He takes a deep breath and slowly releases it as he rubs the rough stubble growing back on his head. He can't leave her here. He needs to get help. Fuck Nina. He's not going to wait for her approval.

He peers into the copper bowl on the hall table, but it's empty. The keys for the Jeep are gone.

Chapter 51

July – 1989

'Where are they, Nina?' Will is waiting for her as she comes down the stairs. She hesitates, the pair of scissors she's been using to cut the bandage on Zoe's arm still in her hand.

'Where are what?'

'The keys,' he says. 'For the Jeep.'

'Somewhere safe,' she replies.

'You're really not going to tell me where they are?'

Nina stares at him. 'Why do you want them?'

'I thought someone should go and get us some food,' he says. 'I know Aiden bought some stuff when he was in Deià, but we're going to need more than that.'

'We'll be fine for a few days,' Nina replies. 'Claire and I picked up some bits when we went in earlier.'

She taps her fingers on the banister. She's lying. He glances upwards as another muffled noise comes from Zoe's bedroom.

'You aren't insured to drive the Jeep anyway,' Nina adds. 'And I think, at the moment, it would be best if we all stayed here together.'

Will hesitates, then shakes his head and tries to walk past her, but Nina puts her arm out and holds on to the wooden finial on the newel post, blocking his path.

'I want to check on Zoe,' Will says.

'She's fine,' Nina says. 'She's sleeping, and Claire's with her.'

Will contemplates pushing her out of the way but is suddenly conscious of how she is twisting the scissors around in her hand, the blades glinting, sharper than he remembered.

'You don't want to wake her up,' Nina says. 'She needs to rest. Let's talk first.'

Will hesitates. He's physically stronger than Nina, but he isn't sure what will happen if she calls out for Seb. Or Aiden.

Think about what's best for Zoe.

He takes a step back. Nina lowers the scissors and takes her other hand away from the post. She smiles as she ushers him towards the sofa and calls out to the others.

He sits down and looks around at the opulent furnishings: the walnut coffee table, the tall wooden shelves that stretch across one wall, adorned with the alabaster statues of those peculiar naked figures, the stone fireplace. The pool filled with turquoise water a few feet away outside. The uninterrupted view straight out over the sparkling ocean.

A piece of paradise in which he now feels as trapped as his brother, hundreds of miles away, in his prison cell.

Chapter 52

July – 1989

The warmth Seb luxuriated in, lying on a sun bed yesterday – *was it only yesterday?* – is too hot to sit out in today. Even this late in the afternoon, it paws at him like a shaggy dog, all hot breath and thick fur, beating him back to the seat beneath the pergola. He sits by the table and fiddles with the deck of abandoned cards, thoughts of Gaby running through his head.

He can see Aiden and Will on the sofas in the living room, glancing every now and again at the news on the television, their figures distorted by the reflection of the pool on the glass of the patio doors. They haven't moved since the discussion with Nina, during which no one mentioned Zoe, her presence sitting alongside them like a ghost.

They were supposed to have come up with a definitive plan but instead the only thing they've managed to agree on is that if anyone asks, they went to the beach party, then came straight back to the villa. If someone saw Nina or Claire buying medical supplies in the pharmacy this morning, they'll use Aiden as an excuse. The cut on his leg still hasn't healed properly from when he scraped it on the jetty.

Nina puts her head out of the patio doors.

'We need to clean the boat.'

Claire stays upstairs with Zoe while Seb follows the others down to the jetty, taking buckets, J-cloths and a bottle of washing-up liquid. The searing heat wraps itself around their throats and burns their skin, as if it is trying to punish them. As they walk down, Seb can see that Aiden's efforts to clean Zoe's blood off the steps have been only partly successful; most of the stains have dried to a rust-brown colour and become indelible, now part of the stones themselves. He hopes no one will look hard enough to notice.

The red smears on the metal handrail of the boat are relatively easy to wipe off; the burn marks across the seat are the only permanent scars. They throw bucket after bucket of seawater across the deck, watching the pink liquid slowly turn clear until Seb isn't sure whether he can see any colour at all, whether the swirls of crimson are all in his imagination.

The damage to the hull is impossible to conceal – deep scrapes have removed the white paintwork in places and replaced it with bright blue streaks. The hole below Nina's name looks larger than it did last night and there's nothing they can do to cover that up. They're going to have to find a way to get it repaired.

'At least it's above the waterline,' Nina says. 'As long as the sea stays calm, it shouldn't be a problem.'

They come back up the steps to the villa and Seb sits down under the pergola and deals out the pack of cards to play Patience. He can't bear to go back inside. Doesn't want to have to listen to the groans of pain coming from Zoe upstairs. Can't stop thinking about Gaby in the water, swimming for the beach. He reaches his hand across his shoulder to feel the scars on his back. The consequences if he fails. *Is he failing now?* He doesn't want to answer that question.

He tries to focus on the cards in front of him, but his head is full of the man – *Señor Lopez* – on the news and the way Zoe's skin had peeled apart, like an overripe piece of fruit, different layers of colour right down to the core. He knows he should get help, tell someone what they've done. But then he imagines his father's face as he answers the call from a Spanish police station, catches the scent of Cuban cigars and burnt flesh, and knows he will do nothing.

And then there's Nina. The two of them intertwined as tightly as strands of barbed wire since that final year at school. She'd found him at the side of the rugby pitch when he should have been back in the common room, sitting on the grass with an empty bottle of Martini Rosso. He'd confessed that he was going to fail his A levels, showed her his scars, what would happen when he did. And she'd offered to help, to do something he knew wasn't legal, providing he didn't tell anyone else.

But Nina didn't do anything for free. In return, she'd requested access to Seb's life. His contacts. The people she wanted to get to know. The friend of his father who was a solicitor in one of the most exclusive law firms in London, who got her work experience and has now offered a training contract, providing she passes her exams.

Seb could have lived with the quid pro quo that constituted the basis of their relationship if it had stopped there. But it hadn't. He'd failed to keep his side of the bargain, hadn't been able to resist telling his room-mate how he was managing to do so well in tests. He'd never expected it to end like it did – lying to a police officer in the headmaster's office; his school shirt damp with perspiration. And now Nina has something she will hold over him for ever.

Whatever he feels about taking Zoe to a hospital, he knows he will end up doing what Nina wants, because he can't face the consequences of the alternative. He stares out over the pool. A few crumpled cerise bougainvillea flowers have fallen into the water, making small ripples in the smooth surface.

'Aiden?' He holds up the cards and shouts towards the living room, suddenly wanting company. 'Fancy a game?'

Aiden looks up from the sofa, where he's watching the TV news bulletin circling around on repeat every fifteen minutes.

'Just give me a minute,' he says.

Seb nods. He never plays cards with Aiden. It's something he and Will always do together. *Always did together.* His brain automatically corrects him. Things are different now. He can't shake the feeling that they are going to hear a knock on the door at any moment and find the police outside.

He deals out two hands of poker and turns over his cards. The eight of clubs and eight of spades. Aces in the same suits, along with the queen of clubs. A dead man's hand. He glances in Will's direction as he sweeps all the cards off the table and pretends to shuffle them before dealing them out again.

Chapter 53

July – 1989

Will stares at the painting above the mantelpiece. The lizards appear to be scuttling about on the yellow canvas and he feels as if something is crawling over his skin. *Focus*. He knows he is being deliberately excluded, pushed out of a circle that is growing ever tighter, and shivers, despite the heat. It suddenly occurs to him that he and Zoe might not be allowed to leave the villa at all.

He waits until he can see Claire talking to Nina in the kitchen before he makes the decision.

Fuck Nina. If he wants to go and see Zoe, he will.

He treads as silently as he can up the stairs, his legs feeling heavier with each step. Through the windows on the landing he can see the sea, a deep midnight blue as the sun drops down past the horizon. He remembers the man's face – *Señor Lopez with his wife and daughter* – on the news, wonders what will happen to the pieces of the boat that sank in the water. Will they just be left to rot?

He pushes down the handle on Zoe's door. The smell hits him as soon as he walks in – something raw and unpleasant that slides down the back of his throat. He moves towards the window to let in some air but realizes it's already open, even though the muslin curtains aren't moving. The heat hangs in the room, dark and heavy.

Zoe is lying in bed, propped up on a few pillows, and Will's first thought is that he can't see any blood on the sheets. He tells himself this is a good thing. The stains on the towels and the sofa are never going to come out.

Zoe stares at him, her green eyes glassy. Pain? The after effects of Ecstasy? Medication? He can't tell which.

'How are you feeling?' he asks.

She doesn't answer. He perches on the side of the bed, notices her wince as the mattress gives slightly under his weight.

'Can I get you anything?' he asks. 'Some water?'

She glances at the bedside table, where a full glass already sits, an almost empty blister packet of pills beside it.

'You're looking a bit better,' he says, the lie falling out of his mouth before he can stop it. He watches her take a deep breath to brace herself for the effort of speaking.

'Need a doctor,' she whispers, her voice beseeching. 'Hurts.'

He reaches for the tablets, convinced he can still see a crimson line under his fingernails from where he'd helped clean the boat. She shakes her head.

'Had them. No more for two hours.'

A tear falls on to the back of his hand as he puts it over hers. She threads her fingers between his, holding on so tightly he isn't sure if he's going to be able to pull away. And he does want to move, despite the fact his heart is splitting open. If he goes back downstairs, he can pretend this isn't happening. Join Nina and the others, stay in their circle.

'How's your head?' Zoe murmurs.

'My head?' he says.

'Claire said you got knocked out when we crashed.'

Will hesitates, swallows his shame.

'It's fine,' he says. 'It ached for a few hours, but it's nothing. Don't worry about me. Just concentrate on getting better.'

His voice echoes in the large room. The others will know he's up here. His legs feel heavy again. He tries to stand up but Zoe is still holding on to his hand and presses her fingers into his skin.

'I need to call my mum.'

'I'll ask Nina if the phone will reach in here.' Will hesitates again. 'Or I can call her and let her know you're OK?'

Zoe stares at him.

'But I'm not OK.' She points at the crepe bandage that covers the top of her arm in a thick layer. 'This is bad, Will. I know it. I need a doctor.'

He knows it, too, but can't think of a way to help her. It's clear she isn't capable of walking the few miles up the track to the main road, and he can't carry her that far. *He could just leave her. Go home and be with his mum. Visit Andy.*

He tries to think of where Nina might have hidden the keys to the Jeep as he peels her fingers off his hand.

'You need to sleep. Let your body rest. Let's see how you are tomorrow.'

He starts to walk towards the door. Zoe stares at him, her green eyes huge in her pale face.

'Promise you won't leave me,' she says. 'Whatever the others do. Don't leave me here.'

He walks back towards her and leans over her on the bed.

'I won't leave you,' he says, unconvincingly.

Is he really going to risk putting his mother through what she went through with Andy all over again? Being ostracized by her friends, the trauma of the court case, another son to visit in prison? *He was driving the boat. He was smoking dope. He was the one who killed someone. He left the scene of an accident. He's taken a father away from his child.*

'Stay here with me,' she says.

He hesitates. 'OK. I'll stay if you focus on getting better.' He smiles, but she doesn't smile back. She leans her head on his shoulder as he sits down on the bed, her breath escaping in shallow gasps.

'Did you come into my room on the first night we were here?'

Her voice is so quiet he has to strain to hear her. That first night. A million miles away from where they are now. *Don't think about it.*

'I wanted to make sure you were OK,' he says slowly. 'You were so out of it after that game of Truth or Dare.'

'I remember you leaning over me.'

He looks at her, but her eyes are shut and he wants to tell her how sorry he is, sorry that he ever came here, sorry that he hadn't known how to tell her about Andy, sorry he hadn't ignored Nina and taken her straight to hospital when they got back to the villa.

'I think Claire might have put something in my drink when we were on the boat,' Zoe mumbles. 'I wondered if she had after that first night. I felt really out of it after the accident and I don't think it was just down to the shock of being thrown into the sea. She's got a load of Es in her room, you know. She brought them with her from home.'

Will doesn't answer. They all know Zoe doesn't touch

Ecstasy after that night out in the Dome. He can still remember the moment she fell; how one minute she'd been walking beside him on the towpath bordering the canal, the next she'd disappeared into the darkness; a rustling noise before a scream, followed by a loud splash and then silence.

He'd slid down the bank after her, grasping for her hand in the water, the reeds so slippery he couldn't get a proper grip, and pulled her towards him as she gasped for breath. The cold had eaten through their skin and spread through their veins, turning their muscles into frozen lead weights and removing their ability to speak.

He'd dragged her up on to the bank, and she'd clung to him, her pupils dilated, as they stumbled home. *She'd been lucky. They both had.* Her teeth had chattered as she told him how she'd thought she was still on the path, that she'd felt like she was floating before realizing she was in the water. He'd curled himself around her in bed that night, lain awake in the dark, feeling the horror of that moment slice through the status quo with one swift, clean, brutal cut, knowing he could have lost her and wanting to hold on to every moment.

For Nina and Claire, a night out isn't a night out without taking something. Speed, charlie, acid – whatever's on offer. But he can't believe Claire would have deliberately spiked Zoe's drinks.

Or is it just easier not to believe it? You drove away from an accident.

Exhaustion sweeps over him like a wave. His shoulder aches from where Zoe's head is leaning on it, but he doesn't want to move in case he disturbs her. The handle on her door moves and he sees Nina's face in the crack of light that filters in from the landing. She doesn't say anything, just watches them for a few seconds and then disappears back into the hallway, leaving them in the dark.

His stomach slithers over itself. His last thought before he falls asleep is that for the first time in as long as he can remember he wishes more than anything that his brother was here. Andy is the only person he knows who can hotwire a car.

Chapter 54

Nina – Now

Nina drops her phone on to her keyboard as she hears the knock on her office door. She scrabbles around to swipe up the screen as her associate appears with the documents she asked for earlier.

'Just leave them on my desk.'

Nina keeps her hands folded on her lap to disguise the fact they are shaking. Her associate stands awkwardly, waiting for further instructions.

'I'm in the middle of something at the moment,' she says. 'I'll look at them later and come back to you.'

The woman glances at Nina's phone, and Nina unclasps her hands and turns it face down. *Has she seen something? She can't have. The screen is blank.*

'Are you feeling OK?' the associate asks. 'You look a bit . . . flushed.'

Nina shakes her head, aware that the bank's artificially controlled environment guarantees optimum working conditions at all times; the temperature is set at twenty-two degrees in every room apart from the gym, and the sensors adjust the lights to ensure the same amount of brightness no matter what time of day or night.

'I'm fine.' Nina smiles, revealing a flash of white veneers beneath her red lipstick. 'Next time I ask you to do something, I'd appreciate it if you can stay in the office until it's finished. Shut the door on your way out, please.'

She scrunches up her toes inside her shoes as she takes a few deep breaths.

Think, Nina.

What solid evidence could the person who sent her this actually have?

There's the photo.

The photo in itself doesn't prove anything. And surely, after this length of time, there isn't anything left to find. Maybe it's just an attempt at blackmail. Whispered rumours that they think she'll pay to avoid hearing them spoken out loud. Why didn't they just say that? Specify an amount and their bank details? She might even have considered it. Hugo would never have to know. But there's only instructions to meet. Something she has no intention of doing whatsoever.

She picks up the documents, but the words swim in front of her eyes. Twenty minutes until her meeting, and she can feel the acid in her stomach bubbling up in her throat. She pulls open her drawer and pops out a couple of Gaviscon tablets, trying not to gag at the chalky strawberry flavour that fills her mouth.

She needs to get out of the office for a minute. Clear her head. Breathe. She picks up her phone and heads for the lift, leaving her throw on her chair. The reception area is now almost empty as she beeps her pass over the turnstile to get out of the building, all other employees already at their desks.

She walks briskly to the nearest deli to pick up a smoked salmon bagel and checks her emails on her phone while she stands in the queue. Nothing new. Ten minutes until her meeting. If the bank finds out about this, she's fucked. *They won't find out. You should threaten to sue. But what if they're telling the truth?* Thoughts chase each other around in her head. Hugo has texted her with a link to the restaurant they are supposed to be meeting at this evening. Another client dinner. The last thing she needs. She shuts her eyes briefly as she holds her phone over the card payment machine and takes the paper bag from the cashier.

She's almost back at the office when she sees him. Blond hair, slicked back. Chiselled cheekbones. The shock is like being punched in the stomach, winding her so she can't breathe. She stops in the middle of the pavement as he walks past, his blue eyes meet hers briefly, then move on, as if she is invisible. Something buzzes in her brain, a hum that slices through time like a scalpel.

She shakes her head, the paper handles of the bag beginning to disintegrate in her sweaty palm. It's not him. She turns around to double-check. He's just a boy. He's barely out of his teens. His features are similar, that's all. She presses one hand against her cheek to cool the redness as she forces her feet to move forwards.

It's not him.

The last time she saw him was thirty-two years ago. And the last she heard, he was back inside.

What if he's not? What if he's out?

If he's still on the same stuff as he was back then, he'll be desperate for money. She shivers.

He wouldn't do that. He has just as much to lose as she does.

And he, better than anyone, knows the lengths she'll go to in order to protect herself.

Chapter 55

July – 1989

'Don't answer it.' Nina stands at the bottom of the stairs and whispers up to Aiden as he emerges on to the landing in his boxer shorts.

The sound of knocking on the front door echoes in the hallway.

'What if they don't go away?' he asks.

'They will if we don't answer.'

Aiden comes halfway down the stairs and peers through the window by the front door. The sun is too bright for him to see properly and the only thing he can hear is the noise of the sprinklers.

Shhh-tik-tik-tik. Get out right now.

The knocking comes again, more insistent this time. Nina clenches her fists into tight balls as she sits on the bottom step of the staircase. She hears footsteps, followed by a voice outside the door.

'Nina, *soy Luis. Estás ahí?*'

She bites her lip, looks up at Aiden. 'I thought you'd told him we didn't need him,' she hisses.

'I did,' Aiden whispers back. 'Yesterday.'

'Nina?' More knocking.

'Someone needs to go and talk to him,' Aiden whispers.

'What if he goes around the back of the villa and sees the boat?'

Nina hesitates, then gives herself a shake and fixes a smile on to her face. She opens the door to find her gardener holding a ragged towel, covered in blood.

Her smile slips momentarily.

'Where did you find that?'

Luis points to the driveway, where Nina can see various empty beer bottles and crisp packets lying on the gravel, along with pieces of torn black bin liner. Stray dogs. Someone must have left the bags out. Fucking hell, does she have to remember everything?

'*Alguien esta herido?*' Luis's eyebrows are pulled together in a frown.

Nina smiles again, a flash of bright white teeth.

'No one's hurt,' she says. 'Claire just had a bit of a nosebleed, but she's fine now.' She glances at what is left of the towel that was pressed against Zoe's arm on the boat. 'It looks worse than it is. Honestly.'

A crease embeds itself into Luis's forehead.

Nina keeps one hand firmly on the door as she calls out to Claire, who comes and stands beside her, gathering her curls into a bun and fixing them in place with a butterfly clip.

'See?' Nina says, placing her arm around Claire's waist. 'She's fine.'

Claire smiles. 'Totally fine.'

Nina holds out her hand for the towel, swallowing her desire to gag as she takes the warm, slightly damp piece of material, the scent of dog urine combined with a sharp metallic tang eating into her nostrils.

She points at the rubbish on the driveway.

'We'll clear that up, Luis. You don't have to do it.' She hesitates. 'In fact, I don't think we need you for a couple of days. The garden is looking great. Maybe you could just come back at the weekend?'

Luis stares at her while Nina repeats what she's just said in Spanish.

'My parents will still pay you, of course,' she adds, hoping that's the reason why he's still standing there. She'll get them to pay him fucking double if she has to.

But Luis doesn't move and she shivers at the thought he can see straight through her – money isn't going to solve this problem.

Chapter 56

July – 1989

'Aiden?'

Luis half shouts his name, and the sound of his voice makes Aiden crumple into a ball at the top of the stairs. He should go down, say something, ask for help. But his legs don't move. *Coward.* He watches the door to Zoe's room, prays the handle will turn and he'll see Will come out. Will isn't a coward. Not like him.

He grabs his headphones, which are still round his neck from where he fell asleep wearing them last night, and switches on his Walkman, turning up the volume as high as it will go as the distinctive synth-pop of Bronski Beat's 'Smalltown Boy' fills his eardrums. He's worse than a coward. By pretending he's not here, by trying to cover up what they've done, he is nothing less than a murderer.

He tries whispering the phrase he'd practised over and over when he was younger in his speech therapy sessions – *My shoes are blue with yellow stripes and green stars on the front* – but can't get past the sixth word without stammering.

'He's not awake yet,' he hears Nina say. 'But I'll tell him you were asking after him.'

'Yes,' Claire adds. 'We'll tell him.'

He can see from the way she glances up the stairs to where he is sitting that she has recognized Luis as the man he was with at the beach party, his tanned hip bones visible above the top of his jeans. He sees her cheeks flush with humiliation and wishes he could just go home, that he'd never come here at all.

Luis doesn't move, but Nina shuts the door anyway. The smile drops off her face the moment the door clicks shut, and the transformation reminds Aiden of a snake shedding its skin.

Claire starts to say something, but before she has a chance to speak, Zoe's bedroom door opens and Will walks on to the landing. Aiden sees Nina put the bloodied towel behind her back.

'You need to come up here,' Will says.

Nina and Claire exchange glances.

'You go,' Nina says. 'I'll be up in sec.'

Aiden hears her walk into the kitchen, open one of the drawers and tear a refuse bag off the roll. Something heavy is thrown into the bin and lands with a thud, then the tap turns on.

His heart thumps in his chest as he prays for Luis to come back.

'You need to go out and pick up the rubbish,' she says as she passes him on the stairs. 'It's all over the driveway.'

He doesn't reply and follows her across the landing into Zoe's room. Zoe is lying in bed and he forces himself to smile to cover his shock when he sees her. Her eyes have sunk into her face. There are two large red streaks on the crepe bandage around her arm, as if someone has scribbled on it with felt-tip pen.

'She's bleeding again,' Will says. 'She really needs to see a doctor.'

'Claire's medically trained,' Nina snaps.

Claire looks up from where she's sitting beside Zoe on the bed.

'I did one term of a medical degree, Nina. I haven't got a clue what I'm doing.'

Claire starts to unwind the bandage from around Zoe's arm, but Aiden notices her hesitate, her fingers trembling as the layers of crepe get thinner, the red streaks larger, until the horror of what lies beneath becomes visible.

The strips of Elastoplast that she'd used to try and close the wounds have come unstuck and hang limply like torn pieces of flesh. Blood oozes from the deep gashes. The skin is an angry red colour, swollen and puffy. He can feel the throbbing heat without even touching it. Claire reaches for one of the pieces of stained Elastoplast and Zoe flinches.

'Sorry,' she says. 'I'm trying to be gentle. I need to put on some more antiseptic.'

Claire soaks a pad of cotton wool in the liquid from one of the small bottles and squeezes it out, but as it makes contact with Zoe's skin she whimpers. Will grabs Claire's wrist to try and stop her, but Aiden can tell everyone has already noticed the smell. Like rotting fruit. It reminds him of the mouldy apples his mum used to discover on a Monday morning in the depths of his lunchbox after they had lain there over the weekend.

'She needs antibiotics and stitches,' Claire says. 'This stuff isn't doing anything.'

Nina walks over to the window and opens it as wide as she can, then stays where she is and rearranges the muslin curtains. Seb sticks his head around the door and smiles at

Zoe, who shuts her eyes in response. Nina holds out her hand, and he envelops her in a hug.

'Zoe's arm isn't going to heal unless I can get the sides of the wound to stay together,' Claire says. 'And if it's infected . . .'

She trails off as everyone stares at her in silence.

'Superglue?' Seb says. 'Couldn't we use that?'

Zoe opens her eyes and stares at him. 'You are not putting superglue on my arm.' Aiden watches her try and wriggle further under the blanket.

'Have you got another bandage?' Will asks.

Claire nods.

'Put that on after you've cut off some more Elastoplast and taped it up.' He turns to Nina. 'We need to take her to a hospital.'

'No, we need to do whatever it takes to get us out of this mess,' Nina replies.

She's pushed her Ray-Bans on top of her head to keep her blonde hair off her face. Aiden is struck by how alike she and Seb look. All angles and sharp teeth.

'Have you listened to the news this morning?' Nina asks.

Will shakes his head.

'You should. It's all over the television. The police are looking for another boat in connection with the accident.'

Chapter 57

July – 1989

They stare at the television screen as it flashes up the same film footage of pieces of wreckage being fished out of the water that they've seen dozens of times already. Will notices Seb close his eyes as the photo of the man appears.

'What's she saying?' Will asks as a reporter speaks in a stream of Spanish.

'The police are appealing for witnesses,' Nina says. 'They are asking anyone who was at the beach party or who thinks they saw anything suspicious to contact them. And they also want anyone who has been asked to do any boat repairs in the past couple of days to get in touch.'

'Fuck.' Seb puts his head in his hands.

Will hears Claire call his name from upstairs. He looks at Nina.

'We can't just leave Zoe here. We need to get her to a hospital.'

Nina points at the television.

'Did you hear what they just said, Will? Don't you think the police will be watching the hospitals? Any doctor is going to realize that the gashes on Zoe's arm were made by a boat propeller.'

'Will? Can you come up here?' Claire's voice echoes down the stairs.

Will hesitates, looks outside to the pool. More bougainvillea flowers have fallen on to the surface, casting small dark shadows that whirl around in the water. It strikes him that Andy probably hasn't seen any flowers for five years. Small things that he takes for granted. Could he cope if he was put in the same situation? He lays his hand on Nina's arm.

'Just tell me where the keys to the Jeep are, Nina.'

Seb steps towards him.

'Chill out, Lawson. Let's not do anything stupid here. We've got to stick together. What Nina is saying makes sense. We just need to wait until things calm down a bit.'

'How long do you want to give it, Seb?' Will jabs his finger at Seb's face. 'Were we just looking at the same person upstairs? You know as well as I do that Zoe's not getting any better.'

Seb pushes Will's hand away, his cheeks reddening. Nina moves between them and holds out her arms.

'Look,' she says. 'After what they've just said on the news, we need to stay calm. Work out what we're going to do with the boat. That's got to be our priority.' She looks at Will. 'Zoe will be OK. Claire is fixing her arm.'

'Claire can't fix anything,' Will snaps back. 'She doesn't have a fucking clue what she's doing. None of us do. Have you seen where Aiden is? Still sitting zoned out at the top of the stairs. We're supposed to fly home in nine days. Or are you planning on keeping Zoe locked up here for ever?'

'Of course not,' Nina retorts, but Will can't help noticing the slight hesitation before she answers.

He shakes his head.

'If you don't want to tell me where the keys are, Nina,

that's fine. But I can't leave Zoe like this. She's getting worse. I'm going to call a taxi to come and collect us. If the hospital asks what happened, I'll make something up. Pretend I don't understand what they're asking, or' – he stumbles in his efforts to find a plausible explanation – 'or, worst-case scenario, I'll say she was hit by a rental boat that didn't stop.'

'Lawson . . .' Seb moves to put his arm around Will's shoulders, but Will shrugs him off.

'Fuck off, Seb. You're as bad as Nina.'

He turns round to find Aiden standing behind him.

'And you're no better,' he adds.

He storms up the stairs, passing Claire coming down the other way. She opens her mouth to say something, but he ignores her, goes into Zoe's bedroom and slams the door.

Beads of sweat have gathered on Zoe's forehead as he sits down beside her. The droplets remind him of her at the beach party, water running off her shoulders in slick streams. But her skin is now a horrible grey colour and she looks as if she's about to faint. At least there are no streaks of red spreading across the new crepe bandage on her arm.

Yet.

He allows himself to hope that perhaps Claire has fixed it, perhaps this time Zoe will heal, but the sickly-sweet smell tells him he's kidding himself.

'It hurts,' she says.

Will looks at the painkillers on her bedside table. There's only one left in the blister pack. He wonders if Nina has any more, whether she'd even tell him if she did.

Zoe's lips are cracked and he passes her the glass of water, helps her to take a sip.

'Do you want me to get you something to eat?' he asks.

'No. I'm not hungry. Just stay here with me.' She rests her head on his shoulder and he resists the temptation to tuck a stray piece of hair behind her ear. They sit in silence for a few minutes as he listens to her breathing – *too fast* – watches her eyes dart around beneath her eyelids, as if she is searching for something.

He remembers how they'd sat like this in his room at university when she'd told him about her sister and he'd felt as if someone had put their hands around his throat and cut off his air supply, his whole world pivoting off its axis in the space of a few seconds. She hadn't understood why he'd started to pull away from her, why he'd spent less time in the house and stayed out with friends, but he hadn't been able to find the words to explain. *That's not true. You chose not to tell her because you knew she'd hate you for it.*

'Zoe,' he whispers. 'I need to tell you something.'

'Mmm?' Her response is so quiet he can barely hear it.

'About my brother. Andy. He's in prison. He killed someone when he was drink-driving. I'm so sorry I didn't tell you before. I didn't want you to hate me.'

He breaks off, his voice choked, and she moves her hand on top of his.

'Doesn't matter,' she whispers.

He waits, but she doesn't say anything else and there is silence apart from the sound of her breathing and the murmurs of conversation he can hear coming from downstairs.

'Zoe, we need to get you to a doctor.'

She doesn't reply, and he gives her a gentle nudge. She opens her eyes briefly, just enough for him to see that their usual bright green colour has faded to a dull grey, before she shuts them again.

'I'm so tired,' she whispers.

'I know, but I'm going to need you to help me. I'm going to call a taxi and I'm going to get you to a hospital.'

Chapter 58

July – 1989

Will looks at what Zoe's wearing. A pair of shorts and one of Seb's T-shirts. Claire has cut one sleeve off so it doesn't get in the way of the bandage.

Should he take something else in case she gets cold? Is she going to be able to get down the stairs if he helps her? What if they don't come back to the villa at all?

He picks up her rucksack off the chair and rummages through it until he finds her wallet.

'Zoe?' She turns her head away. He puts his hand over hers on top of the duvet and squeezes it. Tears well up in her eyes.

'I wish my mum was here. I thought she was, earlier. I felt her hand on my forehead and thought you'd called her and she'd come to take me home.' Zoe's voice is choked. 'But she isn't here, is she?'

Will swallows as he shakes his head.

'I'm going to sort this,' he says.

He feels Zoe give his fingers a faint squeeze as he pulls away, walks to her door and pushes down the handle very slowly, opening it a few centimetres to check no one is outside. He steps silently across the landing, mentally making a list of items he needs to collect from his room.

Please God, let it be there.

226

He doesn't know what he'll do if it isn't. His stomach squeezes itself into a knot as he reaches into the pocket of the jeans he wore when they went out to the bar in Deià. His fingers close around something small and rectangular. A business card from the taxi that brought them home. The relief makes his hand shake as he pulls it out and memorizes the phone number, refusing to think about what the others will do if they find out he has this. Four against two. He'd stand no chance. The numbers blur in front of his eyes.

Wallet. He stuffs it into his bag as he repeats the taxi number over and over to himself until it's fixed in his brain in large, black, solid numbers. He thinks of the others downstairs and throws in his plane tickets, passport and traveller's cheques. He should take some water, but all the bottles are in the fridge in the kitchen. Painkillers. There's only one left by Zoe's bed and he has no idea where Nina keeps them. A spare T-shirt. He crumples one up into a ball and puts that in too. It will be easier to get one of his over Zoe's head.

He walks back across the landing into Zoe's room, his heart thudding so loudly that he can't make out what is being said by the voices he can hear downstairs in the living room. He takes the almost empty packet of tablets from her bedside table and puts them into his bag along with her purse, then rummages through the various pockets of her rucksack until he finds her passport and flight ticket and adds those in too. *Prepare for all eventualities.*

'Zoe.' He puts his hand on her cheek, and she opens her eyes. 'I'm going to phone for a taxi to take us to hospital. You just need to be ready to leave. Are you strong enough to walk?'

A tear trickles down her face as she shakes her head.

'Don't worry,' Will says. 'We'll manage.'

How the fuck is he going to get her downstairs?

He reaches into her wardrobe, pulls out her jelly shoes and then sees the pair of red Converse All-Stars and takes them out instead. He sits on the bed, pushes back the duvet and loosens the laces to get them on to her feet before pulling them tight and tying them into a double bow.

'Maybe you can try getting up?'

She raises herself up from the pillows and shuffles an inch at a time across the bed. Once she's sitting on the edge, she swings her feet around so they're on the floor, grips Will's hand, then stands up for a few seconds before sitting straight back down again. He smiles, his shoulders tight.

'That's great. I'll be back in a minute.'

Will walks out on to the landing, over to the phone that is sitting on the small desk. He picks up the receiver, watches the spiralled plastic coils of the handset cord uncurl as he stretches it out. He can hear the others downstairs, but if he pulls the cord far enough, he thinks he can reach his bedroom and push the door shut so they won't hear him speaking.

He's about to start pressing the buttons to call the number memorized in his head when he realizes he can't hear a dialling tone.

Does it work differently here than at home? There's no sound at all. He goes back out to the landing and jiggles the two black prongs on the top of the telephone, but there's still nothing.

He checks to see if the phone is plugged in, and

something cold crawls over his skin. The wire is hanging away from the wall. Sliced through at the bottom, a couple of inches above the socket. Not frayed or gnawed – a clean cut, one that looks as if it has been made with a knife, or snipped with a sharp pair of scissors.

He slides the receiver back on to the cradle, his heart thumping.

Fuck. Now what?

Seb's voice drifts up from downstairs.

'We can't let him take Zoe to a hospital.'

'You c–c–can't keep them both here,' Aiden replies. There's a moment of silence when Will senses that possibilities not previously uttered are floating through the air between the four of them and finally condensing into something solid.

'Can't we?' Nina says.

'I can't fix Zoe's arm,' he hears Claire say. 'The wounds are infected. The propeller probably had a load of crap all over it and the antiseptic we've got isn't nearly strong enough to deal with it. She's going to end up with gangrene or sepsis unless we get her treated properly.'

The sound of his blood rushes in his ears.

'She could die,' Claire adds.

There's another silence.

'What if we get rid of the infection?' Nina says.

'I can't,' Claire says flatly. 'She needs antibiotics.'

Another silence.

'We don't have any antibiotics,' Nina says. 'But we do have you. What if you amputated her arm? Would that get rid of it?'

Chapter 59

July – 1989

Claire looks at Nina as she leans against the counter twisting a strand of blonde hair around her finger.

'Have you lost your mind?' she asks.

Nina stares at her.

'We all know it's what a surgeon would do,' she retorts. 'And if you'd fixed her earlier, we wouldn't even have this issue.'

'It's one thing not wanting Zoe to go to hospital,' Aiden says, 'but that's just . . .' He shakes his head.

'Haven't you heard those stories of someone cutting off their own limb?' Nina asks. 'Climbers who get stuck in rockfalls, soldiers who are injured on the battlefield, that kind of thing? I bet your dad knows people who have had to do it. Whatever it takes to save themselves.'

'Are you seriously contemplating this?' Aiden asks.

'I'm just suggesting it as a possibility. We need to consider all the options.'

There's a moment of hesitation. A pause long enough to allow Nina's idea to grow. Aiden stares out of the window at the pool and wonders if he dives beneath the surface and stays there he can pretend this isn't really happening.

'Look,' Nina continues, her voice as smooth as the

motionless water, 'we have two problems to deal with. We have Zoe, who Claire says is critically injured, and we have a boat moored by the jetty which anyone can see has been in an accident. Sooner or later, someone is going to tell the police we were at that beach party.'

'Gaby might,' Aiden says.

Nina and Seb exchange glances.

'Or Luis,' Claire says quickly, looking at Aiden. 'He was there too.'

'Or Luis,' Nina repeats. 'Although he'll probably know to keep his mouth shut if he wants to keep working here. But we need to work out what the fuck we are going to do,' she continues, 'and I'm just throwing out suggestions that you're dismissing without thinking them through.'

Aiden holds up his hand.

'Nina, stop. If anyone asks about the beach party, we've already agreed we say we came straight back to the villa.'

'And what if they look at the boat?'

Aiden bites his lip. 'I'll help you repair the boat, paint over the damage or something, but I'm not having anything to do with hurting Zoe.'

He thinks of what he owes Nina, and then of what James Harding is doing now, any plans for his future in ruins. *That could have been you. You owe her.*

'What I'm suggesting would help Zoe, not hurt her,' Nina snaps back. 'We all want her to get better, don't we? Sort out this mess so we can pretend it never happened?'

Aiden stares at her, memories of Luis's mouth against his, knowing that even if he could, he doesn't want to forget.

'Of course we want Zoe to get better,' he says. 'But how

could any of us forget this ever happened if we hacked off Zoe's arm? What you're suggesting is barbaric.'

Claire stares at him, and he puts his hand on his chest, trying to ignore the flutter of panic he can feel below his ribcage. Will she tell the others about what she saw on the beach if he doesn't go along with what Nina wants? He looks at the knives stuck to a magnetic strip on the wall above the counter. One of them has a blade at least twelve inches long. Is that what she's planning to use? *He won't do what Nina is asking.* There's a silence as he waits for her reaction.

'Even if it would help Zoe,' Claire says carefully, 'you can't just amputate someone's arm. It's not as simple as that. You need to know exactly what you're doing. There's the brachial artery, for a start. If I sever that, Zoe will bleed to death. And it's not easy to cut through bone.'

'I think the propeller's done most of the work for you already,' Nina says. She turns to Seb. 'What do you think?'

He swallows. 'I'm not a doctor, Nina.'

'Do you trust me, though?' she asks, tipping her head slightly to one side.

Aiden squints as a shaft of sunlight streams through the patio doors behind her, turning her into a silhouette. He suddenly remembers the name of the painting she reminded him of at the airport when she stretched out her arms and tipped back her head in the heat. *The Nightmare* by Henry Fuseli.

You should have seen this coming.

He watches Seb stare at Nina for a few seconds before he answers. 'Yes, I trust you,' he says. 'I know you'll do what needs to be done.'

Chapter 60

Will creeps back into Zoe's bedroom, feeling as if insects are crawling across his skin. He shuts her door behind him, the wooden surface smooth beneath his fingers. He has never wished harder for a keyhole or a lock, but knows there is neither. He contemplates dragging Zoe's dressing table in front of it, but it's not heavy enough to stop four people pushing it open if they wanted to.

Zoe opens her eyes. 'How long do we have to wait for the taxi?' she asks.

He has no idea what to tell her. *Think, Will. Think.*

Did Nina cut the phone cable? She must have done. Or Seb. Or Claire. He wouldn't put it past any of them. Even Aiden. His stomach swirls in the way it did when he was younger and walked into school to find all his classmates talking about what Andy had done. Whispers that settled around him as he sat on his own at lunch in the canteen, the words slicing his skin.

Zoe is still looking at him, wondering why he's got his back pressed against the door.

'There might be an issue with the taxi,' he says, keeping his voice low, trying to listen for any sound of someone coming upstairs. Her face crumples. *Think.* 'But I'm still going to get you to the hospital. Just give me a minute.'

Zoe opens her mouth to speak, but he puts his finger on his lips.

He tiptoes across the room and looks out of one of the open windows down to the pool. It's a sheer drop to the patio, nothing to break the fall. He might be able to reach the pergola if he jumps out of Nina's bedroom window, but beneath the greenery that covers the structure there is a roof made out of bamboo. The narrow wooden canes would never support his weight. Certainly not his and Zoe's. And she's not going to be able to make it out of a window to start with. Even if she could, they'd have to walk past the pool and the patio doors to get around the side of the villa to the driveway. One of the others would see them.

'Stay quiet.' He mouths the words silently, and Zoe nods as he opens her bedroom door again and steps on to the landing, praying as hard as he's ever prayed for anything, harder than the day Andy went to court and they all hoped he'd get a suspended sentence.

Don't come up here. Please don't come up.

He repeats the words over and over in his head.

The scent of Poison eau de toilette, sickly sweet, lingers in Nina's room. He scans her dressing table, looks in the small drawer of her bedside cabinet, searches through her handbag. Nothing. The first wave of panic breaks in his chest and he has to sit down on the edge of her bed to steady himself.

Breathe. In and out.

His ears ring with the effort of listening for footsteps, every sound amplified in his head.

He reaches into the pockets of her shorts, then her

jeans and jacket, his fingers frantically feeling between layers of material. In the toes of her shoes?

Where have you put it, Nina? There are only so many places you can hide a key.

Another wave rises up as he wonders if she's got it downstairs with her, whether this search is a waste of time, but then he thinks of the carving knives on the wall, their blades sharp enough to cut through bone, and starts looking again, rifling through her underwear, combing through her make-up bag, trying to quieten his breathing, which sounds like the last gasps of a drowning man.

He tries to calculate how long it will take him to run into town if he leaves Zoe here. He's not as fit as Aiden, the dirt track back to the main road has an uneven surface and the sun is at its hottest. Nine minutes a mile, if he's lucky? And it's about five miles, so at least forty-five minutes. And that's before he finds someone to help and gets back again. He can't risk leaving her for that long. He should have gone last night. *Why the fuck didn't you? All that time you just wasted, asleep.* Things have changed irrevocably in the space of a few hours, and now it's too late. Would Nina really do what she's suggesting? *You can't risk waiting to find out.*

He moves Nina's chair from beside her dressing table and puts it next to the wardrobe, steps up on to it and sweeps his fingers across the top of the wood. They encounter something solid and he flinches, knocking it out of the way. He scrabbles around to find it again. The leather fob of the Jeep keys. He picks it up and holds it in his hand, feels tears prick at the back of his eyes in relief.

He slips out of Nina's room, walks across the landing,

opens Aiden's bedroom door and picks up the bag that's lying on his floor before heading back to Zoe, hearing the low buzz of voices still coming from downstairs. She has pushed back the duvet and is sitting on the edge of the bed.

'I found the keys to the Jeep,' Will says quietly.

Zoe looks at him. 'They don't want me to go to hospital, do they?'

The fact that he doesn't answer tells her everything she needs to know.

'Do you think they'll try and stop us leaving?' she asks.

Will stares at her, wanting to scream, *Of course they're fucking going to stop us, and there's nothing I can do about it as there's four of them and only two of us, and you can barely walk,* but he doesn't say anything, doesn't mention the conversation he just overheard, doesn't want to terrify her with ideas that currently exist only in Nina's imagination.

'It might be better if we go without them seeing us,' he whispers.

'How are we going to do that?' she asks. 'They're all in the living room. They'll see us when we go downstairs.'

Will holds open the bag he took from Aiden's room. Aiden had taken the sparklers with him on to the boat, but lying in the bottom are two packets of firecrackers, red and yellow tubes attached to a long line of string.

'We're going to distract them,' he says.

Chapter 61

Claire – Now

The nurse in the dementia care home steps back, dips the sponge in the water and squeezes it out.

'What man from which villa?' she asks.

'The man that keeps following me,' Claire whispers. She glances at the door of her room, as if he's about to walk in.

The nurse runs the sponge over Claire's face, down her neck and across her shoulders, rinses it out before sticking on some shower gel, the artificial scent of jasmine filling the small room.

'There's no one here except you.'

She hands Claire her toothbrush and toothpaste. 'Why don't you have a go at doing your teeth while I finish this?'

Claire takes the brush and squeezes out a pea-sized blob of blue gel. She thinks she remembers doing this for someone else, but that was a long time ago. Small hands holding the brush beneath hers. She knows this woman doesn't believe her, but she's telling the truth. The man must be hiding somewhere. He follows her whenever she goes into the bathroom.

On Tuesday – *was it Tuesday? Or was it last week? She gets a bit muddled about the days in here* – she'd opened her eyes after rinsing out her shampoo and found him standing next to her, a bright yellow T-shirt clinging to his soaking-wet skin, blood dripping from his arm. Staring at her breasts. She'd screamed and wrapped herself in the shower curtain, and then Sandra, not this one – *she likes this one* – had come in and told her off for making a racket. Had said there was no one there, which was clearly not true.

And then yesterday – *or was it Friday?* – she'd woken up in the middle of the night, had gone to get a drink, and the man had been lying in the bath. His eyes were open and he was staring out at her from under the water. She'd screamed then, too, had felt a gush of piss trickle down her leg as she crumpled to the ground then stayed there, her hands clapped over her ears to block out the sound of the waves, until this one had found her.

She's tried talking to them about security, but they don't listen.

No one listens to her any more.

They'd asked if she wanted to change rooms, but this is her room. She doesn't want to go anywhere else. Why should she? All her things are in here. Her clothes. Pictures of Matt. *Is it Matt? She thinks it's Matt.* This one tells her it's Matt. Or perhaps they are pictures by Matt. She can't quite remember and isn't sure who the smaller one is, but she thinks he sometimes comes into her bedroom with Matt too.

This one finishes washing her, dries her off with a hard towel and helps her put her sweatshirt on so she doesn't get it the wrong way round. She does, sometimes, but they always tell her it's an easy mistake to make. She hates the horrible baby-pink colour. It reminds her of the frosted lipstick Zoe wore in Nina's villa before it happened. They'd been out dancing. She used to love dancing. She shuts her eyes, tries not to think about what came after.

The screaming.

She shivers, and this one rubs her shoulder before walking to the bathroom to empty out the bowl.

Claire shuts her eyes as she waits for her to come back, doesn't want to risk the possibility of seeing things she'd rather forget. Dead things. Zoe crying. Steep stone steps. They blur together with her other memories, and she no longer has any idea if they happened today, yesterday, or thirty years ago. All she is certain of is the thick feeling in her throat, the one that tells her that what happened was her fault.

She shakes her head and forces herself to think about Will. He might come and visit her today. She likes Will. He'll talk to the nurses for her, sort out the issue with security. He'd tried to help Zoe when they were at the villa. But Nina hadn't wanted them to leave, and Nina always got what she wanted.

'All done, Claire,' this one says. 'Shall we go and sit in the day room? It's a bit warmer in there.'

Claire nods. 'That would be nice.' She holds on to the nurse's arm as she gets up off the bed.

'Is Will coming to see me today?' she asks.

The nurse frowns as she helps her up. 'Will who?' she says.

Chapter 62

Nina watches Seb twist his signet ring around on his finger, the gold band that his father gave him which he never takes off, despite how much he claims to hate him. He always does it when he's nervous, and she can't deal with it right now. She needs him to be stronger, more decisive. *Is she the only person who can see what's at stake here?* Five people's futures, not just one.

Ever since the incident at Daltings Abbey, she knows she can get Seb to do what she wants, but at the moment, that's not enough. She needs him to take charge for once, to help fix this situation, which is spiralling out of control. She looks at one of her mother's sculptures, a figure of a woman with her arms flung out behind her as if she's in motion, an expression of shock on her face. Like the others on the shelves behind her, the proportions are all wrong. She's not sure why her mother bothered – an artist needs to understand their subject to be able to capture them and, unlike Nina and her father, her mother had never understood people at all. She'd always taken everyone at face value, had refused to see anything dark that ran beneath the surface. When Nina had told her what the girls at primary school said about her ears, her mother had laughed and told her she must have made a mistake.

Focus. They have two problems. They need to fix Zoe. They need to fix the boat. Perhaps she should ask Luis if he knows someone locally who could repair it. Do the job for cash, no questions asked. Her mother said the locals are always complaining about money – Nina could pay a bit extra if he could find someone who'd keep their mouth shut. Or maybe she could get Aiden to ask him. She'd seen Luis slip through the driveway gates when they came back from the bar in Deià, had heard Aiden's bedroom door open a few minutes later, his footsteps down the stairs as he went outside to follow him. Had seen them again at the beach party, their bodies pressed up against each other, one silhouette against the flames of the bonfire. Claire had never stood a chance.

Zoe can't go to hospital. At least not until they've got the boat sorted. Would losing an arm be so bad if it saved her life? She remembers, in one of her history lessons at school, she'd learned about families who had been forced to eat wallpaper and window putty during the siege of Leningrad in Russia when they ran out of food. She'd found the story fascinating and had asked Mr Lebedev, the teacher, about it, but he'd been reluctant to discuss it further, had said quietly that paper wasn't the worst thing they'd had to eat, before changing the subject. At the time, Nina had wondered what could be worse than paper and putty. *Worms? Spiders?* The true horror that they had started eating each other had come to light only when she was older. It had cemented in her an admiration for people who were capable of doing the unthinkable in order to survive.

Seb's ring-twisting tells her he isn't up to the task. But

she already knows that. He hadn't been up to it after what happened at school either. She'd had to sort out that mess as well. And Aiden isn't any better. She'd wanted people around her she could control; she just hadn't realized they would rely on her for every last little thing.

Maybe she should just wait. Zoe might start to get better. *She won't.* Or, if Claire's right and she gets worse, she might just go to sleep – tonight, tomorrow, or the day after – and not wake up. They could say she had an accident, fell off the boat and drowned. Perhaps use her death to explain the damage to the hull. Nina's mind races with possibilities but, for any of them to happen, Zoe cannot be allowed to leave the villa.

Aiden sits on the sofa, one hand covering his mouth.

Claire looks at him. 'Are you OK, Aiden? I think we –'

She is interrupted mid-sentence as an explosion echoes through the living room. Seb flinches as if he's been shot. Nina runs over to the patio doors and flings them open as there is another series of sharp bangs.

'What the fuck was that?' Seb says.

Nina doesn't answer. She walks across the patio, peers behind the bushes in the terracotta pots, then leans against the stone wall and looks out over the cliffs down to the jetty, crushing bougainvillea flowers against her shorts. Seb follows, hovering at the edge of the pool, staring at the water, which looks cloudier than usual.

'There's no one here,' Nina says. 'Not now, anyway.'

'It sounded like someone firing a gun,' Claire says, the panic evident in the shrill tone of her voice, one hand still firmly on the patio door handle. She hesitates. 'Does Luis own anything like that?'

Nina turns to look at her. 'Of course not.'

Claire's shoulders relax but, in truth, Nina has no idea what Luis does or doesn't own. Maybe she'd underestimated how determined he is to see Aiden. There is another series of bangs, and Nina drops to her knees. Claire lets out a shriek and begins to shut the door, but Seb puts his hand on the glass, forcing her to keep it open.

Nina can see Aiden standing motionless in the centre of the living room from where she is crouched down by the wall. He stares at her, then shuts his eyes. She knows he wants to leave too, but he won't go without her permission. He can't. He owes her.

Claire lets go of the door handle and follows Seb outside, runs over to where Nina is curled up on the ground. Seb helps her up and they look over the wall at the rocks below, the familiar scent of rosemary now masked by a different smell. She sniffs. Like rotten eggs. Sulphur.

Chapter 63

July – 1989

Will stands on the landing at the top of the stairs, Zoe's uninjured arm around his neck. His rucksack is strapped over both shoulders and the key for the Jeep is in the back pocket of his jeans. He keeps reaching behind to pat it, runs his fingers over the familiar shape, reassuring himself it is still there.

They should just walk out of the front door. What would the others actually do to stop him? He thinks of Nina holding the scissors, of the knives in the kitchen and the conversation he overheard. The sound of Zoe's breathing – *too fast, too shallow* – as she leans on him, tells him they can't wait.

He'd made Zoe stand at the top of the stairs while he lit the firecrackers and flung them out of her bedroom window. He hoped he'd thrown them far enough to miss the pool, that the fuse didn't go out before they landed, that the others went out to investigate rather than coming upstairs. Every muscle in his body had tensed before he heard the series of explosions. And then he'd seen Nina and Seb go outside, had prayed that Claire and Aiden would follow. But they hadn't.

Zoe had looked at him standing in her bedroom

doorway after the first set of firecrackers had detonated, but Will had held up his hand, a signal not to move. Not yet. He needed her to wait until everyone was outside.

He'd felt a line of perspiration slide down the back of his neck as he went back to the window, lit another set of firecrackers and threw those out as well. Claire had shrieked as they'd exploded and followed Seb on to the patio, but Aiden is still in the living room and will see them coming down the stairs.

He'll be close enough to stop them.

They don't have a choice. He has nothing else to throw. They need to leave. Now.

He holds Zoe around her waist and checks again that he has the keys to the Jeep. She moves her feet slowly, every ounce of her remaining energy focused on getting to the bottom of the stairs.

He grits his teeth as they go down the first few steps. He tries so hard to be quiet, but his trainers squeak on the marble. Zoe's breathing is too loud. The stairs aren't quite wide enough for both of them to fit side by side and he struggles not to let her fall. He watches Aiden in the living room through the gaps in the banisters as they come down the steps, one at a time.

As they stumble down the last few, Zoe's injured arm makes contact with the wall and she gasps. Aiden turns around and their eyes meet. He is standing no more than ten steps away.

Too close.

For a moment, Will hesitates, wonders if he lets go of Zoe, whether she'll be able to stay upright on her own, or whether she'll collapse and he won't be able to get her back up again. Aiden is taller and fitter than he is and Will has no chance against him in a fight. He glances outside to where Nina, Seb and Claire are peering over the wall, desperation clawing at his chest.

For a few seconds, Zoe's breathing is the only sound in the room. A look passes over Aiden's face that Will can't interpret. Pity? Anger? He isn't sure. The hammering in his brain won't let him stop to think. Then Aiden breaks eye-contact, turns back to look out of the patio doors at the others, and Will braces himself, expecting him to call out, but Aiden says nothing.

Will seizes the opportunity and pulls Zoe towards the front door, twists the latch, turns the handle and staggers out on to the porch. The door slams shut behind him. He can see the Jeep parked on the drive, the noise of the sprinklers on the lawn making his heart race.

'As fast as you can,' he says.

Zoe doesn't need any encouragement. She leans on Will's shoulder, keeping pace with him as he half walks, half runs towards the vehicle. He feels the wetness from the sprinklers on his bare shins as he takes a shortcut across the grass, the water cool on his skin.

His hands shake as he pulls the keys to the Jeep out of his back pocket, unlocks the passenger door and helps Zoe inside. The *shhh-tik-tik-tik* of the sprinklers urges him to hurry up. He runs around the Jeep to the driver's side, lets himself in and puts the key in the ignition – *get a fucking move on* – and stalls the engine in his eagerness to get away.

He glances in the rear-view mirror as he turns the key again and presses down on the accelerator pedal. His fingers slip on the steering wheel as the front door opens and Nina steps outside on to the lawn, stares directly at the Jeep and begins to walk straight towards him.

Chapter 64

July – 1989

The hot plastic seat in the Jeep burns Zoe's back. Her left arm throbs as she twists round to reach the door lock, the movement sending a shooting pain across her ribs. She wonders if her mum feels like this – stuck in a body that is conspiring against her, every muscle contraction a hot white streak that flashes across her brain. For a few seconds she can't think; not about getting away from the villa, not about Nina, not about her mum. All she can do is breathe as Nina appears in her wing-mirror and begins to walk across the grass, oblivious to the water from the sprinklers as it hits her legs, peppering them with tiny droplets.

'We have to go,' Zoe whimpers. 'Now.' The pain in her arm screams at her to hurry up.

Will shoves the gearstick into neutral and tries starting the engine again as Nina bends down and tucks a stray hair from her ponytail behind her ear before picking up a large stone from the rockery at the side of the lawn. She continues towards them, her pace never faltering. Zoe can't breathe; it feels as if someone has sucked all the air out of the car. This isn't the Nina she knows; the girl with whom she was downing vodka only two nights ago, whose mascara and lipstick she borrows, whose hands she'd held at the beach party as they'd danced to the same beat.

The Jeep lurches forward down the drive, as if it finally recognizes the danger. Will stops in front of the metal gates, and Zoe wills them to open. She knows the automatic mechanism takes a couple of seconds to kick in, but as she watches Nina getting closer she wonders if it is working at all. Has Nina done something to block it? If she has, there is nothing they can do. The Jeep can't go through metal bars, and the bushes either side of the gates are too dense.

She forces herself to count to three, adding *one hundred* between each number like her mother told her to do when she was younger. The gates finally begin to swing open in a slow arc. In the rear-view mirror, she can see Nina is almost within touching distance of their boot. *They're not going to make it.*

Seb rushes out of the front door and pushes Aiden aside as he runs towards them. Zoe squeezes her eyes shut, willing the gates to move faster. Nina heads for the passenger side. For her. She looks at Zoe through the window, and there is something triumphant in her eyes as she raises the large stone she is holding in front of her.

Zoe wants to scream, but her voice is stuck in her throat. She imagines the rock smashing into her broken arm, wonders if the pain can be any worse than it is already. She puts the palm of her right hand up to the glass, shakes her head as she spreads her fingers, trying to block out Nina's face.

Will puts his foot down, and Zoe shuts her eyes, knowing the gap in the gates is still too narrow for the Jeep to fit through. She hears a crunching noise, the sound vibrating through her arm as the wing-mirror snaps off, hitting her window. She lets out a yelp and then they are out on to the dirt track, the Jeep tyres popping and squeaking on the loose stones as a cloud of red dust rises up around them.

For the first kilometre, she watches Will constantly check the rear-view mirror. She wishes he'd brought some water. The heat of the sun through the glass windscreen is already uncomfortable on her skin. Red spots appear on the surface of her bandage and expand into a large patch of colour, but neither of them mentions it. They just need to get to Deià, or even to the main coastal road. Off this deserted track to somewhere they can make a phone call or stop someone to ask for help.

She loosens her seatbelt and leans forward, the colour draining out of her face.

'What is it?' Will asks.

She doesn't answer.

He glances across at her. 'Try not to worry about your arm. It's not bleeding too badly.' *She knows he's lying.* 'We'll get it sorted at the hospital.'

She stares at him. 'It's not that,' she says, as the engine splutters. 'Look.'

She points at the Jeep's dashboard. Will sees the needle on the petrol gauge is pointing to zero and a red light is on. They have no fuel. Nina must have emptied the tank.

Chapter 65

July – 1989

Seb catches up with Nina on the driveway, stopping a few feet away when he sees what she's holding.

'Nina?' he says, shading his eyes in order to see her properly against the sun.

The rock makes a loud crunching noise as she drops it on to the gravel by her feet.

'They shouldn't have left,' Nina says. She looks up into the clear blue sky and squeezes her eyes shut against the brightness, feeling the heat burn against her eyelids as the sun moves to its highest point. 'They would have been safe here. They only have themselves to blame for what happens next. I can't save people who don't want to save themselves.'

Nina strains to hear the Jeep's engine as it gradually fades away, replaced by the *shhh-tik-tik-tik* of the sprinklers hitting the grass. They'd got further than she expected. She opens her eyes and sees the air shiver with heat, wonders how far someone could walk without water. Seb shuffles his feet, waiting for her to speak.

'As I said, I always do what needs to be done.'

'We need to think what to do about the boat,' he says.

Does she always have to take care of everything?

'We could try and repair the damage.' His words sound hollow; she already knows this. Nina wonders why she thought she needed Seb at all. She shakes her head.

'Forget trying to repair it,' she says. 'I've had a better idea.'

Chapter 66

July – 1989

Claire taps her fingertips against the doorframe as she watches Nina and Seb's animated conversation in front of the metal gates that now won't shut properly. There's a sharp pain as a splinter pierces her skin. She winces as she pulls it out, and a bead of blood rises up on the surface.

'Are you OK?' Aiden asks.

She nods, puts her finger in her mouth and steps back into the hallway, wanting to increase the distance between them, absolve herself of the blame she can sense approaching. Nina strides back across the lawn towards her and sweeps past into the living room, where she paces backwards and forwards beside the sofa with its stained covers.

'Will and Zoe have decided to leave,' Nina announces. 'Does anyone else want to join them?'

Claire glances at Aiden, who flicks the strap of his Swatch against his wrist. She wants to tell him to stop, that Nina hates people fiddling when she's talking, but thinks better of it.

'I'll take that as a no, then,' Nina continues. 'We can't get the boat repaired – I don't know anyone I trust enough not to report it.' She frowns at Aiden. 'But I've had an idea that will solve our boat problem.'

'What?' Claire swallows.

'We sink it.'

There's a silence in the room. A slight breeze moves the muslin drapes against the patio doors, as if someone is letting out a sigh.

'We can't sink it,' Aiden says. 'What will you tell your parents?'

Claire stares at the dozens of ripples on the surface of the pool that are spreading outwards in small circles from the bougainvillea flowers that have fallen into the water. Someone needs to get the net out and gather them up.

'I'll deal with that,' Nina says. 'You just need to help Seb sink it.'

Seb glances at Aiden, his fingers still twisting the end of his watch strap.

'Why me?' Seb asks.

'Because I need you to,' Nina says. She walks over and slides her arm around his shoulders as a reminder. 'Just like *I* helped *you* when you needed it, Seb.'

The gust of wind dies down as quickly as it rose up and the heat rolls back into the room. Claire stares out through the patio doors and watches a huge bird land on top of the wall behind the pool. Her eyes widen and she takes a couple of steps away from the window.

'It's a black vulture,' Nina says. 'They nest around here in the Serra de Tramuntana mountains.'

Claire doesn't mention it's the second one she's seen this morning. Something must be attracting them. It pecks disinterestedly at the bright pink flowers then takes off again, rising into the sky and circling above the cliffs. Thoughts of feathers and sharp talons run through her head.

Nina takes her hand off Seb's shoulder.

'I'll help you with the boat,' Aiden says. Seb looks at him properly for the first time since they got back inside.

'Will you?' he asks.

'Yes,' Aiden says. He turns towards Nina, 'What do you want us to do?'

Chapter 67

Nina – Now

The security guard smiles at Nina when she goes back into the office, but she doesn't smile back. She fans herself with a napkin from the deli in the lift up to the seventh floor, the heat rising in her cheeks whenever she thinks about the email. She can't believe it came from Seb. *But if he didn't send it, who did?* Five minutes until her meeting. She hasn't got time to think about it now. She eats half the bagel, leaves the rest on her desk and grabs an oat latte from one of the barista bars on her floor to take with her.

The head of the equity capital markets section is leaning back in his chair, feet on his desk, shouting at one of the junior associates, who is looking at him blankly, a telephone headset hanging around his neck.

'Steve?'

'Nina!' She knows his delight at seeing her is just for show. Along with most of her colleagues, he would screw her over at the first opportunity. She would happily do the same to him, and is more than capable of it, but at the moment their relationship is mutually beneficial.

'Shall we?' He points to an empty office. As he stands up, he taps the junior associate's laptop screen.

'Get it fucking sorted out, will you?' he mutters. 'I want those figures on my desk when I get back.'

Nina follows him across the floor and he shuts the door behind them.

'How was the honeymoon?' Nina asks. She doesn't really want to know, but her PA made a note of it in her calendar.

'Good,' he says. 'Not long enough, but I've got too much going on here to get away for long. Managed a few days in the Four Seasons at Cap Ferrat. You ever been?'

Nina shakes her head.

'Gorgeous place. Incredible views. Bill Gates has a place there. We hired a yacht for the day, got the crew to take us over to Monaco.'

Nina shifts slightly in her chair.

'You sail?' he asks.

Nina swallows and shakes her head, keeping a smile fixed on her face. Does he know something about the email?

Don't be so paranoid.

'It's not really my thing,' she says, twisting her three-carat diamond engagement ring around on her finger. 'Hugo and I are more city-break people. Or safaris. Dunes Lodge in Namibia is to die for.' She takes another sip of coffee, the hot liquid burning her tongue as the face of the man she saw outside flashes up in her brain. 'Anyway,' she says quickly, 'enough about holidays. What do you need my opinion on?'

He hands her a list of investor names.

'I wanted to check there weren't any issues from a legal standpoint if we give these guys a copy of the advance draft of disclosure document for this IPO.'

She glances through the list, but the names blur and she

sees the words in the email instead: *Saturday after next, 6 p.m. I'll be waiting.*

She blinks, clears her throat. *Get a fucking grip, Nina.*

'I'll need to double-check a couple of them,' she says, 'but I'll confirm if there's a problem by the end of the day.' She hands him back the piece of paper, hoping he doesn't notice her hand is shaking. 'Does that work for you?'

He nods. 'As efficient as ever. I'll email a copy of everything through to you.' He stands up and opens the door. 'Pleasure, as always, Nina.'

'Pleasure's all mine,' she replies. 'Merilyn's a lucky lady. Hope you get the chance to get away for a bit longer once this deal is done.'

He shrugs as he holds the door.

'Once this one's finished, we'll be straight on to the next. You know what it's like. Never stops.'

'Well, at least you're on top of it,' she replies. 'There's nothing worse than coming back after a holiday to a nasty surprise.'

She drains the last of her coffee and drops the cup in the bin as she strolls across the floor, past the junior associate, whose forehead is shiny with sweat.

Blond hair, slicked back. Chiselled cheekbones. She tries to scrub the image out of her head as she walks back to her office. But Seb isn't the only one who knows what they did. Despite the Gaviscon, acid bubbles back up from her stomach, stinging her throat.

What if the email is from one of *them*?

Chapter 68

July – 1989

The water below the wooden boards on the jetty has turned a dark navy as the sun sinks below the horizon. The afternoon, which passed in a matter of minutes when they first arrived at the villa, had today stretched out into an indeterminate period of time, smothering them in sticky heat and flying insects. Claire looks at the waves below her through the gaps between the slats, rougher this evening than when they went to the beach party. She shivers as they splash against the cliffs and wraps her arms around her chest.

Seb unties the rope that attaches the boat to the jetty, throws it to Aiden and climbs on board to join him. Aiden passes it through his hands in a loop. Claire feels something pull inside her chest.

What if Aiden doesn't come back? What if he's just another inconvenience that Nina has told Seb to deal with?

She'd knocked on his bedroom door earlier, but he hadn't answered, and when she turned the handle it had moved only a fraction, as if he'd put something heavy up against it. She'd put her ear to the wood to listen, but there was nothing but silence. She'd felt an emptiness inside her that seemed to spread through her bones as she swallowed down the urge to cry.

She'd wanted to explain why she'd borrowed his Walkman. Tell him what Nina had confessed in their game of Truth or Dare about that boy's death at school. How she'd covered it up. Someone needed to know. But Aiden hadn't opened his door so she'd had to creep back down the corridor to her own room, her throat tight. She'd crawled under the duvet and hoped Nina wouldn't come and find her.

Despite the way her heart races when she looks at the boat, part of her wants to go with them; anything would be better than being left here on her own with Nina. They've barely spoken this afternoon; Claire has taken everything out of her drawers and wardrobe, packed her bag so she's ready to leave the villa first thing in the morning.

She'd tipped the bottle of Es down the toilet and flushed the chain until she was certain they'd all gone. Nina will be furious when she finds out, but Nina isn't the one who is going to have to risk carrying them back through the airport and, right now, more than anything, she just wants to get home.

She watches Aiden start the engine and move the boat away from the jetty, turning off the one working light that's attached to the stern. He heads out to sea, the boat a white shape that slides into greyness, finally turning to a dark silhouette that merges with the water and vanishes completely.

You're not going to see him again.

Claire's stomach shrinks and she tells herself not to be so ridiculous, but when she looks at the way Nina stares at the boat as she gathers her hair up into a ponytail, something tells her she's not being ridiculous at all.

Chapter 69

July – 1989

Seb glances at the rubber dinghy lying on the deck. Nina had got it out of the pool house earlier, and he's still not sure whether it's big enough to hold them both. Nina had insisted they wait until it was dark so they couldn't be seen, but the thought of being out in the blackness that stretches down metres and metres below him makes goosebumps rise up on his skin. *You'll be in a dinghy. Not in the water. Don't panic.*

He contemplates suggesting they drive the boat some-where down the coast, away from here. But where would they go? Nina had come into his room earlier, had picked up his passport off his chest of drawers and told him she'd look after it, keep it with hers so it wouldn't get lost. He'd opened his mouth to object then closed it again when he saw the way she looked at him. He wonders if she has Claire's and Aiden's as well. Leaving isn't an option. *Don't be a pussy.* His dad's words echo in his head. He needs to get this over with, and then they can all go home. He turns around to look at the jetty, now a tiny spot of light in the distance, and taps Aiden on the shoulder.

'Are we out far enough?'

Aiden shrugs. 'You tell me.'

There's an edge to his voice, and Seb narrows his eyes,

trying to see Aiden's face more clearly in the darkness. The outlines of everything are blurred, apparitions that could fade away to nothing at any moment.

'Let's do it here.' Seb turns off the engine.

'We need to make sure we don't leave any air pockets in the boat anywhere,' Aiden says. 'We'll be in even more of a fucking nightmare if it doesn't sink right to the bottom.' *Planning is indispensable.* He remembers another one of his father's favourite phrases as he walks around the boat opening all the doors and hatches.

'Ready?' he asks Seb.

Seb nods. Aiden picks up the carving knife Nina gave him and cuts the hose to the engine-cooling water inlet. Seb watches the water start to gush into the engine compartment. Aiden stands up and leaves the hatch door open so it can reach the rest of the hull.

'How long will it take, do you reckon?' Seb asks.

Aiden shrugs. 'Twenty minutes? I'm not hanging around to find out.' He drags the dinghy along the deck towards the metal steps at the back of the boat. They both stand still, listening to the sound of the ocean rushing into the hull. Aiden pushes the dinghy into the sea and jumps in after it, landing half in the small rubber boat and half in the water next to it before pulling himself in over the side.

Seb stands frozen on the deck. Aiden is leaving.

Don't panic, don't panic.

What if he rows back to the jetty without him? Seb has a sudden flashback to being in the water after the accident, his eyes stinging from the salt, the pressure in his lungs as he fought for air.

'Come on, Seb, hurry up!'

He can hear Aiden – *his dad* – and watches the outline of the dinghy blur as it floats further away into the darkness, but he can't make himself move. The smell of burning flesh and cigar smoke rises up along with the water on the deck beside him. *Don't panic.* His feet are stuck.

'Seb, get a fucking move on!' Aiden shouts.

If you stay here, you'll drown. Seb takes a deep breath and jumps off the back of the boat. He gasps as he hits the water – *don't panic don't panic don't panic* – the waves now a series of black shapes coming for him in the darkness. The dinghy has vanished.

He disappears below the surface and kicks his legs frantically at the thought of what could be below him, his arms flailing as he comes up again, gasping for air. He pushes aside imaginary pieces of wood as his father's hands press down on his shoulders, forcing him under again.

'Stop fucking panicking.' Aiden – *not his father* – has hold of his T-shirt and shouts something he can't make out as he tries to pull him over the side of the dinghy. The rubber squeaks as he slides across it and lands in a heap, his whole body shaking.

'What the fuck are you doing?' Aiden screams the words as he shoves one of the oars Nina gave them earlier at Seb. 'You fucking idiot. If you go back in, I'm not going to rescue you. Take this. Start paddling. You do the right; I'll do the left.'

Aiden's features melt into one another and Seb drops the oar. Aiden shuffles forward so his face is an inch away from Seb's.

'You're hyperventilating. Breathe slowly. Pick up the

oar and paddle. Look, you can see the jetty. It's not that far.' He points into the distance, but Seb can't see anything. He's not even sure he can see Aiden. Everything has faded into the darkness.

Nina's boat is already sinking in the water behind them, the metal steps at the stern almost fully submerged. He tries humming to block out the noise of the water rushing to fill every empty space in his head. He lifts the oar Aiden has given him, puts it in the sea and moves it backwards and forwards, pretending he can't see the pair of hands desperately clinging to the side of the dinghy that disappear when he shuts his eyes and reappear when he opens them.

Pussy. Pussy.

He repeats the word over and over, his strokes getting weaker and weaker until finally he lets the oar drop on to the floor of the dinghy and stops paddling at all.

Chapter 70

July – 1989

Claire stares out into the darkness and swats away another mosquito that lands on her arm, attracted by the lights on the jetty. Bloody things. A small lump rises up beneath her fingers.

'They've been gone ages,' she says.

Nina bites her lip.

'It hasn't been that long.'

'It's been almost an hour and a half,' Claire says. 'We thought it would only take them five minutes or so to get out far enough, then about half an hour to get back. What the fuck are they doing? They took a torch, but I can't see a light.'

'Seb's a strong rower,' Nina says. 'They'll be fine.'

'And what if they're not, Nina? What if something's happened to them? Do we call for help? Or are we just going to pretend everything is OK, like we did with Zoe?'

Claire scratches her arm, leaving red weals on her skin as she glances towards the steps back up to the villa.

Nina hesitates. 'We can't phone anyone, Claire. I cut the line. You'll have to walk down the track to the main road and flag someone down if you want to get help.'

Claire stares at Nina, her face hidden in the darkness.

What kind of a person cuts a telephone line?

She remembers Nina's words from earlier, about a person who will do whatever it takes to save themselves. Claire is gripped by a sudden certainty that Nina knows Aiden isn't coming back. She takes a couple of steps away from the edge of the jetty, slaps at another mosquito.

'Look.' Nina points into the blackness. Claire wonders if she should try and run up the steps to the villa, can't remember if they left the door unlocked. Would Nina catch her before she got there? Claire has never been a runner. Not like Aiden.

It's a hell of a drop.

Isn't that what Nina had said? Which would be worse? Falling or drowning? She backs away across the jetty, the waves rising up under the boards beneath her feet.

'I'm serious, Claire. Look.' Nina moves towards her, her arm outstretched.

Claire's body is rigid with fear. She knows it is futile to try and avoid the inevitable, but Nina doesn't attempt to grab her.

Claire turns her head slowly to see where she's pointing. A tiny light winks at them in the distance and Claire holds her breath as she makes out the faint sound of splashing, an oar going in and out of the water.

Chapter 71

July – 1989

Aiden steps out of his wet shorts, hangs them over the bathroom towel rail to dry and slides the chest of drawers across his bedroom door before climbing into bed. The suitcase he borrowed from his mother lies empty on the landing, all his clothes shoved inside a holdall that Nina has lent him.

More practical to walk with.

Her words, not his, but he hadn't objected. He'll have to tell his mother hers broke. Another lie to add to those he has already told.

He looks at his watch. Seven hours until they leave the villa. In twenty-four, he'll be home and will never have to see Nina or Seb or Claire again. His arms ache when he moves them. He didn't tell Nina he'd been the only one rowing, that Seb had almost fucked up the entire plan. He's learning from her. Seb owes him now; he's not the only one who has a debt to pay and something he'd rather the others didn't know hanging over him.

Nina wants them to get an early start for the long walk up the track to the main road. Before the sun gets too hot. She thinks they'll be able to hitchhike into town and then get a taxi to Palma airport.

Get as far away from this fucking villa as possible.

As he listens to the humming of the cicadas through his open window, his thoughts slide to Luis and the beach party. His features are starting to slip from Aiden's memory; he can't picture the exact colour of his eyes, can't remember the subtle shades of brown on his torso. Can't taste the saltiness of his skin, recall the exact places his tongue ran over his body. Will he disappear completely at some point? He tries to memorize every inch of him in his head, desperate to hold on to every detail.

Chapter 72

July – 1989

Every time Seb shuts his eyes he sees the man in the water. He can't seem to get warm, no matter how far he buries himself under his duvet. Maybe he shouldn't have let Aiden pull him into the dingy. Maybe he should have let himself slip away into the waves, but the thought of his body ending up floating in the same stretch of water as the man from the boat makes him shudder. He gets up and walks silently across the landing into Nina's room.

She lifts up the corner of her duvet and he slides in beside her, feeling the warmth of her body next to his in the dark. If he ignores the fan circling on the ceiling above them, he can almost persuade himself none of this has happened and they are back in their university house in Birmingham.

'I wasn't sure you'd come back,' Nina says.

'Me neither,' he replies.

He thinks of Gaby, and the guilt presses down on his chest until he can't breathe.

'Nina,' he whispers.

She doesn't reply.

'I killed him,' he says, after a pause. 'The man in the water. He tried to hold on to me after the accident to stay afloat and I pushed him away.'

His confession dissolves into the darkness. Nina is silent. He can feel her breath on his skin.

'You did what you had to do,' she says, finally.

'I keep seeing his face,' he says. 'I should have tried harder to –'

Nina slides her hand into his, intertwining their fingers.

'If we'd saved him,' she says, 'everyone would have found out what we'd done. It's better this way.' She slides her arm across his stomach and puts her head on his chest. 'Sometimes you have to be more like me and let things go, Seb.'

'That's easy for you to say, Nina, but it wasn't you. It was me.'

She hesitates.

'It was us,' she says. 'It's always us. You and me. Together. His pulse was so weak I could barely feel it.'

He stares at the ceiling as her words sink in, feels the steady beat of warm air against his face like a heartbeat, making up for his own, which seems to have stopped. Nina moves closer to him, but he barely feels her. His body is frozen and he can't think of anything but Gaby, a small, white dot in the dark water.

Chapter 73

Seb – Now

Seb can't work out how beachparty89@me.com has found him. He doesn't have a job and he's not on social media. He's spent most of the last thirty-two years inside for dealing various illegal substances, one stretch followed shortly by another. Every time he got out, he promised himself he'd reform but succumbed to the lure of temptation after rediscovering that the odds of getting a job with a criminal record were highly unlikely.

As he walks home up Camden High Street from Nina's office in Chancery Lane in order to save the tube fare, he wonders if she sent the email. He wouldn't put it past her to make him suffer, but she, more than anyone, would want what they did kept quiet. Perhaps, if the boat has been traced back to her, she doesn't have a choice. Is going to take the opportunity to blame one of them.

Unless it's someone from his past. One of his cellmates, perhaps. There've been enough times when he's been stoned off his face in one of the many prisons he's had the pleasure of staying in when he might have mentioned something he shouldn't have. And if whoever sent this email knows his contact details, they probably know his address. It's only going to be a matter of time before they pay him a visit if he doesn't do what they're asking.

The scars on his back itch; the four burns have faded, along with memories of his father, cremated two years ago in the middle of his last sentence. The warden had offered to let him out for the funeral, but he hadn't bothered. His father had never been to see him inside, and the rest of his family had made it clear his presence wouldn't be welcome.

Other blemishes now cover his skin instead: scars left by stitches from knife wounds on his back, slashes from a razor blade on his chest and a puncture wound from a pair of scissors on his hip. He scratches at the most recent one through the cheap material of his T-shirt as he cuts across Regent's Park through Primrose Hill, relishing the open space. Swathes of green that stretch into the distance, the colour more vibrant than ever after the monotonous grey he has been used to seeing day after day for most of the last three decades.

He looks at the image attached to the email again. *How much does this person actually know? What can they prove?* What could be left after all this time?

Ashes to ashes, dust to dust.

He shivers, remembering the taste of salt in his mouth. He wonders if the others have been sent the same email too.

Those who are left.

He looks down at the Walkman that Aiden gave him and runs his fingers across the plastic surface, the once embossed black buttons now smooth from the number of times he's pressed them.

He needs to go back to Mallorca. To the villa. See what beachparty89@me.com wants. It could be his last chance to put things right.

Chapter 74

July – 1989

Claire smells the smoke as soon as she opens her eyes. She must have drifted off to sleep, despite her efforts to stay awake.

Nina is already outside, standing in front of the large metal grille of the brick-built barbecue, where something is burning. Claire watches her out of her window as she bends down, picks up an armful of clothes from the pile in front of her and throws them on to the fire. The air shivers in the heat of the flames, distorting the view of the cliffs and the sea behind.

Claire squints, a knot hardening in her stomach as she recognizes the items on the ground: Zoe's bikinis, her white jelly shoes, the dress she wore out to the bar in Deià. Will's shorts and T-shirts. Everything they brought out here with them, together with Aiden's suitcase, cut up into several pieces, and the cream cushion covers from the sofa. A petrol can with its top off lies nearby.

Claire turns away silently, goes out on to the landing and opens Will's bedroom door, then Zoe's. Both their rooms are completely empty, the beds stripped down to the mattress. Even the towels in the bathroom have gone, along with the horrible sweet smell of decay.

It's almost as if they were never here.

Chapter 75

The sprinklers are on when they leave, covering the tough grass in thousands of tiny droplets of moisture. Their *shhh-tik-tik-tik* reminds Nina of magpies chattering in her garden at home, warning of imminent danger.

The sound follows her to the bottom of the driveway and out of the gates. She looks back at the villa, the glass panes watching her like giant blank eyes. This place knows what they have done. Their secrets are smeared across its rooms, their blood stains its foundations, and she wonders if she will ever be able to face coming back.

She watches Claire fall behind as they walk up the track in single file. The strap on her bag looks like it's digging into her shoulder, and she's limping; one of her trainers must be rubbing against the back of her heel. She should have put socks on. There are some in Nina's bag somewhere, but she's not going to offer to stop. They need to keep moving.

The dust rises in small clouds around them and settles on her white shorts. Its reddish hue makes her think of the towel wrapped around Zoe's arm, and she tries brushing it off, but it stains her fingers. She's so busy looking down at the loose stones, watching her feet – *God forbid she twists her ankle and gets left behind* – that she doesn't notice the two vultures until she is almost on top of them.

She stops dead. The birds look up from where they are pecking at something on the ground, studying them for a few seconds before they spread their massive wings and fly off. She, Seb and Aiden stand in silence.

'What the fuck is that?'

Seb's voice trembles as he peers at what the vultures have left behind.

'Looks like part of an animal,' Aiden says, after a pause. 'A sheep's leg or something?'

'They're big bones for a sheep,' Seb says.

No one moves as Claire catches up with them.

'What are you lot looking at?'

She breathes heavily and wipes her forehead with one hand, leaving behind something that resembles a bloody smear. Perspiration mixed with dust.

Nina shuffles her feet as she points to the remains.

'Something the vultures were eating,' she says.

Claire frowns. 'They look like arm bones,' she says. 'The radius and the ulna.'

No one speaks.

'They could be from a deer or something,' she adds.

'The vultures have almost stripped them clean,' Nina says. 'Aren't those –'

She breaks off suddenly as she spots what the others have already seen. A splash of blue that looks out of place amid the white and red. Something shiny. Neon.

She swallows and takes a couple of steps forward, the bile in her stomach rising up in protest at the rotting stench of something that has been left out too long in the sun, a sour, putrid smell that climbs inside her nostrils and scrapes at her throat.

'What is it?'

Aiden leans over the mess on the ground, trying to keep his feet as far away from it as possible. He picks up a small branch from the side of the track and pokes at the shiny material. It resists his efforts, stuck to the mess beneath, until he prods more vigorously and then it gives way, captured on the top of the stick. He steps backwards and holds it out to show the others. Blue neon fabric sewn on top of a circle of elastic. He swallows.

'It's a hair scrunchie,' Claire says. 'Like Zoe's.'

They stare at it. Nina can't bring herself to touch it. Aiden drops the stick and the neon material falls to the ground.

'We don't know it's hers,' Nina says.

She looks at the remains, something icy cold slipping around in her stomach.

Claire puts her hand over her mouth.

'They're not –'

'Of course they're not,' Nina says, her voice uncertain. 'They're from an animal. They've probably been out here for weeks.'

She wants to get away, carry on up the track, but she doesn't want to have to walk around whatever is lying in front of her. *God, what if it's part of Zoe? It's not Zoe. What if it is, though? What if she didn't make it to the main road and the vultures found her?* She remembers watching a documentary where they'd stripped the carcass of a zebra in minutes. Nina starts to edge around the bones, but she can't leave the track as the scrubby grassland either side is full of thorn bushes, too difficult to walk through without scratching her legs.

They can't afford another accident.

The sun burns down on the top of her head and she's suddenly acutely aware of how far they still have to walk and the lack of shade. The cicadas start to hum in a loud chorus and the sound vibrates in her brain, as if they are trapped inside her skull. The smell is making her dizzy, but she can't drag her eyes away from the strips of discoloured flesh hanging off the end of one of the bones.

The humming reaches a crescendo, a terrible, high-pitched whine that makes her want to cover her ears – *it could be part of Zoe* – and she sways, then stumbles.

She sees the look on Seb's face – *he thinks it's Zoe* – as he reaches to grab her arm, catching hold of her as she sinks down into the darkness.

Chapter 76

Aiden crouches on the ground beside Seb. He's tempted to take the opportunity to run while Nina is incapacitated. He can outpace any of them – he would come into his own, after all those hours of training – but his passport is in Nina's bag. Would Seb actually stop him if he took it? Is it worth the risk? Nina looks harmless enough right now, sitting in the dirt as Seb rubs her shoulder, but Aiden knows animals are at their most lethal when they're vulnerable.

Claire glances at him, and he feels the flutter of tiny wings in his chest. He wonders if she's contemplating the same thing. Before the beach party he might have tried to signal to her somehow – they could have made a run for it together, taken Nina's bag – but not now. He can't trust her. And Seb would catch her before she'd gone ten paces.

Nina gets to her feet and takes a sip of water from the bottle Seb hands her. A few drops escape, turning the earth by her feet a deeper shade of red.

'You OK?' Seb asks.

Nina nods. 'It's just the heat. Let's go.'

They hoist their holdalls back over their shoulders and edge around the remains that are lying on the ground. Nina walks faster than ever. Aiden glances behind them after a couple of minutes and sees one of the vultures land back next to the bones, peck at the scrunchie and then discard it. He shivers.

The sun beats down, the air thick with the smell of pine trees. It's like breathing in mouthfuls of car air-freshener, and he is reminded of the one that hangs off the rear-view mirror of his dad's Saab Turbo: feu orange. Like a mini traffic-light. He can see Claire is falling further behind, limping as she tries to keep up with them.

He hears Will and Zoe's names in the humming of the cicadas. What if the remains are part of them? *Don't be stupid. The Jeep would be here too, and there's no sign of it.* What if Will had driven it off the side of the track and abandoned it in the forest somewhere? Decided to walk through the trees. Will is sensible. He'd have thought to stay in the shade. His thoughts buzz around in his head, making him dizzy.

When he finally hears the faint noise of tyres on asphalt on the main road he wants to cry with relief. Seb is holding Nina's hand, and part of him thinks he should have waited for Claire, offered to help her, but then he thinks about Luis and keeps walking.

Seb flags down a taxi and asks the driver to take them to Palma airport. They sit in silence, the remains they saw on the track lying on the floor between them. He glances at their faces, all covered in a layer of red dust, like something from the correfoc. He wipes his with the bottom of his soiled T-shirt in an attempt to get rid of it but only succeeds in smearing it further across his face.

The driver stares at them curiously in his mirror. Seb puts his hand firmly on Claire's knee to stop it jiggling. He wonders if anything else has been on the news about the accident, whether Will and Zoe have come forward – *or been found dead* – or whether the attempt to sink the boat didn't go to plan and it's been discovered.

Photos of them could already be circulating; photos the taxi driver has seen. Seb turns away from the window to avoid looking at the sea, focusing instead on objects in the car: the small flip-down ashtray overflowing with cigarette butts, the stains on the floor mats, white circles that feel sticky under his trainers. The man's face floating in the water.

What the fuck have they done?

Chapter 77

July – 1989

Aiden follows Nina into the airport terminal. He stands a short distance away, Seb beside him, as she heads straight for the customer service desk. *Who leaves a holiday eight days early?* He listens to her speak in fluent Spanish to the agent, smiling as she hands over their passports. He is reminded of the man he saw at Gatwick, the flash of white teeth.

He can't bear to watch as Nina's eyes well up. Can't bear to listen to more lies about 'her mother', 'heart attack', 'very sudden', words he can pick out from her stream of Spanish. He has to move, and paces around in circles as the other passengers mill about listening to the announcements in Spanish over the tannoy.

Seb goes over to join Nina and Claire at the desk. He turns on a charm offensive – slicks back his hair, twists his signet ring, puts his Gucci wallet down on the counter – and Aiden sees the passenger service agent nod before she picks up the phone.

Aiden turns to look at the large television on the terminal wall. Familiar news footage fills the screen, although the sound is muted. Pieces of wreckage floating in the sea. His chest feels as if it is full of freezing-cold water. He glances at the others, but they haven't noticed; they are too focused on sorting out the airline tickets.

The photo of Señor Lopez with his family flashes up. Aiden is about to get on a plane, and this man is dead. He can't drag his eyes away as the screen returns to the newsreader silently mouthing the words on the autocue. A photo of another man appears, dressed in a yellow T-shirt that Aiden has seen before. Not Señor Lopez this time. Someone else.

He drops his holdall on the floor and shuts his eyes as something inside him falls away, but he knows the man's face matches the one already in his head. The one he'd convinced himself he hadn't seen in the water as the boat headed back to the villa after the accident. A man wearing a yellow T-shirt, his arm up amid the waves. The one the others said wasn't there. He had been alive, and they had left him to drown. *He* had left him to drown. Henrique Martinez. His name appears at the bottom of the screen, along with video footage of grieving friends and relatives.

Seb turns around at the desk and raises his thumb, but Aiden can't bring himself to respond. He suddenly realizes how young the four of them are, how much more life they have ahead of them. How every second of every minute of every hour, he will have to live with what he has done. No matter what happens in the future, it is never going to go away. He wishes Luis was here.

He puts on his headphones and presses play on his Walkman, needing something to stop his mind breaking apart. Alice Cooper's rasping voice fills his head as 'Poison' blasts from his headphones, and he watches Nina step away from the desk, smiling, holding up their passports and four boarding cards. Aiden knows he should be relieved – this means he can go home – but the image of

Henrique Martinez flashes up again on the TV screen and he feels as if he is drowning.

He turns around to see a couple of local police officers in their black uniforms standing near the check-in counter. He looks at them, then back at Claire, feels the familiar flutter beneath his ribs. Does she give him a tiny shake of the head, or does he imagine it? Either way, it doesn't matter. It's too late. Nina beckons to him.

One of the police officers looks in his direction, his gun clearly visible in a holster strapped around his waist.

I cannot be a better man. I am a coward.

The thought burns in his brain. Seb shouts his name, but Aiden ignores him and starts walking across the floor of the terminal, straight towards the officer, his eyes fixed on the man's belt.

Chapter 78

Nina – Now

Nina stares out of the window of her London office at the building opposite. It's the same height as the one she's sitting in; another modern construction made of glass and concrete. The sun reflects off the tinted windows with a glare so bright it's painful, but she forces herself not to look away.

Now what?

She blinks away tears, and the smell of a barbecue and something floral fills her nostrils, making her stomach turn over. *It's not real. Just breathe.* The email attachment on her laptop is open in front of her – a double-page-spread article in the *Daily Bulletin*, the English-language paper picked up by all the tourists in Mallorca.

Her father had driven to Deià to buy it, Nina sitting next to him in the front seat of the car, whenever they'd stayed at the villa. He'd drilled it into her that it was vital to stay abreast of the news. In their first summer there, they'd done the same journey every morning; she remembers the heat of the plastic seat on the back of her legs and, on the way back, her fingers gripping the white stick of the Chupa Chups lolly she would be allowed to choose in the shop. A sickly-sweet stickiness that made her nauseous.

She shakes off the memory and reads the headline again as something flutters in her chest.

BOAT RETRIEVED IN SALVAGE OPERATION.

At the top of the page there is a photo of the retrieved boat, upended, suspended in the cradle of a floating crane, held above the water by four long yellow straps that squeeze it like a belt.

The image is clear enough for her to see that the fibre-glass hull is covered in algae and barnacles. It looks like one of the motorboats tourists hire to sail around the island, except she knows it isn't. The shape of it, the rusted metal handrail, the dark hole she can see in the prow just below where the letters of her name would be if they hadn't faded away, it all screams at her with a horrible familiarity. The fluttering in her chest grows stronger; a kaleidoscope of butterflies trapped beneath her ribs.

Nina scans through the article, knowing she should be focusing her attention on checking the investor names on Steve's list for the IPO. A property developer had discovered the boat when underwater cables for a new hotel were being laid. It had been traced as the source of an oil leak and a marine salvage company had been paid to retrieve it. The developer was quoted as having been 'Sufficiently concerned by pollution issues to organize the operation as a goodwill gesture to the local community.'

She doubts a developer would have paid to recover a boat because they were worried about the environment. She googles the firm, finds that it is based in London and builds boutique luxury hotel resorts in Europe. She knows a developer would want their new venture to be operational as fast as possible and be smart enough to understand that any negative publicity if the leak had got worse would cost them more than a salvage operation.

She peers more closely at the photo, then rereads the article, wondering if there's something she has missed. There is no mention of the owners of the boat, just a quote from the salvage company commenting on the success of the operation, together with a map showing where it was found. But Nina doesn't need to see that. She knows exactly where it was. Where Seb and Aiden had sunk it.

Fuck.

She shifts uneasily in her Herman Miller Aeron chair as she closes the attachment and rereads the email she was sent that morning for what feels like the hundredth time. A few words below the sender's address: Beachparty89@ me.com. She's sure whoever wrote it knows exactly where this boat has been and what they did; their request is an instruction she can't afford to ignore.

Unless you want everyone to find out what you did that summer, you must return to the villa. Saturday after next, 6 p.m. I'll be waiting.

The message isn't signed. Surely, if it was from Seb, he would have just come straight out and asked her for money? Why would he want to go back to the villa? She has no idea how to reach him. She could use one of her many legal contacts to find out where he is, trace him through the prison system, but that might cause more problems than it would solve, especially if Hugo found out. She can't see her husband having any sympathy for her wanting to get in touch with a convicted drug-dealer, especially as she's never mentioned him before.

What if it's not Seb?

Other possibilities run through her head and she feels a line of sweat run down her back, despite the air-conditioning.

Don't think about that.

She can't just go to Mallorca. The deal she's working on requires her to be in the office at weekends and she'll have to take time off work. And what will she tell Hugo? An old friend's wedding? Not enough notice. Invites would have come out months ago and he'll wonder why he wasn't asked. A last-minute business trip? She doesn't normally have to travel, but she could say she has to go for the IPO. That she's got meetings with her US counterpart and has to fly out for the weekend. Hugo doesn't have to know where she is and she'll get her assistant to cover for her in the office.

She checks her diary. She's supposed to be going to a client dinner with Hugo a week on Saturday, with one of his barrister colleagues, but she'll have to miss it. He won't be happy, but what other choice does she have?

Focus, Nina. She prints out a copy of the email and the attachment, folds up the pieces of paper and puts them in her bag, then deletes both and empties her trash folder. She opens the message from Steve and stares at the investor names on her laptop, but the letters swim in front of her eyes. Steve is going to have to wait.

She picks up her phone, types a few words into the Google search bar and waits to see what comes back.

Whoever sent that email has seriously underestimated what she is capable of if they think she's just going to hand over a load of cash. Everyone knows blackmailers don't give up after one request.

They always come back for more. Unless someone stops them.

Chapter 79

Will – Now

The letter arrived yesterday, but Will still hasn't opened it. He knows who it's from. He put it on the coffee table in his sitting room, the room he uses least. Out of sight, out of mind, as his mother would say. Except that's not the case. He hasn't been able to think about anything else since he picked it up off the doormat.

He spots the envelope again this morning as he carries out his usual checks around the house, making sure he's turned off the television and all the lights. Unplugged as well as switched off all electrical items. Sprayed anti-bacterial spray across the kitchen surfaces. He always leaves fifteen minutes in the morning to complete the routine before he leaves for work, half an hour if he knows it's a bad day and he's going to have to do it twice. And seeing the letter unopened on the coffee table makes today a bad day, so he goes upstairs and runs through the entire process again, then surrenders to the urge to tap four times – *always even, never odd* – on the handle of the front door before he opens it.

It's only a fifteen-minute drive to the prison from his house, but today it seems to take so much longer. His mind is blurry, still full of the dreams he had of Zoe last night, and when the first bars of that song by the Human

League come on the radio he flicks to another channel before the lyrics have a chance to start.

He catches a glimpse of himself in the rear-view mirror and forces himself to take a deep breath as he grips the steering wheel, reminding himself that he cannot change the past. He is about to give the same advice in the anger management session he is leading this morning, but now realizes how trite the words sound.

Will walks down the corridor of the prison to one of the rooms he uses for his sessions, his shoes squeaking on the linoleum flooring. There are five inmates in the group today, all of them wearing grey jogging bottoms and trainers, all convicted of violent crimes with sentences exceeding eight years. Some of them have been making good progress, particularly the youngest, who was sent down for grievous bodily harm with intent at nineteen after getting into a fight in a pub and attacking someone with a broken bottle.

Most of the men arrive at HMP High Down with the same rage Will saw in his brother when he was first sent down – a fierce resentment at being deprived of their liberty – but over time most of them begin to accept responsibility for what they've done, and he hopes at some point they might be able to reintegrate into society. Unlike Andy, who he found out last week has just been handed another custodial sentence for burglary. Will might be a psychologist, but he can't perform miracles, as much as his mother would like him to be able to.

He goes back to his office after the session and looks at his desk; files and research papers stacked neatly in a letter tray on one side. The rest of the surface is empty, just as he likes it. Space to think. Except, at the moment, his brain keeps flicking back to the envelope lying on his coffee table at home. He walks over to his shelving unit and takes out a book he'd promised to give to a colleague. A photo falls out from between the pages and his stomach lurches as he picks it up.

He'd been sent it years ago by the same people who wrote the letter that's sitting at home. They thought they were being kind; the accompanying note said they already had a copy, but thought he might want one. As a reminder. As if he could ever forget. Will hadn't wanted it then, and he certainly doesn't want it now. He'd hidden it away on his shelf and, at some point, it must have got caught up inside the book.

He opens the drawer of his desk and puts the photo on top of his paperwork. Their faces stare back at him. He traces over Zoe's with one finger and experiences a sharp pain, as if something inside him has split open. She's laughing. They all are. Nina is posing for the camera, Claire is looking at her, a cigarette between her fingers, her smile revealing her dimples. Seb is wearing his Ralph Lauren polo-shirt, a bottle of beer in one hand and his other arm around Aiden. Taken the night they went out to the bar in Deià.

Seeing all of them together makes him feel as if someone has stripped off a layer of his skin. He barely recognizes the boy with the buzz cut who is smiling at him. His mother always tells him how proud she is of him and his achievements, but he knows deep down he is no better than his brother. Worse than Andy, in fact. He remains unpunished, his guilt sitting inside him like a dusty arte-fact in a tomb, waiting to be discovered.

He moves a pile of envelopes in the drawer and sticks them on top of the photo, his fingers shaking. He can't bring himself to destroy it. It serves its original purpose as a reminder, but not for the reason it was sent. He taps the top of his desk, twice, as he shuts the drawer, knowing what he has tried to leave at home always manages to find a way to follow him here.

Chapter 80

Will – Now

Will stays late to do some work that he could have easily put off until tomorrow. The distant cacophony of the men's voices from the landing and the sound of slamming doors are preferable to the silence waiting for him at home.

He takes out the photo again, catches a glimpse of Zoe's red hair as he slips it into his bag. In his head, she hasn't aged, and neither has he, the two of them entwined for ever in that summer. Despite the gut-wrenching horror, there is still a small part of him that would be prepared to relive it all over again – that wants to, even – just so he could see her.

He strolls back through the maze of corridors, plaster peeling off the walls, the smell of unwashed male bodies and stale cigarette smoke clinging to his jacket. The security guard smiles at him as he passes under the metal detector and his fingers tap the pass hanging around his neck before he steps out through the main door. He keeps the radio turned off as he thinks about Zoe on the way home, a fifteen-minute reward at the end of each day, his coping mechanism for going back to an empty house filled with a gnawing sense of regret.

The envelope is still on the coffee table when he gets

home. He takes the photo out of his bag and puts it face down on the table, then pours himself a large whisky and feels the fire slide down his throat as he swallows a mouthful. He tears open the envelope and pulls out the piece of paper. The words are written in the same blue fountain pen as last year. He takes a deep breath before he begins to read.

Dear Will,

As I'm sure you are aware, the anniversary is once again fast approaching, and we just wanted to send our best wishes and thank you for your efforts in fundraising for our charity this year. The cause is so important to us, as obviously you know, and we are delighted to have you as an ambassador and for all that you have done.

Losing someone so young is a tragedy we wish we'd never had to experience, but from the emails and letters we have received from others who have benefitted from the charity's work, we feel some good may have come from Aiden's death and that at least he will not be forgotten.

We know that you are very busy, but we will be holding our usual memorial event and you are more than welcome to attend. Aiden used to talk about you a lot — he was clearly very fond of you, and we are glad that one of his last memories would have been of the wonderful holiday he had with his friends just before he passed away. We will obviously never know what led him to make the decision he did that day, and we still find it so difficult to accept that he didn't feel he could reach out for help, even to his closest friends. This is why we feel the work done by our charity to encourage young people to talk is so important, especially those in the armed forces.

We will continue to ensure any funds raised are donated to programmes that inspire communication, and hope they will help to ensure that other parents do not have to endure what we have been through. I do hope we will see you at the memorial,

Col. Bob and Sandra Buckley

Will downs the remaining liquid in his glass, turns over the photo on the table and forces himself to look at it. He touches one finger on Aiden's face and shuts his eyes as a tear slides down his cheek.

Chapter 81

Seb – Now

Seb looks up at the three tower blocks that block out the sky in front of him, twenty-three storeys of concrete facade covered in dirty white panels and small brown windows, the odd wilted pot plant and cheap MDF table visible through the panes of glass. The place he currently calls home. The hard ball that sits in the bottom of his stomach gets a little heavier each time he comes back here.

He follows one of the other occupants through the main entrance and takes the lift up to the twentieth floor, ignoring the smell of stale smoke with its distinctive musky undertones. The metal doors slide back with a jolt and he heads down the corridor to his flat. Number 172: a studio, identical to all the others on this floor in the block.

The small room smells of damp and tobacco and something else – *don't think about that* – as he opens the door. His post is lying on the floor – a few junk-mail leaflets and one envelope that he picks up after putting down the cheap bottle of sun cream and roll of two hundred small plastic bags he's just bought in Poundland.

He opens the envelope. His old passport is inside; it's been sent back with the corner cut off. His new one is in his bedside drawer – it only arrived yesterday. He takes it out and an unfamiliar photo stares back at him. His once blond hair hangs around his face in greasy brown streaks and his face is puffy; all those angles he'd once had are now buried under a beard and loose flesh. He compares it to the old one – looking at the two of them side by side, he wouldn't be able to recognize them as the same person.

But the question is, will she?

Something sticky catches on the soles of his shoes as he walks across the carpet, its edge frayed where it doesn't quite meet the wall. He sits down on a wooden chair that is missing two of the four struts at the back and gets out his phone, an ancient model that he picked up off eBay. He scrolls through his emails to find the one he's looking for and opens the attachment so the photo fills the screen.

Each time he does this, he remembers the feeling of being in the water, of fighting to stay above the surface, the terror that he was going to be left to drown. He knows the boat is the same one he and Aiden sank. The map showing where it was found puts it in exactly the same spot, and if that wasn't enough of a coincidence, there's a hole in the prow below where Nina's name used to be.

He rubs his forehead as he rereads the instructions written in the email. He could ignore them, but it's not like he really has a choice. He wonders what Nina has been doing for the last nine days since he saw her, what she is doing at this exact moment.

Does she ever think about him? About them?

Maybe she no longer thinks about that holiday at all. She'd cut him off when he was first sent down thirty-two years ago. Had changed her phone number and returned his letters unopened. He looks at his bare leg through one of the holes in his tracksuit bottoms, remembers how their skin used to touch.

He pulls out all of his clothes from his chest of drawers – one pair of jeans and a pair of jogging bottoms, three T-shirts, a few pairs of socks and boxer shorts – folds them up and packs them into a bag. He adds in his toothbrush and a tube of toothpaste and throws his new passport in on top.

All packed and ready to go.

Nina could have helped him after his dad threw him out. She knew how much he'd hated working for him in that City job. The nausea he'd felt in the pit of his stomach each morning when they'd left the house to start their commute. Packed into the tube like sardines, fighting to breathe. The pages of figures he didn't fully understand. The monotony of the reams of paperwork, surrounded by people just like his dad. He hadn't been able to face doing it for the next forty years and had quit after just six months. His dad had kicked him out. *Ungrateful little arse. Nothing but a waste of space.*

He'd asked Nina if he could stay with her for a few weeks. She knew he had nowhere else to go. But she'd refused. And when the chance had come up to sell a few grammes of coke to his ex-work colleagues, who were all snorting lines of the stuff in the bars of Canary Wharf anyway, he'd taken it. At the time, it had seemed like the easy option, just a stop-gap until he was back on his feet in a new career. He'd only been providing a service. But a couple of years later, after a prison sentence and a criminal record, it had become the only option available; a lifestyle he'd signed up for but had never really wanted.

He glances at the one small table in the room, its surface covered in piles of tablets and screwed-up pieces of clingfilm. A habit that seems to stick to him, impossible to shake off, however hard he tries.

He thinks about the conversation he'd had on the phone with his brother this morning, the awkward interaction they put themselves through once a year to *keep in touch*, although they haven't seen each other face to face for over ten. He had hesitated before answering the question as to whether things were looking up, had thought of the photo of the boat and the tablets lying in small piles around him.

'I'm exploring a few options,' he'd said. 'Just got to work out which one would be best.'

He'd pictured his brother nodding, unable to get off the phone fast enough.

He has no idea.

Seb tears plastic bags off the roll and puts them on the table, sits down and starts dividing up the tablets between them. He glances out of his window at the people in hoodies hanging around in the usual spots on the forecourt below, small dark specks on the grey concrete.

Not long to wait.

He fumbles as he picks up a glass of water, swallows until he can feel the liquid reach the hard ball in his stomach, then picks up his phone, opens a new email and begins to type.

Chapter 82

Will – Now

Will puts his car keys into the small bowl on the mantel-piece, taps it twice and walks into his cloakroom to wash his hands. He can't bear to touch anything in the house until he's done that first; it's a ritual to remove all traces of his day and a way to eradicate the smell of disinfectant that lingers from his visit to the care home – a cloying citrus scent, artificially sweet.

Claire had turned away from the television to look at him when he'd arrived. She hadn't done that before. He'd been in to see her twelve times in the past year, a regular visit once a month, reality slipping a little further away from her each time.

Her husband, Matt, had traced him through Birmingham University's alumni network and asked him to go and see her. Told him that Claire had started talking about a villa in Mallorca where someone had died, and that Will had been there with her. Matt had said that, obviously, he knew it wasn't true, that it was all part of the tragic, inevitable progression of the disease, and that Claire had started to 'remember' all kinds of things that had clearly never happened, but it was still distressing. He'd wondered whether a visit from Will might help reassure her.

One of the nurses had taken him through to the

residents' area the first time; his palms had been slippery at the prospect of seeing her again. He couldn't help thinking about the number of secrets she held in her head, ready to slip out at any moment. His bunch of roses and stocks had wilted in the overheated room as he'd stared at the vacant faces looking back at him. His eyes had met hers without any sign of recognition, and he'd been forced to admit to the nurse that he couldn't find who he was looking for.

Her long brown hair, once a bounce of curls, was now poker straight, cut to just below her chin, thin, wispy strands that were stuck together in clumps. She'd smiled at him, had held out her hand for the flowers, her face puffy. Her eyes were still recognizable, but the early-onset Alzheimer's had eaten most of her away.

'Are you here to do the garden?' she'd asked.

Will had shaken his head, struggling to speak as he sat down next to her. He'd been expecting a monster, but there was nothing left of the person he remembered from over thirty years ago. None of her exuberance, her constant chatter, her desire to be noticed. He couldn't picture this woman dragging on a Marlboro Light, leaving baby-pink lipstick marks on the tip. Always the first one to get up and dance on the table. Even her dimples were no longer visible. This woman was a washed-out shell of a person. The Claire he knew had completely disappeared.

He'd fidgeted through that first visit, picking at the threads on the thin seat cushion, trying to prompt a conversation about Mallorca and the villa, but she had just wanted to talk about what was on television. He'd stood up to leave and she'd caught hold of his arm.

'I know who you are,' she'd said.

Will had felt something cold grip his insides.

'Do you?'

'Yes,' she'd said, smiling. 'We went on holiday together. To this amazing villa. You didn't want to leave. There was a waterfall and we swam naked in the pool and drank tequila shots.'

Will had frowned. Matt had warned him what to expect, but her confusion was still hard to hear.

'And we killed that man,' she'd added, dropping her voice to a whisper. 'The one in the boat. But I'm not supposed to talk about that.' She'd raised a finger to her lips. 'It was nice to see you. Thank you so much for the flowers. I hope you'll come again.'

And Will had. Once a month for the past year. Just to keep an eye on her.

Chapter 83

Will – Now

The radio disguises the silence in his kitchen as he cooks himself baked beans on toast for dinner. If you could even call it cooking – he'd never bothered to learn to make anything more complicated.

What's the point when he'll forever be making meals for one?

He listens to the news about fires rampaging in the Amazon rainforest as he pushes the food around his plate before scraping most of it into the bin, and taps the lid four times after he closes it. He wonders if Claire is back in her room, staring at the pictures of Matt and Ollie propped up beside her bed and stuck to her walls, trying to work out who they are.

He pulls out his laptop and logs on to finish replying to his emails, filing the ones that need to be dealt with tomorrow in a to-do folder, wanting to get his inbox clear before he stops for the night. He can't sleep properly if he leaves anything unfinished. *When did he ever sleep properly?*

The last email was sent from an address he doesn't recognize. Beachparty89@me.com. He opens it and his fingers freeze over the keyboard, his veins beating a visible pulse beneath his skin.

He reads the words, then opens the attachment and stares at the photo of the boat, his heart thumping in his chest. He lowers the lid of his laptop, walks over to the back door and turns the key, pressing the handle down six times to check it's really locked.

He knew what they'd done would catch up with them eventually – he just thought he'd have more time to prepare.

The email sits in his head throughout the parole hearing he has to attend the next morning. He offers up his professional opinion to the board, but it's the first time he falters while delivering his speech. *Should he recommend that this inmate be let out? How long is long enough to pay for what he's done? Ten years? Twelve? Thirty?* He fiddles with one of the Sharpie marker pens he has brought with him, taps the nib on his notes, tiny patterns of dots in groups of four that look like freckles on the page, realizing when he's finished that what he's drawn resembles the letter 'Z'.

He doesn't want to go back to the villa. He can't face it. He's spent over thirty years trying to leave the past behind him.

He walks past the security guards at the end of the day, out into the car park, where he is forced to shade his eyes against the evening sun. He reaches into his pocket for his car keys and presses the button to unlock the doors.

A notification pops up on his phone as he puts it into the holder on his dashboard. Another email from beachparty89@me.com.

> Just in case you were thinking of not coming, I should remind you that I have your mother's contact details and won't hesitate to get in touch.

Fuck.

If he wasn't sure before, now he is. Nina must be sending these. For a moment he feels a stab of hatred towards his brother for everything he has done to make their mother so fragile, for leaving Will to take sole responsibility for her. She wouldn't be able to cope with finding out what he did with Andy already in prison. But, deep down, he knows this isn't Andy's fault. It's his. *Theirs.* And as much as he hates the idea, he needs to go back to the villa, face Nina and finish this.

Chapter 84

Will – Now

Will stares at the screen in Gatwick's departure lounge as he waits for his gate number to appear. He's been here a few times over the past thirty-three years, but still half expects to see one of the old phone booths from which he'd called his mother before they left for Mallorca, feeding ten-pence pieces into the machine to avoid being cut off.

He texts her to say he'll call after the weekend. His flight home is booked for Sunday lunchtime, which should give him enough time. He chews the skin at the side of his thumbnail, a metallic taste seeping into his mouth. A young girl walks past him, the white lead of her earphones trailing down to the phone she's carrying, her red hair falling around her face. His heart squeezes before he remembers the woman he is looking for would be fifty-four now, not twenty, and has been gone for just over thirty years.

His gate flashes up on the screen and he pulls open the handle on his small wheelie case. He's packed light; just the essentials he needs for one night. He checks the hotel booking on his phone; the cheapest he could find in Deià at short notice.

Time to go.

He rereads the instructions on the email one more time and stares at the photograph, the image of Nina's boat imprinted on his brain as he walks across the departure lounge to catch his flight.

The hire car is waiting for him when he lands at Palma – *did it really have to be silver?* – and he heads west in the shimmering heat until he reaches the winding coast road. He drives past the Torre del Verger and stares out of the window at the hundred-and-eighty-degree view of the ocean. From this height, the water looks like a sheet of blue silk, smooth and inviting. It's not until people reach the bottom of the cliffs that they see the strength of the waves and realize how easy it is to be pulled under and swallowed up, leaving not so much as a ripple on the surface.

A high stone wall borders the road on the passenger side of the car, holding back the gorse bushes and pine trees that threaten to spill over on to the tarmac, their woody aroma distinctive through his open window. On the other side of him, the rockface slopes steeply away into the ocean. Every now and again the vegetation thins out and the sea flashes into view again. He imagines the six of them out there on Nina's boat, sitting on the deck like they had all those years ago, downing bottles of vodka, music blaring from the speakers.

He is so busy thinking about the past that he only sees the front grille of the lorry when it fills his windscreen. His heart explodes with a rush of adrenaline and he yanks the steering wheel to put the car back on the right side of the road. The image of a black vulture flashes before his eyes as the lorry shoots past his open window, horn blaring. So close that he feels the hot air press against his face. A line of perspiration runs down his back.

Focus, Will, for Christ's sake.

He misses the turn off the main road the first time and has to double back. He's not even sure this is the right way; the track is more overgrown than he remembers – *no shade to hide from the scorching sun* – the red earth now barely visible among the patches of tall grass. He drives slowly, checking the petrol gauge again – *three quarters of a tank* – his heart thumping at the thought he might stall. Was it really this far down? He's about to turn around when he spots the familiar metal gates in the distance.

The car door is unpleasantly hot as his arm brushes against it when he gets out, even this late in the afternoon. He takes the keys with him and walks towards the gates. They aren't fully shut – there's a gap between them as if they have started to open but got stuck. Just wide enough for him to squeeze through. He heads down the paved driveway, which looks as if it's just been laid, a mixture of gravel and large slabs of sandstone. He rings the bell, but there's no answer, then tries the handle, but it's locked. He peers through one of the windows; the hallway is empty, no sign of life.

He takes the photo of them in the bar in Deià out of his bag and traces over their faces with his finger. If he shuts his eyes and tries hard enough, he can still see the six of them in the empty hallway, can hear them laughing, can smell the musky odour of weed that lingered on Seb's fingers after he'd skinned up at the beach party.

He makes his way around the side of the villa, through the unlocked gate that leads to the terrace at the back.

'Hello? Anyone here?'

Silence.

The pool is the same aquamarine blue that he remembers, the stone wall behind is covered in the same bright pink bougainvillea flowers. He remembers Nina floating on a lilo in her polka-dot ra-ra skirt, Claire swimming beside her, and him waking up with the taste of tequila in his mouth after that first night, the weight of regret sitting in the bottom of his stomach like an anchor.

There are new outdoor sofas where the old ones used to be. He runs his hand over the grey fabric; the labels are still attached. The rusted metal grate on the barbecue has been replaced by one that doesn't look as if it has been used. He peers inside the villa through the patio doors; the living room has been redecorated. The wooden shelves are gone, the paintings have been taken down and the walls are covered in large, colourful canvases that match the rug and cushions. Only the muslin curtains look the same.

He walks around behind the pool. The wooden posts and rope handrail beside the steps are still there. The shrubs that used to fill the terracotta pots on the patio are bigger and the lemon tree is heavy with fruit. But there is still no sign of anyone.

He stares out over the stone wall. The ocean, with its countless shades of blue, stretches out into the distance, and he can see the jetty sticking out into the water below him.

Where the fuck is Nina? It's her villa. *Who else would have asked them to come here?*

The steps drop away sharply in front of him. The pale

grey surface of the first few is mottled with rust-coloured marks, and he can't help remembering the splashes of blood that dripped from the towel he'd wrapped around Zoe's arm.

Should he just turn around and go home?

He can't. He's come this far. Despite the fear that crawls in the bottom of his stomach, he'll wait. And while he's waiting, he'll climb down to the jetty. See whether the nightmares that haunt him match up to the reality of what is still there. He takes a deep breath and starts down the steps, concentrating so hard on gripping the handrail that he's oblivious to the sound of someone walking across the patio behind him.

Chapter 85

Will – Now

The steps are steeper than Will remembers and his knees ache with the effort of having to turn sideways to get down each one. *You're not in your twenties any more.* He goes slowly, keeping a tight grip on the rope and staying as close to the wooden posts as possible. His trainers squeak on the smooth surface – one slip and he'll tumble straight to the bottom. He feels for his phone in his pocket.

You won't be capable of using it if you fall.

A vision of his body lying in a bloodied mess on the jetty runs through his head, and he can taste iron in his mouth – memories from thirty-three years ago or just his imagination, he isn't sure. He wonders if he should have told someone where he was going, just in case he doesn't come back. *Don't be paranoid. Of course you'll come back.*

The jetty comes slowly into focus as he reaches the bleached wooden boards that jut out a small distance from the side of the cliff. A few slats are loose; they creak and shift under his feet, and the relief he'd felt at getting down here evaporates, replaced by thoughts of trying to make it back up to the villa with a broken ankle.

He looks at the posts, evenly spaced at intervals along the edge of the boards. The wood has been varnished recently; he can smell it. The rusted metal light fixtures from all those years ago have gone, replaced by small LED-type bulbs inset into the top of the posts themselves. A brand-new lifebuoy is hanging up. No sign of a boat.

He wonders which of them sank it. Did they all sail out, or did Nina nominate a volunteer? Was it floating down to the seabed while he was still in the Jeep with Zoe – *that godawful smell coming from under her bandage* – listening to her moan in pain whenever they hit a bump before that terrible silence?

He shivers despite the heat of the late-afternoon sun beating down on his head. The sea is a dull grey colour here, the silt stirred up by the current. The thought of being out on it again, of searching in the dark amid pieces of wreckage, makes his heart thump in his chest. Spots flash in front of his eyes and he crouches down, taps his fingers on the ground twice, then six times, then twenty, focusing intently to block out the sound of the waves.

For a second, he senses he is being watched and instinctively looks up. There's a noise behind him and he whirls around to see a huge bird sitting at the bottom of the steps. A black vulture. It spreads out its wings and he steps away from it, towards one of the wooden posts, wanting something to hold on to. The bird stares at him, and he feels a sense of connection; it's as if it knows something terrible happened here. He swallows, not daring to move. Then, as quickly as it came, the vulture flies off, and he starts back up the steps, part of him wondering if it was ever there at all.

He's panting when he reaches the top. A figure is standing by the patio doors, staring through the glass into the living room, and he squints, wondering if he's hallucinating. They turn around slowly and he grips the rope handrail more tightly than ever, feeling as if he has been plunged into freezing-cold water.

'Hello, Will.'

Her eyes haven't changed at all. Still the same green colour he sees in his dreams.

'Hi,' he says. 'It's been a long time.'

Chapter 86

Will – Now

She walks towards him with her arms folded. He looks at her hair, remembers how it spread out around her head when she floated beside him in the sea. He gives her a hug, conscious of the unnaturally smooth skin on her arm that he can feel beneath his fingers and resists the urge to bury his head in her hair.

She smells just like he remembers.

He hasn't seen her since Aiden's funeral; his guilt at what happened had cut almost as deeply as the boat propeller, and he'd broken off contact. The wounds have never healed, the scars invisible but still as painful all these years later.

You never told her what you did.

His conscience stabs at him like the sharp beak of a bird.

'Where's Nina?' she asks. 'I presume she was the one who asked us to come.'

Will shrugs. 'That's what I thought too, but she's not here.'

Zoe looks back at the villa. 'I was just thinking about Aiden,' she says.

He nods. Zoe had stood beside him in the wooden pew of the church at the funeral; flashbacks of their drive from the villa to the main road had run through his head, the hymn book shaking in his hand. He'd remembered the noise of the Jeep engine slowly dying as it spluttered up the last few kilometres, of hitting the steering wheel in desperation as Zoe leaned her head out of the window in an effort to stay conscious.

The congregation had sung 'Abide with Me', which he knew Aiden would have hated, his father in full military uniform at the front of the church. Will had tried not to think of his broken body lying at the bottom of the clock tower.

He hasn't been able to face going back to Birmingham since.

He'd heard the news about the floods in Sant Llorenç after the funeral and it had seemed appropriate that the country in which Aiden had been only a few weeks earlier was itself suddenly in turmoil; entire streets buried underwater as if the whole place was submerging itself in grief for him too.

He stares at Zoe and knows they are thinking the same thing. They had both pretended not to see Aiden's silent plea to take him with them when they walked out of the front door here thirty-three years earlier.

If he'd come back with you, he might still be alive.

He clears his throat. 'What did your email say?' he asks.

'Just that I should come out here. There was a photo of the boat.'

'Like this?' Will gets out his phone, finds the email he received and shows it to her.

Zoe reads it. 'Yes. I got exactly the same one. Word for word.'

315

'From the same email address?'

She nods. 'I wasn't going to come,' she says. 'But then I didn't want to risk Nina turning up at my house.'

She steps back, glances at the smooth surface of the pool and then back at Will.

'I have a son,' she adds. 'Alex. He's fourteen. And I don't want him knowing anything about what happened here. I have to protect him.'

Will sees the way her face softens when she mentions his name. He swallows as he looks at her fingers. No rings. *Maybe she just doesn't wear one.*

She smiles. 'Divorced. About five years ago. And no, he has no idea about what we did out here either.'

The blood rushes back through Will's veins.

'I don't understand why Nina asked us to come,' he says. 'She has as much to lose as the rest of us if this comes out.'

Zoe stares at him, and he runs his hand through his hair, so much longer than the buzz cut he had when she last saw him.

'Claire came to see me a few years ago,' she says. 'She has early-onset –'

'I know,' Will interrupts. 'I've been to visit her in the care home.'

Zoe tilts her head to one side, and Will hears the question she doesn't ask.

Why her and not me?

'She told me about something that happened on the first night we were here,' Zoe continues. 'I was so out of it after all those shots, do you remember?'

Will nods, feeling a sharp pull in his stomach, like the thread on a hem unravelling.

She knows.

He walks over towards the outdoor sofa, knowing if he doesn't sit down, his legs might give way.

'Claire told me about something Nina said,' she continues. 'And if Nina has brought us here to threaten me, or my son, I'll take what I know to the police.'

Will bows his head briefly.

She doesn't know about Claire. You're going to have to tell her.

He looks through the glass patio doors again into the living room. At the brightly coloured paintings that now cover the walls.

'It looks so different, doesn't it? Not how I imagined Nina's taste,' he says.

A shadow passes over Zoe's face as they hear the sound of a car engine outside the villa and then a door slam.

'I assumed it was Nina who sent those emails,' she says, moving closer to him. Will has a sudden flashback to the face of the man in the news, his wife standing next to him by the boat on the stone quay. 'But what if it wasn't her at all?' Zoe asks.

Chapter 87

Zoe – Now

Zoe's insides twist when she sees the two of them walk across the terrace. The same gut-wrenching terror she'd felt when she was standing at the top of the stairs in the villa, convinced they wouldn't make it out. Thirty-three years vanish in a moment, until she's back in a silver Cherokee Jeep watching Nina pacing towards her across the grass, the sound of sprinklers screaming in her head.

Her first thought is that she hasn't changed at all. The same girl from all those years ago, just playing dress-up in a designer outfit and a sleek haircut. Then she looks closer and realizes of course she's changed; her sculptured features are still evident, but they have an air of artificiality. Botox and fillers, no matter how expensive, aren't able to restore the skin of a twenty-something-year-old. She's thinner, almost angular, her body honed, no doubt by a personal trainer. Still wealthy, judging by the diamond rings and expensive clothes.

She squints at the man walking behind her. Is that Seb? She glances across at Will and can see her uncertainty reflected in his face.

Why had she presumed Nina would come alone?

The man's face is puffy, his once blond hair now a dull brown colour. She wouldn't have recognized him in his scruffy grey jogging bottoms peppered with small holes. She has a sudden flashback to him whirling sparklers around on the boat, white streaks of light falling past her face.

Her arm tingles, and she wishes she'd brought a cardigan. She has covered up her scars with a layer of acceptance over the years, one that has grown thick enough for her to start wearing T-shirts again. But the shiny pink patch, larger than her palm and the colour of candy-floss, still has the ability to make her flinch if she catches a glimpse of it in a mirror. On the other hand, she thinks, they should bear witness to what they did to her.

'Zoe,' Nina says.

The sound of her voice makes Zoe want to turn around and walk straight out of the villa and drive back to the airport. It's as if someone has scooped out her insides, leaving behind a hollow space. She swallows the stifling taste of red dust that filtered through the windows into the Jeep as Will drove away from the villa all those years ago.

'Nina.'

Zoe's arm burns as Nina's eyes run over it. She looks at Seb.

'Did you come together?' she asks.

Nina shakes her head.

'We bumped into each other outside, when the taxi dropped me off. I got an email asking me to come.'

She pulls out her phone and shows Zoe the screen. 'This one.'

Zoe glances at Will. She can't tell if Nina is lying, but her body tenses in anticipation of what is to come. She hears her saying, 'Didn't you know?', when she told her about Claire wanting to change flights thirty-three years earlier, feels the sting as acutely as if she had only just spoken the words.

'You didn't send it?' Seb asks.

If Zoe was unsure before, she isn't now. Seb's voice is still the same, although so unmatched to his outward appearance. The disconnect between the two makes her feel as if she's trying to force together pieces of a jigsaw puzzle that don't fit.

Nina laughs. A high-pitched screech that scrapes down Zoe's insides and takes her straight back to their very first day in Mallorca. She sees Will tap his fingertips on the leg of his chinos, pause for a moment, then repeat the same action, over and over again.

'Of course not,' Nina retorts. 'Why would I ask you to come back here? I don't have anything to do with this place any more. My parents were forced to sell up in the crash in '08. Hugo, my husband, bought it and rents it out.'

She looks at Seb. 'And he has no idea I'm here. I've told him I'm on a business trip.'

'Well, whoever sent it,' Will says, 'has photos of the boat being dredged up.' He looks at Nina. 'I presume you sank it after Zoe and I left?'

Nina hesitates, then nods.

'Is there any way someone could trace it back to you?' Will asks.

Nina shakes her head. 'I don't think so. Usually, the hull identification number would have all the registration details. All boats have had to have one since 1998, but the model my parents bought was made ten years earlier and didn't have one. There's no serial number on the motor either, and anything on the paintwork will have worn away.'

'Are you a boat expert now?' Zoe asks.

'No,' Nina snaps back. 'I asked someone who is. I told them it was to do with a case Hugo was working on.'

Nina stares at her, and Zoe notices her lipstick is now red rather than bubble-gum pink; the same mask, just a different colour.

'If they can't prove it's yours, then there isn't a problem, is there?' Zoe says.

'Well, I guess that depends on what else they know,' Nina replies.

She looks at Zoe's arm.

'Did you get treated by anyone in Mallorca for that?' she asks. 'Because if you did, there'll be hospital records showing the date. And someone might have realized your altercation with a propeller was suspiciously close to when the boat accident happened.'

Zoe feels as if everything her life has been built on is suddenly very fragile, like an eggshell, ready to crack open at any moment. She walks over to the outdoor sofa and sits down on the grey cushions.

'But it wasn't my boat,' Zoe says.

Nina shrugs. 'Unless someone can prove it belonged to my parents at the time, the only thing that links any of us to that accident is you.'

Chapter 88

Will – Now

Will's face pales as he stares at Nina. The shock of seeing her here, of seeing her at all, feels like being stabbed in the chest with an icicle, a bitter cold that spreads out gradually into his limbs. Nina tucks a loose strand of blonde hair behind her ear and smiles, revealing her perfect white teeth.

She brushes something invisible off the front of her trousers. He swallows as she takes a step closer to him and he catches a whiff of her perfume. Expensive. Cloying. *Like something rotting.* He remembers the deer running on to the track as he and Zoe drove out of the villa up to the main road. The bump as the wheels of the Jeep ran over it and Zoe's scrunchie escaping from her hair and falling out of the open window. The terror in her eyes as the petrol light continued to blink at them, knowing what would happen if they stalled.

Nina stares at him, her head tilted slightly to one side, and he feels as if she is reading his mind. Sliding her nails into his brain and scraping out his secrets.

'I only did what needed to be done,' Nina says.

Her voice doesn't falter, but he sees her curl her fingers into a fist then uncurl them when she notices he's watching.

He realizes how much she has to lose. But so does he. His job. His mother. The same things he was terrified of losing thirty-three years ago, only now he's more attached to them than ever. He sits down on the sofa beside Zoe.

'Claire isn't coming,' Nina says.

He stares at her.

'I didn't know you two kept in touch.'

'We did for several years after the . . . we came back from Mallorca. Not recently. Her husband, Matt, told me she'd developed Alzheimer's. He said she'd gone into a care home and that I was welcome to visit, but it's tricky to find the time, you know?'

Will doesn't respond, resists the temptation to agree with her, a habit that lingers even after all this time. Something turns over in the bottom of his stomach.

'You've never been?' he asks.

'I send flowers every month,' Nina says quickly. 'But it doesn't sound like she'd know if I was there or not.' She smiles again, and he wonders how often she's seen Seb in the last three decades. Whether they're still as close. *Entwined like snakes.*

His fingers twitch as he taps the cushion. 'I didn't want to come back,' he says. 'Not after what you did.'

'What do you mean, *after what I did*?'

Her voice rises an octave, then she glances at the smooth surface of the pool and continues more quietly.

'I saved us on that holiday, Will. I was the only one who had the balls to do what needed to be done. *I* was the one who got us back to the villa after *you* killed someone.'

'It was an accident,' Will retorts. 'And if Zoe and I

323

hadn't left when we did, you would have let her die. I heard you downstairs. You were contemplating cutting off her arm, for fuck's sake.'

His voice seems to reverberate in the heat.

'Don't be ridiculous,' she snaps. 'I wasn't being serious.' She drops her leather bag on the ground by the sofa as she sits down opposite him. 'I was just trying my best to keep us all safe.'

'You emptied the Jeep's petrol tank. We were lucky to make it out to the main road.'

Nina stares at him, spots of colour on her cheeks.

'I was there, Nina,' Will says. 'I remember what happened. What you did. What we all did. You weren't trying to keep us safe,' he continues, 'you were trying to save yourself. *You* are your number-one priority, Nina. No one else. You didn't even come to Aiden's funeral. Zoe and I sat through that on our own. Lied to his parents about how we'd had such a great time here. Why did he do it? What did you say to him?'

Nina shakes her head.

'What happened to Aiden wasn't my fault. He couldn't cope with the fact he'd spotted Henrique Martinez in the water but hadn't stayed to help him. It was announced on the news when we got to Palma airport that they'd found his body, and Aiden lost it. Seb had to drag him on to the plane. Aiden couldn't live with himself, that's why he killed himself.'

Will's heart crumples a little further. The look on Aiden's face – *desperation* – that he'd misinterpreted when he and Zoe had walked out of the villa.

I shouldn't have left him behind.

'Did you speak to him after you got home?' Will asks. 'Did he tell you how he was feeling? Ask for help?'

Will notices the tiny hesitation before Nina shakes her head.

'You wanted to get back to the villa after the accident as much as we did, Will,' she says. 'If you're looking for someone to blame, then you're as responsible for Aiden's death as I am.'

Will hates the fact that she's right. He gets up off the sofa and walks over to the stone wall, his hands trembling as he stares out across the Mediterranean.

I shouldn't have left him behind.

He senses something is coming undone and there isn't anything he can do to stop it, a ball of wool unravelling in one thin, long, fragile strand.

He walks back past the pool and up to the patio doors, tries the handles again, but the doors are still locked. He cups his hands either side of his face to block out the sun as he stares in through the glass. There are six chairs positioned around the large rectangular wooden kitchen table at one end of the room and, as he sees what is lying on one of them, his stomach sinks.

He turns around to the others. 'Have you seen this?'

They walk over and stand beside him, pressing their faces up to the hot glass.

'What?' Zoe asks.

'Look on the table,' Will says. 'On the far left.'

He hears her intake of breath as she sees what he's looking at. A bottle of Absolut vodka stands next to a photo frame on the table and something green and silky is flung over the kitchen chair beside it.

'What is it?' Nina asks.

Seb takes his face away from the glass.

'It looks like the dress Gaby wore the night we went to Deià.'

He puts his hand on Nina's arm and pulls her away from the window. 'But that's not possible,' he says. 'Is it? Because you told me Gaby was dead.'

Chapter 89

Gaby – Now

Gaby drives down Deià's main street, which winds around the edge of the hillside, cutting through the valley down to the sea. The beige-coloured stone buildings with their painted shutters still feel familiar, even though she hasn't been here for years.

Just like thirty-three years ago, this place still attracts the wealthy. Spacious luxury villas with huge pools and manicured lawns are hidden behind high walls and only used once or twice a year as second homes. The price of everything is kept deliberately high to maintain an air of exclusivity and keep out people like her. Artificial beauty with a sharp edge.

Where she lives now is busier, houses and apartments of all different colours crowded together on narrow streets. The tourists still descend in high season, like swarms of flies, crawling into the bars and over the beaches, leaving behind their litter, empty bottles and used condoms, but there is a sense among the locals that they are something temporary to be endured for a short period during the blistering heat of summer. The community holds its breath and tolerates their presence while swallowing their euros, starting to breathe again when they return home. The same pattern repeated year after year.

She glances at the two photos from the beach party lying beside her on the passenger seat. Their faces stare back at her. Nina is the one that stands out, eclipsing the others, as if someone is shining a spotlight on her. Back then, she exuded a confidence only money could buy; Gaby sees it in some of the guests that visit the Amara hotel, where she works. Nina's hair is pulled off her face in one of those side ponytails they all used to wear back then, her bubble-gum-pink lips pouting for the camera. Seb is beside her, his arm around her waist, and they are all standing behind a bonfire, the flames filling the foreground of the photo. A group of twelve of them – the six from the villa and Gaby's friends – their hands raised in the air. She remembers the DJ, the heat, the feel of the sand on her skin. A night that is burned into her memory, even after all this time.

In the other photo, she's perched on Seb's lap in her white bikini, her arm slung around his shoulders. He's clutching a bottle of Absolut vodka. She remembers the burn of the alcohol on her lips when they'd kissed. The smell of shampoo in his hair. Swimming through the sea in the dark, a sky full of stars, sand stuck to her skin, a boy's mouth on hers. She can just make out the panel under the seat behind their tanned legs, a round, stainless-steel padlock fastened around a metal catch.

She remembers Seb pulling her out of the water on to the metal steps of the boat. The feel of his hand on hers. She hadn't mentioned his name when the police asked her who was at the beach party. Hadn't wanted her mother to know she'd met up with him that night, hadn't wanted to face the humiliation that he hadn't got in touch with her afterwards, as he'd promised.

She'd let herself believe that he would come looking for her when she didn't turn up in Deià the night after the party. Check she was OK, like some twisted modern-day version of *Romeo and Juliet*. For days she'd held on to the slim hope, but the disappointment when she realized he wasn't coming had cut as sharply as a knife. She should have known better.

She turns both the photos face down on the seat.

Focus.

The bar they went to that night is just up ahead, and she lowers the car window as she goes past, blurred memories of fancy cocktails, too many cigarettes and sweaty bodies crammed together on a dance floor. It's now a tapas restaurant, the veranda filled with circular tables, dark blue chairs and dozens of candles in silver speckle-glass votive holders. The smell of cooked chorizo and pimientos de padrón makes her salivate. She imagines it would still be very much Nina's kind of place.

Gaby winds up her window and carries on, the past tasting bitter in her mouth. She grips the steering wheel, needing something to focus on. She, better than anyone, knows that tragedies can occur in a matter of seconds. They come out of nowhere, like being slammed into a concrete wall. Or being hit by another boat in the dark.

She turns on the radio and listens to the headlines before the first few notes of an instantly familiar pop song ring out, the sound of the synthesizer pulling her back into the past. She turns up the volume and sings along to the lyrics, remembers the strobe lights of the club, the feel of her green silk dress against her skin, dancing until her feet hurt. A different life.

She's waited thirty-three years for this. And if they've followed her instructions, she'll get the chance when she reaches the villa. They'll be waiting for her.

Chapter 90

Gaby – Now

The unmistakable *shhh-tik-tik-tik* of the sprinklers switching on makes the four of them turn around as Gaby walks across the patio in the evening sun. Her hair is still as dark as it was back then, still long enough to fall over her shoulders and down her back. The odd streak of white at the front is the only visible sign of how much time has passed. She's wearing an emerald-green T-shirt and white trousers and watches the colour drain out of Nina's face as she gets closer.

'*Hola,*' she says. 'Thank you for coming.'

'I thought you were . . .' Nina trails off.

'Dead?' Gaby smiles. 'No, still very much alive. I live just up the coast, in Sóller.'

'We were told that you'd drowned,' Nina protests. 'After the beach party. Your photo was on the news and the pharmacist in Deià said you'd died.'

Gaby stares at her. 'Was that the only reason you were so sure it was me?'

Nina doesn't answer as she fiddles with her engagement ring.

'Did you send the emails?' Zoe asks, changing the subject.

Gaby nods. She takes her iPhone out of the pocket of

her linen trousers, swipes up to find her photos and shows Zoe the screen.

'I read in the local paper about a boat being dredged up and couldn't stop thinking about it. How similar it looked to the one you took to the correfoc party. So I went to the salvage yard and asked to see it.'

She enlarges the photo and points at the panel under the seat. 'See? That padlock is the same as the one on Nina's boat. I remember because Seb had trouble opening it to get to the vodka. I had to do it for him.'

She looks at Nina.

'That's why you thought the girl who died was me, wasn't it? Not because of anything Antonio said. It was because of the vodka. You'd spiked one of the bottles. I was lucky – I'd almost made it to the beach before it hit me. My friends had to drag me out of the water.' She hesitates. 'It was you, wasn't it?'

Nina doesn't answer.

Zoe stares at her. 'You?' she says. 'I thought it was Claire.' She wraps her arms around herself, hiding her scar.

'You weren't supposed to drink it,' Nina snaps. 'It was for me and Claire.'

Gaby reaches into her bag, takes out the photos she had with her in the car and puts them on the table.

'Once I was sure the boat was yours,' she continues, 'I went hunting for my old photo albums. And found these.'

Nina stares at the picture of them on the beach. *Of Seb with his arm around Gaby.* There is an ache in the back of her throat.

'I took them into Deià and asked around to see if anyone remembered you. And Antonio Furedo did.'

Nina swallows.

'He's retired now,' Gaby continues, 'but his son runs the pharmacy. He said your family used to come here every summer but he hadn't seen you for years. He thought the last time must have been around 1989, because his wife, Juliana, died in '91, and he knew it was before that.'

She glances at Nina.

'He said how fond of you he was. How you always used to go behind the counter in the shop to talk to Juliana.' She hesitates. 'But he doesn't know what I know.'

Nina scrapes her hair away from her face and Gaby notices the damp patches on her T-shirt. *Guiris never get used to the heat.*

'He said the last time he saw you, you were with Claire. You told him one of your friends had hurt themselves. Scraped their leg or something. He was worried about you, as you didn't stop to talk to Juliana, like you normally did.' She lets out a derisive laugh.

Nina looks over at the pink bougainvillea. A few of the flowers tumble across the patio into the pool, making small ripples on the surface.

'He asked me to send his regards,' Gaby adds. 'I told him I was trying to get back in touch. And once he'd told me your surname, it wasn't hard to find all six of you on the internet. Even those of you who are dead.'

She turns to Zoe.

'There were photos of you in a newspaper at Aiden's funeral. I saw your arm was in a cast.'

Zoe edges closer to Will. She opens her mouth, but Gaby continues before she can speak.

333

'And don't try to tell me it was from some other accident,' she says. 'You were fine at the beach party.'

Zoe swallows. It doesn't seem that long since she was last here. She remembers the tang of salt and lime on the terrace, the clink of shot glasses and Will leaning over her in bed that first night, her duvet on the floor. She stares at them all watching her, waiting to see what she's going to say.

Nina adjusts her designer sunglasses and wipes the perspiration off the bridge of her nose.

'So, we're here,' she says to Gaby. 'Just like you asked. What exactly do you want us to do now?'

Chapter 91

Gaby – Now

Gaby stands up, takes a hand-held fan out of her bag, unfolds it and waves it in front of her face. The pergola needs a new roof. The bamboo canes have long since rotted away and there is nothing to shade the table. Nina squints at her in the heat, waiting for a reply.

'Shall we go inside and discuss it?'

'The doors are locked,' Nina says. 'My husband rents out the villa. I told you, I don't have anything to do with it any more.'

Gaby picks up the photos off the table, puts them in her handbag and takes out a key.

'I know that,' she says. 'Hugo has been charming to deal with.'

Nina blinks furiously behind her sunglasses.

'I've got a flight booked early tomorrow morning,' she says stiffly.

Gaby shrugs. 'That'll give us plenty of time to sort this out. It'll be like home from home for you.' She glances at Nina's bag, lying by the sofa. 'The bedrooms are all made up, if you want to stay.'

'I've booked a hotel in Deià,' Nina says.

Gaby shrugs as she glances at her watch.

'Your choice. But the offer is there if you want it.'

Nina glares at her as the four of them follow Gaby around the side of the villa, avoiding the sprinklers, and head in through the front door. The smell of fresh paint fills her nostrils as she walks into the living room. She stares at the artwork on the walls, runs her finger across one of the large canvases as if she's checking it's really there.

Gaby puts her handbag down on the kitchen table, holds a glass against the dispenser on the fridge and fills it up. The ice cubes knock against the sides of the glass as she takes a sip.

'I didn't know Hugo was planning to redecorate,' Nina says.

Zoe walks across the living room, past the new taupe sofas, which have replaced the cream ones she lay on all those years earlier. She picks up the photo frame lying on the table next to the bottle of vodka.

'What's this?' she asks.

Nina frowns and snatches it out of Zoe's hand, her fingers trembling.

'Don't you recognize it?' Gaby asks. 'You should do. That picture was all over the news at the time.'

She stares at the little girl in her father's arms wearing a pink sundress, the two of them standing next to her mother, the three of them smiling. The photo that was shown on the television after the accident. Some journalist had taken it from their house and used it without her mother's permission.

Sometimes she thinks she can remember it being taken. Her father lowering her down to the ground and kissing her mother while she ran off across the beach to play at the edge of the waves. *Maybe you just think you remember.*

Maybe you're just making it up. She knows her mother kept the pink sundress hanging in her wardrobe long after she'd outgrown it.

'That's Mateo Lopez.' She points at the photo.

Her father exists as a jigsaw, a person reconstructed from memories. Some, she knows are her own: his dark beard, his big hands that smelt of chlorine and a huge smile. Some are from others, who have told her Mateo Lopez was the life and soul of the party, a man who hugged everyone and liked a beer. Her mother says he was the love of her life, but Gaby understands that death washes away everyone's faults. All she is really certain of is that the person who stares back at her from the photo is a stranger, a man who has been absent for much of her life. And the people standing before her are the ones responsible.

'My father was one of the men who died after the beach party,' Gaby says. 'When you ran into Henrique Martinez's boat. That's why I went missing for a couple of days after the correfoc. I had to get away. I couldn't face it.'

Nina doesn't reply. She puts the photo frame back down on the table, pulls out a kitchen chair and sits down. Gaby takes a few more sips of water and watches Nina fiddle with her sunglasses, her neck now covered in red blotches.

'Didn't your father work here?' Zoe says slowly. 'I remember you saying he looked after the pool?'

Gaby nods.

Zoe looks at Nina. 'You must have known who he was. Back then, I mean. *You knew* he was Gaby's father when you found him in the water. Mateo Lopez cleaned your fucking pool for years, and you didn't say anything. Bloody hell, Nina. How could you?'

Nina's knuckles are white as she grips the seat of the chair.

'It wouldn't have helped the situation.' She glances at Seb. 'He was already dead.'

'Gaby stayed at the villa with us.' Zoe spits out the words, her face white. 'She was on your boat that night. You knew she'd drunk the vodka that *you* spiked. And you said *nothing*.'

Nina presses her lips together.

'How would telling you I knew who Mateo was have helped us?'

Zoe shakes her head. 'It's always about you, Nina.'

'You ruined my life,' Gaby says. 'All my friends went off to college, and I stayed behind to look after my mother. She was so overwhelmed with grief she could barely function. Thirty-three years on, and she still rarely leaves our apartment.'

Gaby's eyes swim with tears, and she swallows. *She won't cry.* She sees people like Nina where she works all the time. She can tell who they are before they've finished checking in. The way they look at the staff, the veiled threats they make when they aren't offered an upgrade, the way they assume she's a receptionist rather than the general manager. Their entitlement has soaked so deep into their skin it can never be washed out.

'What are you going to do?' Nina asks.

Gaby stares at her.

She doesn't care.

'My father's death is just another accident with no one to blame,' she says. 'I know you are responsible, so I'm going to the police. I asked you back to the villa to give you a chance to do the decent thing and come with me.'

Chapter 92

Nina – Now

There's a silence after Gaby stops speaking. Nina can feel Seb staring at her. She wonders when he was released from his latest prison stretch. He'd been sent down for the first time in 1990; a year after they'd come back from Mallorca. She'd followed the reports in the local paper but couldn't bring herself to attend court in person; wasn't going to risk anyone finding out she was friends with a convicted drug dealer. She'd taken down the photos of the two of them at university, torn them up and thrown them away.

You can't always save someone.

She's lost track of how many times he's been inside since then.

And then she'd met Hugo. Seb's looks, without a self-destruct button. *Boring*, a small voice whispers in her head. She thinks of her luxury Mayfair apartment, the fancy restaurants she dines in every night, her wardrobe of designer clothes. *Secure*, she hisses back. Hugo is brilliant at his job and supportive of her career.

As long as it makes him look good.

He'd stood by her when her parents lost everything, including the villa, in the financial crash, had even bought them out when they'd had to sell their house *to save him the embarrassment of having in-laws who were homeless.* She's not going to risk him finding out about this. If he does, she'll lose him, as well as the life she's so carefully constructed for herself. It's the only reason she's here.

'I'm not going anywhere with you,' Nina says, looking at Gaby. 'What happened was an accident. I'm very sorry for your loss, but it wasn't anyone's fault.'

'Of course it was,' Gaby snaps back. 'None of you should have been on that boat. I bet you didn't even have a licence. You'd all been drinking and smoking God knows what. Claire was off her face. You fled the scene and tried to cover up what you'd done.'

'We never intended . . .' Seb starts to say, but he trails off when he sees the expression on Nina's face.

He should be grateful. If it hadn't been for her, they would all have gone to prison.

She thought they'd covered every eventuality – until Gaby's email had arrived. That fucking boat. It had been a nightmare to get rid of it the first time. And she'd had to lie to her parents when she'd arrived back in England, telling them she'd left the keys outside when Luis had been gardening and he must have taken them. She'd persuaded them not to file a police report or an insurance claim as Luis would only deny it and she didn't want him to get into trouble. Her parents had reluctantly agreed and fired him instead.

Nina looks at the objects that are sitting on the shelves at the back of the living room. Her mother's alabaster nudes are nowhere in sight. She wonders whether Hugo got rid of them without telling her. The falling women. She shivers. A couple of hand-carved wooden fishing boats stand in their place, their red sails like splashes of blood against the white walls. She realizes her parents had never asked what had happened to the sofa.

'We were trying to save Zoe,' she says.

'Maybe if you hadn't spiked the vodka in the first place,' Gaby replies, 'she wouldn't have needed saving.'

Nina ignores her. 'Zoe was barely conscious. We needed to get her back to the villa, not focus on someone who was already dead. I'm sorry about what happened to your father, I really am, but if you're going to talk about blame, then perhaps you need to look a bit closer to home.'

Gaby frowns.

'What are you talking about?' she asks.

Nina hesitates, her red lipstick slick.

'The night of the beach party,' she says, 'your father came here, to the villa. He told me you'd had a big argument about you going out to meet Seb. I said you weren't here and told him to leave.'

Gaby puts the glass down on the counter as if it has suddenly become too heavy to hold. Nina knows no one likes hearing something about their past that twists it into something unfamiliar.

'I didn't know Mateo was going to try and follow you,' she says. 'He must have gone to find Henrique after he left here and persuaded him to take out his boat. If you're searching for someone to blame, Gaby, you need to look at yourself. Your father was only out that night because he was looking for you. He must have turned all the lights in the boat off when he got close to the beach party because he didn't want you to see him. If he'd kept them on, we might have spotted him. That's down to you, not us.'

Gaby stands motionless for a few seconds. Her green dress slips off the back of the chair and falls on the floor, but she doesn't make any attempt to pick it up.

'And let's just say you go to the police,' Nina continues, turning the photo frame face down on the table. 'You can't prove any of us were actually driving the boat that night. Zoe's scars aren't proof of anything. There's nothing to show the boat even belonged to me. And even if the police believe your story, all of this happened a very long time ago.'

She walks over to the patio doors, unlocks them and throws them open on to the terrace. The slight breeze hits her face, cutting through the heat in the living room. Gaby's frown deepens.

'Thirty-three years ago, to be precise,' Nina says.

Gaby looks at the bottle of vodka on the table.

'Which means,' adds Nina, 'the statute of limitations in Spain has expired so there would be no prosecution. No one is going to charge any of us with anything.'

Chapter 93

Nina – Now

Nina leaves Gaby staring after her as she steps outside on to the terrace. Ripples run across the surface of the turquoise pool and she remembers how Zoe's blood had dripped off the towel into the water and disappeared.

Like everything does, eventually.

She walks over to the gap in the stone wall that leads down to the jetty. The gate has gone and the Mediterranean stretches out in front of her. She thinks she can see the coast of Spain in the distance, but perhaps it's just a mirage. The shimmering heat makes it difficult to be sure of anything, and she knows how easy it is to misjudge distances. Her father always used to say that things often turn out to be further away than you thought.

The jetty sticks out from beneath the cliff, and she can see a white boat tied up beside it which vanishes when she blinks. She shivers as she hears footsteps behind her and turns around to find Seb standing there.

'Is that really true?' he asks. 'About the statute of limitations?'

She nods. 'They wouldn't prosecute after all this time.'

'Why are you worried, then?' he asks.

She ignores his question.

'Did you see the way Will was looking at Zoe?' she asks. 'Some things never change.'

He shrugs.

'When did you get out of prison?' she asks.

'This time?' He smiles sardonically. 'A few months ago. I looked you up. Found an article that was written about you – a feature on successful women working in the City. Saw a photo of your wedding. Of your husband. Looks like you have the perfect set-up.'

Nina hesitates before she answers.

'Yes,' she says. 'Hugo and I have a great life.'

She doesn't tell him that Hugo's skin is cold when she pecks him on the cheek before she goes to work, that when she switches off the television at night the silence in their apartment fills her room as her husband sleeps by himself across the hallway. She doesn't tell him that when she stands in front of her en suite mirror and rubs La Mer cleanser over her face she can't help thinking that, despite her job, despite all the flash lunches and dinners, she has never felt so alone.

'He's a criminal defence barrister?' Seb asks.

Nina nods. She's glad she has her sunglasses on. Seb's face is bloated and his grey jogging bottoms have holes in, but she only sees the one boy she has always wanted. Ever since they met at Daltings Abbey.

I would never let anything come between us.

She remembers the words she said to Gaby as she glances at the steps that lead down to the jetty. Steeper than she remembers.

She hadn't liked Eduardo da Silva from the day he'd started sixth form. He hadn't seemed to understand that

Seb was *her* friend and there was no way she was going to let someone who'd only just moved to the country take her place.

His face had a tight, pinched look, as if he'd swallowed something sour. She'd taken to mimicking him – pulling in her cheeks whenever he appeared, making sure Seb saw. She'd hated the way he'd corrected her Spanish; Profesora Garcia fawning over him as if he was something special.

Nina has pushed what happened to the back of her mind. Hidden it away. She has so many versions of the event in her head it's difficult to remember which one is actually the truth.

There's the account she'd given the headmaster on the day it happened – that she hadn't seen Eduardo since lunchtime. That she hadn't really had a chance to get to know him.

Or the version she'd repeated to the police when she'd been interviewed, the one that included a few extra embellishments to cover any holes in her original story – how she'd stood behind him in a drama class that morning; small details that would explain any traces of her DNA on his sweater.

Or there's the version she'd told Seb – that she'd seen Eduardo fall after he collapsed suddenly in front of her. That she'd had the presence of mind to go straight back to their boarding house and retrieve what Seb had been stupid enough to give him in the first place, before the investigation and searches started.

She'd never mentioned the argument to anyone. Had never disclosed that Eduardo had only staggered backwards after she'd shoved him, how his body had tumbled down the stone steps, the crack his head had made as it hit the bottom. How she'd left him there. Memories that occasionally still stab her in the gut, reminding her that even she has a conscience, no matter how deep she tries to bury it.

She knows that sometimes events have to be re-told, things omitted or added; whatever it takes to save ourselves. Because isn't the truth often just what we make it?

'Why did you come here,' Seb asks, 'if you knew the police wouldn't be interested?'

'Because there are people who can't find out what happened. My husband, my boss. Allegations can be as damaging as a court case, even if they aren't proven. And besides,' she adds, 'I wanted to see you.'

He stares at her.

'You haven't wanted to see me for over thirty years, Nina. Let's face it, I haven't been difficult to find. You could have come and visited me anytime.'

His voice still has the same deep baritone she remembers. She thinks about how they'd danced together in the club in Deià, of how his arms had felt around her on the beach. Of how he'd run his fingers through her hair at university when she lay across his lap. There is a physical pain in her stomach and she wishes she could go back, do it all over again, just differently this time.

She looks at the steps. The rust-coloured stains Aiden tried to erase are still visible. She wonders whether a similar pattern remains at the bottom, or whether the spray from the sea will have worn those away.

'I didn't come and see you because it would have been too difficult,' she says.

'For you, or for me?'

She can smell his skin; it's not an artificial scent like one of Hugo's expensive aftershaves, but something earthy and plain that makes her take a step towards him. He leans away, a movement so tiny she almost wonders if it was deliberate until she sees the muscles tense in his neck. In that split second, she knows she has misjudged the situation, and her cheeks flush in embarrassment.

'I already know the answer,' Seb says. 'You haven't changed, Nina. You didn't come and visit me because, as someone training to be a solicitor, it wouldn't have looked good. All the things you did back then, they were only ever for you.'

The movement as he steps backwards triggers something in her head. Two silhouettes against the fading evening sun. She sees a foot slip, a hand grasp for a rope that isn't there, hears the dull thud of flesh as it hits stone, over and over and over again, followed by a long silence.

She swallows.

Blinks.

Swallows.

Time falls away and she is eight years old, back to that evening in the villa. Swallowing to try and get rid of the lump in her throat, like a piece of the birthday cake her mother had given her had got stuck on the way down. She had found it later, squished into a ball, her fingers curled around it as if she hadn't wanted to let it go.

Her dad had told her it wasn't her fault, but she'd known it was. She'd been given specific instructions not to go outside and annoy the grown-ups at the party but had gone anyway, had wanted to give some of the cake to the birds. She'd seen her father try to kiss Juliana and had watched her push him away. He'd caught hold of Juliana's wrist with the look on his face he always had when he scolded Nina. Eyebrows knitted tightly together, lips pursed in fury, the blood leeched out of them.

Nina had stepped out of the shadows, and the shock of seeing her had made him let go. Juliana had stepped backwards, her foot missing the top step, and Nina had watched her fall, a look on her face that seemed to say she had always known it was going to end that way.

Her father had tucked Nina into bed after the police left, had smoothed out the wrinkles in her duvet and told her what had happened was a tragic accident and she needed to remember that if anyone asked. It wasn't anyone's fault. He hadn't mentioned kissing Juliana, and Nina had wished he would leave her alone so she could go to sleep and pretend she hadn't seen it at all.

No one had told her until much later that Juliana would be in a wheelchair for the rest of her life. That she couldn't remember anything about the party.

Seb is staring at her. She looks at the bougainvillea, the cerise flowers more vivid than ever. Things have a habit of turning full circle. The heels of Seb's trainers protrude over the edge of the step. She can hear Gaby talking inside the villa, can feel the sun beating down on her skin. The image of Juliana's face keeps appearing in her head like a persistent fly that won't leave her alone.

'It wasn't only for me, Seb,' she says. 'We both know that, without my help, you wouldn't even have gone to university. Sometimes you have to do something terrible to stop something even worse happening, don't you?'

Chapter 94

Zoe – Now

Zoe can see Nina talking to Seb by the pool when she steps out through the patio doors. Will follows her and leans against the wall, the heat now more bearable. The sky has turned a deeper shade of blue, still as cloudless as she remembers, and when she looks out towards the horizon she realizes it's impossible to see the exact spot where it merges with the water. The cicadas have started their evening chorus, a hum that makes her feel dizzy. She stares at Nina, her bright red lips pressed tightly together.

'Gaby wants you to come back inside,' she says.

Nina turns to look at her, her eyes hidden by her over-sized sunglasses.

'I guess she's going to tell us how much she wants to keep quiet.'

Money isn't going to fix this, Zoe thinks. Gaby is not the kind of person who can be bought, at any price. She glances at the steps to the jetty, a shiver running down the back of her neck as she remembers how Aiden struggled to carry her. Will taps the wall in a weird irregular beat, a kind of Morse code.

The thought of Alex finding out that she was involved in Mateo's death sends a sharp pain through her chest.

She will not let that happen.

'Do you remember our first night here?' she asks.

'I don't think now is the time for reminiscing, Zoe,' Nina replies.

'I'm only asking because Claire came to see me before she went into the care home,' Zoe says. 'She told me what you'd said when we played Truth or Dare. Do you remember? About what you did to that boy at your school. She tried recording what you said on Aiden's Walkman but said there was too much noise to hear you properly.'

A flush spreads across Nina's cheeks as she adjusts her sunglasses.

'I don't know what you're talking about.'

'I think you do,' Zoe says. 'Just like you know exactly what you did to me here. We're not talking about it because we all want to forget about it. So I'm bringing it up now because if we go back inside and find out what Gaby wants, I expect you to deal with it. Give her whatever she asks for. Or I'll make sure everyone knows about what happened at Daltings Abbey. And before you say it, I know I don't have proof, but we all know how much damage accusations can do.'

She stares at the two of them. Seb shuffles his feet but doesn't speak. Nina smiles.

'If we're going to be truthful about what happened on that first night,' she says, 'then I presume that applies to everything?'

Zoe looks at her blankly. Nina shoots a glance at Will, and Zoe sees her mouth twitch. Will's fingers tap the wall even faster, the cerise flowers nodding to the beat. A knot tightens in her stomach.

'Claire told you what she thought I said that night, but did she tell you what *she* did?' Nina asks.

Zoe swallows. 'What?'

'She slept with Will,' Nina says smoothly.

Zoe experiences the sensation that she is being pushed backwards and is falling through the air, just like she did on the boat. She tries to catch her breath as she looks around for something to cling on to. She glances at Will but then wishes she hadn't – *it's true* – and wonders whether in fact she's always known – *that niggling feeling something wasn't quite right*. It's been over thirty years. They weren't even together at the time. *So why does it hurt so much?*

Nina puts her hand on Seb's arm.

'Shall we go back inside?'

Nina brushes past her, so close that their skin almost touches, but Zoe doesn't take any notice. She's too busy replaying the night of the beach party in her head, looking for clues she missed at the time, wondering how she could have got it so wrong. She flushes at the memory of Will's fingers holding on to hers as she looked at the stars. She'd been going to tell him she thought about that moment more often than her wedding day.

It serves her right. What price did she expect to pay for taking a life?

Chapter 95

Will – Now

Will doesn't say a word as Nina and Seb walk across the terrace towards the villa. He thinks about kissing Zoe in the sea, the last time his heart wasn't trying to beat while being squeezed by guilt, a guilt that has continued to grow over the years, slowly compressing his veins and arteries until he barely feels alive.

'I'm so sorry,' he says finally. 'I should have told you.'

Zoe stares at him. 'Yes, you should.'

'I was going to, but it never seemed to be the right time, and then there was the accident . . .' He trails off. 'It's no excuse. I should have told you.'

He taps the bougainvillea as he looks at her. He has lived so many more years of his life without her than with her, but he can't help feeling they are still connected.

'I know it doesn't matter now,' he says, 'but I thought it might help me to forget about you. Back then, I mean. I knew it was only a matter of time until you found out Andy was in prison for killing someone while driving drunk and I thought you'd hate me because of what happened to your sister, and I know it was stupid – so stupid – but . . .'

He breaks off, his voice choked, and rubs his forehead.

'I need to show you something,' he says. 'If you'll let me?'

Zoe hesitates, then nods and follows him as he walks

past the pool, over the grass towards the gate that leads to the front of the villa.

He opens the door to his hire car and gets into the driver's seat. Zoe slides into the passenger seat beside him as he roots around in his bag and pulls out a copy of the mix-tape Bob Buckley sent him thirty-three years ago, along with Aiden's camera, which is now sitting in the drawer of his bedside cabinet at home.

'It's for you,' he says as he gives it to her. 'I asked Aiden to make it before we came away and never got a chance to give it to you.'

Zoe smiles as she reads the back of the plastic cover, Will's handwriting still familiar, the J-card covered in song titles and tiny doodles in black pen.

'I wanted you to hear this,' he says as he turns on the engine, plugs his phone into the USB socket in the car and flicks through the playlist to find the song he wants. The intro to 'Love Will Tear Us Apart', with its distinctive synthesizer and bass guitar, echoes around them in the small space.

Too true, Aiden. He thinks. *Too true.*

He senses Zoe move towards him and, as her lips meet his, thirty-three years slip away and he is back on the beach, watching her float in the water, her hair spread out around her face in the dark, and it feels as if he has come home.

He doesn't want to let go, wants to hold on to this moment that he has imagined more times than he can count. Memories of nights they spent together at university flash through his head. Their bodies moulded together in his single bed, sheets sticky with perspiration, his hands stroking her bare skin.

She finally pulls away, smoothes down her rumpled T-shirt with one hand.

'When are you flying back?' His voice is thick.

'Tomorrow morning.' Her green eyes are brighter than ever. 'I had a hotel booked in Deià, but if I stay here, will you stay with me?'

He tucks a loose piece of hair behind her ear, feels her shiver as he kisses her again, runs his hand down her spine.

The song finishes, and the humming of the cicadas is the only thing he is aware of in the silence that follows.

'Of course I will,' he says, finally.

Chapter 96

Will – Now

Will can hear Nina talking loudly on her mobile as she paces up and down the drive. Something about share prices. He takes his bag out of the boot and carries it upstairs, being careful not to slip on the polished marble steps.

As he walks across the landing, he notices that the table where the telephone used to be has been replaced with a grey chaise longue. A memory of seeing the wire hanging slackly against the wall flashes into his head. He goes into the bedroom next to the one Zoe disappears into, restrains himself from following her inside.

There are three quiet taps on his door, and he adds an extra one with his foot on the floorboard as Seb walks into his room.

'We need to talk.'

Seb walks slowly across the floor and grimaces as he lowers himself to sit beside Will on the bed. *He looks nearer seventy than fifty.* Prison does that to a person; Will has seen the same thing with Andy.

'There's something I need to tell you,' Seb says.

Will can hear a wheezing sound in Seb's chest when he breathes. He rubs his beard and Will notices his fingers twitch in a muscle spasm before he puts his hand between his knees. He suddenly realizes how gaunt Seb's frame is beneath his faded black T-shirt and sees the lesions on the back of his hand.

Neither of them says anything. Will can hear the sound of the sprinklers outside as the sun slips below the horizon.

'Not long, is the answer,' Seb says finally. 'Cancer.'

Will stares at him.

'Don't look like that,' Seb says. 'You know what my life is like, Will. You work in the place I've called home for most of the last thirty-two years. I've fucked it all up. This is my chance to put things right. As much as I can, anyway. I should never have let things go that far with Zoe in the villa. I went along with it; I always went along with whatever Nina wanted, but that's no excuse.'

'Aiden saved us, you know,' Will says, after a pause. 'He could have shouted when he saw us coming down the stairs, but he didn't. He let us walk out the front door.'

Seb nods. 'I know.' He leans forward to adjust his position and briefly shuts his eyes before opening them again.

'It's my spine,' he says. 'Throbs like hell.'

'Does Nina know?' Will asks.

Seb shakes his head. 'I haven't told her. Not yet.' He hesitates. 'Do you think she's changed?'

Will taps the duvet with one finger, hoping it's subtle enough for Seb not to notice. He shakes his head. Seb lowers his voice so it's barely above a whisper.

'Nina won't ever change. What Claire told Zoe was true. Nina got hold of Ritalin for me when we were at school. I was under a lot of pressure from my father to do well in my A levels and she said it would help me study more effectively. You've heard of it?'

Will nods, his body rigid. 'Methylphenidate. Stimulates your central nervous system. Used to treat ADHD, among other things.'

'Exactly. Obviously, you can't get hold of it to use as a study drug, so Nina got hold of some illegally through her father. She used to write herself prescriptions for all kinds of stuff. I took it, and it helped me to concentrate, but my room-mate, Eduardo, caught me taking it and decided to try some. He found out where I kept it and took a few tablets without asking. Quite a few, in fact.' Seb hesitates. 'Do you know what the side effects of Ritalin are?'

Will swallows. 'Agitation, anxiety, dizziness, nausea, increased heart rate . . .'

'Indeed. Which is exactly what happened to Eduardo. Our school was a posh boarding school. Old stone buildings, lots of wood panelling and stone staircases. You know the kind of place. Eduardo had some kind of seizure at the top of one of the staircases and fell.'

Will shuts his eyes.

'Tumbled all the way to the bottom, apparently. But Nina was with him and, instead of going to get help, she decided to leave him and go back to the boarding house so she could get rid of the Ritalin. She knew there would be an investigation and made the decision to save herself and, unintentionally, me.'

'What about Eduardo?' Will asks.

'He was unconscious when they found him about twenty minutes later,' Seb says. 'But he died later in hospital.'

'Can you prove any of this?' Will asks.

'No,' Seb says. 'Zoe said Nina told Claire about it when

they were playing Truth or Dare on the first night we were here, but it's all hearsay. The police wouldn't be interested.'

Seb glances at the clock on the bedroom wall as he gets slowly to his feet.

'Is there something you want me to do?' Will asks.

Seb shakes his head. 'Let's just say I believe there's always karma if you wait long enough in life.' He smiles. 'Even for Nina.'

Chapter 97

Nina – Now

Nina watches Gaby take a knife off the magnetic strip above the counter and cut a lemon into thin slices. She wipes her fingers with some kitchen roll, picks up one of the slivers from the chopping board, puts it into a glass of water and takes a sip.

Nina has suggested a figure, but Gaby hasn't accepted it, or turned her down. She can go higher if she needs to, but there's no point in giving money away for free.

She wonders whether she should check into the hotel she booked in Deià, but she wants this sorted before her flight tomorrow morning. *Should she just stay over?* She might not have a choice if Gaby doesn't make a decision soon. Seb has already said he's staying, and she remembers how he used to look at her, the way he used to come up behind her at university and thread his thumbs through the belt loops on her jeans. The lights come on outside the villa, illuminating the terrace and the pool, turning the water a familiar shade of neon blue.

'Where is Seb?' she asks.

Gaby shrugs. 'I don't know.'

She pours Nina a glass of water and pushes it across the counter.

'Are you going to take what I'm offering?' Nina asks.

Gaby frowns. 'What do you mean?'

'Oh, come on, Gaby. You know you can't go to the police. How much more do you want to keep quiet about what happened?'

'*What happened* is that my father was killed,' Gaby says. 'It's not a thing – he was a person.'

Nina stares at the knife lying on the chopping board, the blade covered in juice and lemon flesh.

'It was you, wasn't it?' Gaby says quietly.

'What are you talking about?'

'It was you who killed him. My father was still alive when you found him in the water, wasn't he?'

Nina swallows. 'Of course not. I checked his pulse.'

Gaby looks at her as she picks up the knife and fiddles with it, drawing circles in the pool of liquid on the board.

'I think you're lying.'

Two spots of colour appear on Nina's cheeks, but she doesn't reply.

She can't prove it.

'I don't know how you carry it around with you,' Gaby says. 'All the guilt. The weight of it will crush you in the end, you know.'

She picks up the board, scrapes the leftovers into the bin and carries it over to the sink before turning around. Nina is standing slightly closer to the counter than she was before.

'People like you think you are better than people like me,' Gaby says. 'But my father was worth so much more than you ever will be. Tourists like you come to my country for the summer, you expect us to be hospitable when you treat us like shit and then you go home again and we are left to pick up the pieces.'

She raises her glass towards Nina as if she is making a toast. 'I am going to sleep on your proposal,' she adds.

Nina can see Seb's figure silhouetted outside by the pool.

'I don't need a lecture from you,' she says. 'What happened to your father was an accident. You can't bring him back. But I am offering to give you something to make your life a bit easier. Just think about it.'

She shuts the patio door firmly on her way out.

Chapter 98

Seb – Now

Seb stares at the dolphin mosaic lit up on the bottom of the pool. For a second, he sees Aiden underwater, blowing a stream of bubbles on his way up to the surface, his eyes wide open and a goofy half-smile on his face. He blinks and Aiden disappears, the surface now smooth and still.

'You told her, didn't you?' Nina says.

Seb frowns. 'Told who what?'

'You told Gaby that Mateo was still alive when we found him. You're the only person who knew.'

Seb rubs his beard. 'Gaby is just throwing out accusations to see how you react.' He sees Nina frown as she notices his tremor. 'And even if she does know, as you said, you won't be prosecuted. It all happened too long ago.'

'Are you all right?' she says. 'Your hand . . .'

'I'm fine. It just spasms every now and again when the muscles get tense.' He puts it in his pocket. 'We need to sort this out so we can all get on with our lives.'

'What, like you've done?' Nina gives him a tight smile.

Seb thinks of his flat. Of the one small room with a table covered in dozens of plastic bags, all full of pills. 'Actually,' he says, 'things have been looking up recently.'

'Have they?'

He nods.

'I guess it's all about waiting for that one opportunity, isn't it? Something that comes along at just the right time.'

He stares at Nina, remembers how much he used to want her to want him, how he would have done anything for her.

'I'll talk to Gaby,' he says.

'You're going to have to do more than that,' she says, lowering her voice. 'I can't have Hugo finding out about this. Or my boss. Any hint of a scandal and I'll lose my job.' She holds out her hand, and he hesitates, then takes what she's offering.

'I'm going to have to stay over.' She sighs and runs her hand through her hair. 'Gaby is going to let me know what she thinks of my *proposal* tomorrow morning.'

With Nina safely inside, Seb allows himself to look over the wall and down the steps to the bottom of the cliff. Gaby is standing on the jetty by one of the posts, her arms wrapped around herself, staring out to sea. She obviously can't sleep either. He glances back at the villa. A light is on in Nina's old room.

Is she watching him?

Their past is so closely intertwined that it had taken him being sent to prison to physically prise them apart. Now they are back together he wonders if they could stay like that. The two of them. Just the way they were. He knows what she wants him to do; she doesn't have to spell it out. He has learned to predict what someone wants even before they open their mouth from living with his father.

He puts his hand on the wooden post at the top of the steps. The new rope snakes down the side of the cliff in a series of symmetrical loops, lit up by the lights inset into the steps. He remembers how he'd clung to the old one like a lifeline when he came back from sinking the boat. He'd been so terrified of disappointing Nina, had spent hours wondering whether Aiden was going to tell her that he'd given up paddling and had almost stopped them from making it back at all.

He's not going to disappoint her this time. He grabs hold of the rope, feels the weight of the knife Nina handed to him earlier in the pocket of his jogging bottoms, and starts the walk down to the jetty.

Chapter 99

Nina – Now

'Nina.' Seb whispers her name as he puts his hand on top of her duvet and presses the shape that is curled up underneath. 'Nina, wake up.'

She opens her eyes slowly and frowns when she sees him sitting on her bed in the darkness.

'What?' she mumbles.

He holds his forefinger up to his lips.

'Sssh. I need your help.'

She sits up, reaches for the cord on her bedside light and squints at her phone beside her. Four fifteen. Seb's eyes are wide, and she notices he's spilt something down his T-shirt; there's a large wet patch on the front of the dark material.

'What is it?' she whispers. 'What's the matter?'

'It's Gaby,' Seb says. 'I need you to come with me.'

Chapter 100

Will – Now

Will wakes in the middle of the night to a loud thump. Memories swim in his head – of Zoe, of floating pieces of debris, of a man staring at him from underwater, eyes wide open.

What the fuck was that? He lies still in the darkness, listening, but there's no sound other than the fan rhythmically circling above his head.

The illuminated clock on his phone shows that it's four thirty. Five hours. Better than his average night.

He turns over on his side to see Zoe's face on the pillow beside him, her hair fanned out around her face. It's almost as if she's still floating in the water. He touches the ends of the red strands with his fingers, needing to check that they are real and that she is actually there. With him.

He watches her as she sleeps, half wanting to wake her up but also not wanting to disturb her when she looks so peaceful.

The noise is the first thing he remembers when he opens his eyes a couple of hours later. He must have fallen back to sleep without realizing. He slides out from under the duvet and pads across the wooden floorboards as quietly as he can, stopping to pull on his boxer shorts and a T-shirt before he steps out on to the landing.

Silence.

He walks past Seb's room. Then Nina's. He's at the top of the stairs before he realizes her bedroom door isn't shut properly. He doubles back and stands outside it, puts his ear to the crack and listens.

Nothing.

He pushes it open very slowly, preparing to shut it again as soon as he sees her, but as the light from the landing illuminates the room he notices her bed is empty, the duvet arranged neatly over the plumped-up pillow. No clothes, no shoes, no bag – nothing. Almost as if she was never there.

He walks back up the corridor to Seb's room, wondering if Nina has copied Zoe, creeping across the landing to sleep somewhere else halfway through the night.

Behaving like teenagers. Almost like they've never been apart.

He turns the door handle, switches on the light. Empty. He checks all the other bedrooms – all of them are empty, apart from Gaby's. Her clothes are strewn over the floor and her make-up bag is on the dressing table, but there is no sign of her anywhere.

Where the fuck is everyone?

Will heads down the stone stairs, taps the banisters and tells himself not to panic as he reaches the living room. *Empty.* There is broken glass on the floor by the kitchen table, a crimson stain on the newly painted kitchen wall and a soaking-wet tea-towel in the bin. The hairs lift on his arms as he checks the patio doors: all locked. The pool glows neon blue in the darkness.

He slumps down on to the sofa, accidentally sitting on the remote control, which has buried itself between two cushions. The TV blares out the local news, uncomfortably loud, and Will hurriedly fumbles for the control to mute the volume so as not to wake Zoe. He stares blankly at the subtitles, his mind elsewhere.

The harsh light spills out into the living room, casting shadows across the floor. The edge of the rug isn't quite equidistant between the two sofas and he feels an urge to adjust it, but he doesn't want to disturb the atmosphere that sits heavily around him, blurring the edges of reality like thick smoke.

The newsreader mouths silently and he stares at the screen as the photo of a man appears, his name written underneath. He blinks, unsure if he's imagining it, but the picture remains, and for a few seconds it is as if the sofa beneath him has vanished, leaving him suspended in mid-air. His body tenses, braced for the gut-wrenching feeling of falling that he is familiar with in his dreams, but the plummet he's anticipating doesn't happen. He finds the volume button on the remote control and turns it up, now desperate for Zoe to come downstairs and see this.

The subtitles blur in front of him into something unintelligible. The man in the photo stares back at him. His unkempt beard covers most of his face, and one side of his mouth appears to be swollen. Almost unrecognizable. Almost, but not quite. Even without his name on the screen, Will would still know exactly who he is. He thinks about what Seb was capable of doing all those years ago – would he have cut off Zoe's arm if Nina had insisted? Nausea swills around in the bottom of his stomach.

'. . . *the man responsible,*' the subtitles spell out at the bottom of the screen as the newsreader talks, '*has been detained at Palma airport.*'

The remote control shakes in Will's hand.

Where's Gaby? What the fuck have you done, Seb?

Chapter 101

Nina – Now

Nina's plane touches down on the runway at Gatwick five minutes ahead of schedule. She glances at her watch as it taxis to the stand, waits for the doors to open. If they get a move on, she can be through security and home by lunchtime. Spend a couple of hours with Hugo – *if he's speaking to her* – and clear her backlog of emails before she goes into the office.

She shakes off any thoughts of Seb, of how he'd shouted to her when he was handcuffed and led away at Palma airport. She'd turned her back when they took him out of the check-in queue, had clutched her passport and waited for the kerfuffle around her to die down. *What was she supposed to do? She'd helped him get to the airport – what more did he want?*

Sometimes, we have to save ourselves.

She waits for the seatbelt signs that are still illuminated in the cabin to be switched off. *How long does it take to find a stand?* The man sitting next to her flashes her a smile, and she responds. He looks as if he can't wait to get off as well.

The tannoy crackles. She doesn't take much notice of what is being said until she hears her name and a request to make herself known to the crew. Seb must have said something. *Fuck.* She presses the call button and watches a stewardess in a bright orange jacket walk down the aisle.

'Nina Thornton?'

The man sitting beside her looks at her as she nods.

'Can you follow me, please?'

Nina stands up, goes to open the overhead locker, but the stewardess puts out her hand to stop her.

'My colleague will get your bag in a second. Just walk straight ahead, please.'

Nina adjusts her cashmere throw. 'What's this about?'

The stewardess doesn't answer. Nina can feel the other passengers staring at her as she follows the woman down the narrow aisle, hears muttered comments about preferential treatment and knowing someone on the flight deck. A few of the crew are standing by the exit in silence. She smiles, but no one smiles back. One of the stewards opens the plane door and she is confronted by two uniformed police officers.

'Nina Thornton?'

She nods, confusion spreading across her face.

Chapter 102

Nina – Now

'I'm PC Reynolds. I'm arresting you under Section 2 of the Suicide Act 1961. You do not have to say anything, but it may harm your defence if you do not mention when questioned something which you later rely on in court. Anything you do say may be given in evidence. Do you understand?'

Nina nods. *What the fuck is going on?*

The stewardess who had stopped Nina getting her bag out of the overhead locker reappears with it and hands it to one of the officers.

'I'm going to need you to accompany me to Crawley police station.'

The PC handcuffs her and takes her down the steps of the plane, where she can see a police car waiting.

'I don't understand what I'm being arrested for.' Nina's voice is sharp as she follows the officer towards the car.

'Just follow me, please.'

'Is this to do with Sebastian Hughes? I know he was arrested at Palma airport.'

PC Reynolds opens the door of the car, and she slides into the back seat. The other officer gets into the driver's seat, and the car pulls away across the tarmac then stops at a security gate. PC Reynolds rummages through

Nina's bag to find her passport, holds it out of the window, and someone checks it.

The car drives on, out of the airport and past suburban streets lined with terraced houses and cars parked nose to tail against the kerb. The sun reflects off their paintwork and Nina squints, her back uncomfortably warm against the seat.

'Can you tell me what this is about?' she asks. 'If it's to do with Seb, I can explain.'

PC Reynolds and the driver exchange glances.

'You'll find out when we get to the station.'

She shuffles forward in her seat. 'You must be able to tell me something?'

'You really want to know?'

Nina nods. *Hugo is going to be livid.* At least, if she knows why she's being arrested, then she can work on a strategy to get out as fast as possible and he'll never have to know.

PC Reynolds rummages around in his rucksack and pulls out an iPad. He flicks through a couple of screens to find what he is looking for then turns up the volume so Nina can hear it in the back of the car. They sit in silence as a recording plays and a couple of voices echo in the small space.

Nina swallows when it finishes. 'Who sent you that?'

PC Reynolds shuts the iPad and puts it back in his bag.

'We'll talk about it more when we get to the station.'

This is nothing to do with Seb. She's been caught committing an offence that has a penalty of up to fourteen years in prison. Encouraging suicide. And, unlike in Mallorca, the fact that it happened thirty-three years ago is irrelevant. There is no statute of limitations in the UK.

PC Reynolds says something to his colleague, but Nina isn't listening. She wonders whether Hugo has been sent the recording, can imagine the look on his face when he hears it. She thinks of Seb and what he said in their last conversation.

I guess it's all about waiting for that one opportunity, isn't it? Something that comes along at just the right time.

He hadn't been talking about a drug deal, as she'd assumed. He's had this for years and has just been waiting for the chance to use it.

Chapter 103

Seb – Now

Date: 22 June 2022
To: PCReynolds@GatwickPolice.co.uk
Cc: Hugo.Thornton_QC@connaughtchambers.com
From: Seb.Hughes@gmail.com

Dear PC Reynolds,

Please find enclosed an .MP3 formatted copy of a cassette tape recording made by Aiden Buckley in August 1989, six weeks after he returned from a holiday in Mallorca. Aiden sent this to me – it was recorded on the day he died – the date and time is confirmed in the news report you can hear playing in the background. The tape contains a conversation between Aiden and Nina Thornton (nee Devine). I believe what was said constitutes an offence under Section 2 of the Suicide Act 1961 and, as such, I am sure the police will be keen to open a full investigation into whether Nina encouraged Aiden to take his own life. If you wish to talk to her, she will be on the 09.30 flight from Palma to Gatwick on Sunday, 26 June.

Regards,
Sebastian Hughes

(Recording plays)

'We could have saved Henrique, Nina.'

'No, we couldn't, Aiden. It was almost impossible to see anything, it was so dark. And even if we had, what would we have done with him? Taken him back to the villa with us? Waited for him to tell everyone that we hit his boat? We've been through this so many times. He would have ruined everything for all of us.'

'Did you see him in the water? After I told you I thought I could see something?'

(Pause)

'I don't know what I saw. It could have been anything.'

(Aiden crying)

'You might be able to live with it, Nina, but I can't. I keep seeing his face. Everywhere I go.'

(Sound of clock tower chiming in background)

'Look, Aiden, we have been over this again and again. You can't keep phoning me. I don't want to talk about it. What's done is done. We're home, that's the main thing. You have to learn to live with it.'

(Aiden crying)

'I can't. I told you I can't. I meant what I said.'

'Where are you?'

'In a phone box near Old Joe. Visiting some of our old haunts. Do you remember we had a photo taken here after we graduated?'

(A woman's voice can be heard in the background. She calls out Nina's name)

'Aiden, I don't have the energy to deal with this right now. It's late. I have to go. My mother's calling me. Go home.'

(Short silence)

'I'm telling you, Nina. I can't take this any more.'

(Nina's mother calls her again, this time repeating her full name and surname. In the background a television can be heard; a man's voice announces the time and date and says they are joining ITN for the news, followed by the headlines)

'For fuck's sake, Aiden. If that's what you really want, I'm not going to stand in your way. If you really can't cope, then stop talking about it and just do it.'

(Aiden crying)

'Do you think I should? Because I will, you know. I'm so tired of it all. I can't live with it.'

(Pause)

'Actually, Aiden, I do. You can't go on like this, and I can't keep saying the same things to you over and over again. If you can't deal with the situation, then there are always options you can take. We've talked about this before. I told you it can be painless. I offered to get hold of something that would help. I think we both know it might be for the best.'

(Silence)

'Look, Aiden, I have to go. Don't call me again tonight, OK.'

(Phone goes dead)

Chapter 104

Seb – Now

Seb closes his eyes as Gaby drives over the bumps on the track leading off the main road back to the villa. She's got the air-conditioning turned up full blast, but he can still feel the heat through the glass on his skin. He rubs his beard. *Not much further.* It always seems to take longer than he remembers.

When the juddering finally stops and the pain in his back recedes enough for him to breathe normally, he opens his eyes and looks at the tattoo on his arm – a clock with no hands. He had it done after his first stretch inside – a reminder that time in prison doesn't pass at the same rate as on the outside. Hours had felt like days, every minute spent trying to find things to do to ease the boredom. Now he wonders how much longer he has left.

He'd deliberately engineered his arrest at Palma airport. Had told Nina he'd stabbed Gaby on the jetty and that they needed to leave. He'd driven his hire car down the coastal road at such high speed it had been impossible for someone not to notice. The police had collared him while he was waiting in the check-in queue after he'd dumped the car outside the terminal. Nina had carried on ahead without him, but then he'd never expected her to do anything else.

As he walks into the villa, he catches the scent of her perfume lingering in the hallway – Balade Sauvage by Dior. He'd spent a whole afternoon in Selfridges trying out the testers at the perfume counter until he found it; different scent, but the same designer brand she'd worn thirty-three years ago. *Old habits, Nina.*

Gaby goes to shut the front door, but he puts his hand out to stop her.

'Leave it open,' he says. 'The place could do with some air.'

Zoe comes down the stairs with Will behind her. Seb has to blink twice before he sees them as they are, not how they were all those years earlier.

Time is slipping. Maybe it starts to go backwards close to the end.

'Where the fuck did you go?' Will asks. 'We saw on the news that you'd been arrested.'

'Seb got into a bit of trouble at the airport,' Gaby says. 'I had to go and help. It's fine now; we sorted it out. They let him off with a fine and a speeding ticket.'

Seb looks at her. '*Esta todo arreglado,*' he says.

Gaby smiles. 'Exactly that. It's all fixed. You're learning.'

'Where's Nina?' Will asks.

'She went home,' Seb says, 'but I'm staying here. Gaby has asked me to hang around for a while.'

Will stares at them.

'What happened?' he asks.

Seb opens the patio doors to the terrace and shuts his eyes briefly as he feels the warmth of the sun on his face.

'I got in touch with Gaby after she emailed us when the boat was dredged up,' he says. 'We talked, and I told her

Nina was the person responsible for pushing her father back in the water.'

He turns away to look at the pool as his back spasms, not wanting them to see his face. Aiden is in the water again, sitting cross-legged on the bottom in his green swimming trunks. Seb thinks he sees him hold out his hand before he disappears.

'When Nina gets home,' he says, 'she's going to find something waiting for her.' He glances at Will. 'Karma,' he adds.

Zoe stares at him. 'So all this was about her? Why did you get us out here as well?'

Seb looks at her. 'Because I wanted the chance to apologize in person. Before it was too late.'

He can see from the look on her face that Will has told her about the cancer.

She doesn't say anything, but nods, briefly.

'We need to go,' Will says. 'Or we'll miss our flights. I'll get my bag.'

Their footsteps echo on the ceiling above Seb's head. *Same room.* He smiles.

Will comes back down a couple of minutes later holding a pack of cards.

'One last game?'

Chapter 105

Seb – Now

Seb lies on the sofa outside on the terrace and looks up at the sky as it deepens in colour until it reaches a velvet blackness, sprinkled with stars.

Gaby has switched on the lights in the living room, and he can see the artwork she's chosen for the walls through the windows. Large, bright canvases that suit the house so much better than the paintings that were there before. She says she wants to start on the bedrooms next – new en suites, and maybe a small balcony so he can sit out and look at the sea when managing the stairs gets tricky. She's more optimistic than he is about the time he has left, but he finds comfort in watching the never-ending motion of the waves – they were here long before him and will still be here when he's gone.

Gaby brings out two glasses filled with ice, a bottle of vodka and a carton of cranberry juice. She sits down next to him and pours him a drink, knowing the tartness of the cranberry takes away the taste of his medication. It's a ritual they've carried out every night since he arrived four days ago with his one bag containing everything he owned. They'd needed some time to visit a lawyer in Palma and finish the renovations in the villa. He raises his glass to hers.

'To Mateo,' he says.

'To my father.'

He takes a large sip as they listen to the *shhh-tik-tik-tik* of the sprinklers, the evening heat wrapping him in a warm blanket. Another twenty minutes, and he won't be able to feel the pain in his back, at least for a few hours – he smiles inwardly at the irony of wanting time to both speed up and slow down.

He thinks about Nina's husband, how surprised Hugo was when Seb had contacted him about the possibility of buying the villa. Hugo had kept very quiet about the amount of renovation work that was needed; the fact that one of the bathrooms had damp and the entire place needed rewiring were things he couldn't have failed to notice, but he hadn't mentioned them when he'd accepted Seb's cash offer on the spot.

He wonders how long it will take Hugo to tell Nina what he's done. Whether he'll wait until she's serving what he hopes will be a prison sentence. She'll find out eventually; part of him wishes he could be there to see the look on both their faces when she realizes the money has come from the proceeds of a drug deal. By then, Seb knows, it will be too late for Hugo to do anything about it. He will be gone, and the meeting with the lawyer in Palma means Gaby is now the legal owner of the villa.

He takes another sip of his drink, thinks of Mateo, of Aiden, of Zoe, and hopes he has done enough.

The sprinklers switch off for the night and the hum of cicadas fills the darkness, together with the faint sound of waves breaking against the rocks by the jetty. The scent of jasmine hangs in the air. Seb stares at the smooth surface of the neon-blue pool and sees Aiden laugh as he jumps in, splashing him with water.

He shuts his eyes and wonders if he will still be there when he opens them.

Acknowledgements

Writing a book and getting it published is never an easy thing to do, and sometimes circumstances arise that make it harder than ever.

I would like to thank my agent, the wonderful Sophie Lambert at C&W, for her great kindness and support during the writing of this novel – the fact that she believed in me meant more than I can say. In addition, I would like to thank Harriet Bourton for her excellent advice during difficult times – as Eleanor Roosevelt said, 'Women are like teabags. We don't know our true strength until we are in hot water.'

I am very fortunate to have had two editors on this book – Harriet and I have worked together before, but I would also like to say a massive thank you to Vikki Moynes, who has been a total joy to work with and whose incredibly intuitive edits made this book so much better than it would otherwise have been. May we swap many more spreadsheets going forward!

I'd like to thank the rest of the team at Viking, who I am absolutely delighted to have as my publishers, and who could not have worked harder on this book. To Ellie Hudson, Lydia Fried, Jane Gentle, Poppy North, Ellie Smith, and no doubt many others behind the scenes – I am so grateful for all your efforts.

Thank you to Charlotte Daniels for my favourite-ever cover, to Sarah Day for her brilliant copy-edits and Alice

Hoskyns at C&W, who read an early version and gave such insightful feedback.

A big shout out to all the other authors who are a huge part of my life and have shown me so much support. In particular, Laura, Lauren and Zoe, who started off as Harrogate housemates (and will continue to be for ever) and are now friends for life – you know I couldn't have written this without you. Our WhatsApp chats make what can be a lonely job much less so. To the D20s, who were a critical lifeline during lockdown and the pandemic, and who continue to brighten my weeks. And to the Ladykillers, who keep me entertained, and who are some of the kindest and most supportive women I know.

This book is set in Deià in Mallorca – a place I never knew existed until I visited it with some of my oldest girlfriends back in October 2019, when we were oblivious to Covid and what was about to hit us. Anna, Ceril, Els, Lynn and Nanna, I am so lucky to have had you as friends for over twenty years and can't wait for our next trip.

I would like to thank Graham Bartlett, my go-to crime fiction advisor, for his help regarding various aspects of police procedure – he corrects my somewhat-vague ideas and lets me know what would actually happen in that situation!

A big thanks to Philippa East: through her various connections she put me in touch with Jason Borthwick, Anna Biesty and Will Ellison, who gave me so much useful information about boats, how to sink them and retrieval of wrecks from that area of coast in Mallorca. Any inaccuracies are entirely my own.

A massive thank you to all the bloggers, reviewers and

bookstagrammers who have championed this book – I am so grateful for your support. And thank you to all my readers – without you, I could not do this.

I'd like to apologize to my whole family for the many occasions during the writing of this novel that I was too busy to chat, or was 'zoned out', as my two daughters often told me – sometimes it's the only way I know to work out the plot! All my love, as ever, goes to you, Charlotte and Liberty; you are already the women this book is dedicated to, and I hope you always continue to be so. And all my love to my husband, Martin – we are so very lucky to have each other.